THE
CLASS
Of 1968

L.J. Rowan High School
Hattiesburg, Mississippi

A THREAD THROUGH TIME

DORIS TOWNSEND GAINES

EDITOR

CAROLYN HALL ABRAMS

CO-EDITOR

PAGE PUBLISHING, INC.
Conneaut Lake, PA

First originally published by Page Publishing 2021

ISBN 978-1-64628-730-7 (pbk)
ISBN 978-1-64628-731-4 (digital)

Printed in the United States of America

CONTENTS

FOREWORD

"The Russians are coming! The Russians are coming!" Those of us who lived during the Cold War era and the fears of retaliation after the Cuban Missile Crisis remember vividly the Civil Defense Drills, running to the school buses to board and ride, with no shelters in sight for the students of a segregated society, just a drill to prepare for the inevitable—a ride to nowhere. Fifty years ago, we mourned over the loss of our classmates, snatched by the "lottery" and propelled into a war thousands of miles away in a sweltering place called Vietnam. As U.S. casualties rose in Vietnam to over 543 Americans killed in 1968 and over 2,547 wounded, we pondered how so many young Black men were drafted to serve and die while others successfully evaded the pick of the draw. Did anyone wonder about the makeup of the Selective Service Boards that did the "selecting"?

The Class of 1968 watched in sorrow the clips of the assassination of Dr. Martin Luther King in April 1968, followed by the assassination of Robert Kennedy a few months later. We wept, we cried, we doubted, and yet we survived. We knew then that if we were to conquer the world and make it a place for all people to live in joy and peace, we would have to "shake it off" and strive to be twice as good as the next student, the next employee, and our competitors. We were trained to take on the world. Our teachers encouraged us: "The world is yours. You change it and make it great." Our music inspired us… "I Heard It Through the Grapevine"—(Marvin Gaye), "I'm Black and I'm Proud"—(James Brown). This is what propelled us. This is what held us up when it was so much easier to fall down; this is what made us want to change the world that we lived in. This, fellow classmates, is what we now celebrate: our resilience…our fortitude…our quest for excellence…our refusal to take second place. Class of 1968 can you hear the chants again, now in 2020, "The Russians are coming! The Russians are coming!"? They infiltrated our election and they're preparing to infiltrate it again. (Sound familiar?) The world has changed to the extent that falsehoods are deemed to be truths. Lack of morals is okay… Integrity has gone astray.

As you read the stories of 1968, remember that they are true. Some are funny. Some are hurtful. Some are unbelievable, but believe them. We must tell our stories, for if we are not vigilant, if we do not remember our history, it will truly repeat itself. Let's take up the mantra again: Let's teach the children… Let's tell them our history so they too can know that they *can and will rise*!

—Chancellor Deborah Jones Gambrell Chambers
Class of 1968 Locker High School—Wiggins, Mississippi

ACKNOWLEDGMENTS

First, we must thank the team of classmates who have worked to make this project a success. Although we are listed as the editors, by contributing your stories and experiences, you have made this book possible and deserve recognition. Thank you for your efforts and unwavering support, contacting others, making arrangements, running here and there, and providing support in so many ways. Without you, this would not have come to fruition. Additionally, we are grateful for the support of the Honorable Judge Deborah Gambrell Chambers, the Class of 1968, Locker High School, Wiggins, Mississippi, who enthusiastically agreed to contribute the foreword for our book without hesitation. Others who deserve recognition include Attorney Michael Adelman who has been extremely helpful and instrumental in forming our corporation, Rowan Book Project: Class of 1968, LLC., Rick Taylor, LaToya Norman, the Hattiesburg Tourism Commission for their continued support, McCain Archives at the University of Southern Mississippi (USM), the Library of Hattiesburg and Forrest County who provided free meeting space, and Randall Williams who assisted with photography. For their assistance at the beginning of the project in offering advice on interview questions, technology, and legal concerns, we are also grateful to Andrea Abrams, Stacey Abrams, and Leslie Abrams. This gratitude extends to Grady L. Gaines for his time attending meetings and for general support, and to LaNita Gaines Hargett, Leslia M. Gaines Osakuade, and L. Brooke Gaines for their help in editing, proofing, and providing general assistance. Thank you also to Ms. Olivia Moore, a doctoral candidate studying History at the University of Southern Mississippi who willingly helped with ideas in the compilation of documents, editing, and contributed her experience and time to the project. Ms. Moore is fast becoming an expert on Hattiesburg history, and has conducted several interviews with local activists. She is currently writing her doctoral dissertation on the fractures that started to develop within the local civil rights movement toward the end of the 1960s. We also thank Ms. Moore for writing the Preface and the italicized introductions for Chapter 7. Additionally, thank you to Miss Emily Smith, a master's student in History and Library Science at USM who willingly contributed her experience and time to the project. It is also important to acknowledge Dr. Thomas V. O'Brien, a distinguished professor at USM who specializes in the study of race and education in the American south. Professor O'Brien saw our vision, and contributed his energies and know-how to our efforts. Thank you for sharing the gift of time, and encouraging us throughout the process of getting our book to the publisher.

We pause to also acknowledge those members of the Class of 1968 who, in the school year 1967–68, chose to attend Blair Center (Hattiesburg High School) under the "Freedom of Choice" policy. Integration of the public schools in Hattiesburg was instituted in stages, with twelfth graders being eligible in the 67–68 school year. Their actions fundamentally changed the people who lived during those times. We can only imagine what they endured and witnessed, since there are no known documented accounts of their experiences. We honor them for their courage and bravery in integrating Blair Center during the fall of 1967. Our descendants stand on their shoulders today. We now take this time to recognize and salute these students who paved the way for others. Thank you: Georgia Ann Adams Hunter (deceased), Glenda Brown, Ethelyn Fairley Reid, Harvell Harris, Jr., Bessie Howze Mackabee (deceased), Betty Johnson Slusher (deceased), Charles Killingsworth, Sr., Louis Payton (deceased), Claudia Polk Bivins, and Richard Turner.

LIST OF CONTRIBUTORS

Carolyn	Atkins
Thelma	Bacchus
Deborah	Barrett Jackson
Patricia	Berry Blake
Hayes	Boles, Jr.
Katherine	Bouie Boyd
Betty	Bournes Hill
Stella	Brooks Clark
Teleceno	Carr, Jr.
Deborah Jones Gambrell	Chambers
James	Chatman
Willie Don	Denard
Lillie	Dwight
Ethelyn	Fairley-Reid
Grady	Gaines
Patricia Ann	Griffin
Carolyn	Hall Abrams
Alma Jean	Hall Henderson
Tommy	Hall, Jr. **
Beverly	Harris Abrams

Dianne	*Hart Breland*
Margaret	*Hill Burger***
Ann	*Holmes Sowell*
Mattie	*Hudnall Ponder*
Ella Sue	*Jackson***
Mildred	*Johnson Watts*
Eva	*Lenyoun Crosby*
Juanita	*Mayes Walker*
Willie Ruth	*McDonald Sanders*
Doris	*McNeill Collins*
Melvin	*Miller*
Mildred	*Miller Short*
Rose Mary	*Montgomery Harrell*
Olivia	*Moore*
Thomas V.	*O'Brien, Ph. D.*
Bernita	*Parker Johnson*
Lionel	*Peyton*
Claudia	*Polk Bivins*
Willie	*Sanders*
Barbara	*Thomas Ross*
Doris	*Townsend Gaines*
Richard	*Turner*
Patricia	*Turner Bradley*
Linda	*Turner Harris*
Vernette	*Wallis Andry*
Randall	*Williams*
Hattie	*Williams Knight*

** Deceased

NOTE ON STYLE

In editing this book, we generally follow the guidelines set by the Chicago Manual Style (CMS) and Page Publishing. In several instances, however, we break with the guidelines in order to convey the true meaning of specific words and phrases. For example, to confirm the level of respect we afford to our elders in our families and community, we deliberately capitalize the first letters of "Mother," "Father," "Aunt," "Uncle," "Grandma," and other similar titles rather than adhering to the CMS practice of using all lower-case letters. Likewise, we capitalize the terms "Black" and "White" when they refer to Americans of African descent and Americans of European descent, respectively. Also, our pride compels us to refer to ourselves as the "Class of 1968" rather than the "class of 1968." Additionally, local street names that are numbers (sixth street, for example) are designated using numerals rather than spelled out, conveying the way we read them on street signs in the 1960s (6th Street), and as we still understand them today. Finally, we proceed with the utmost of care when considering changes to a contributor's story. We resist intrusive edits on this front, and change the text only in specific instances to help clarify meaning. We make no revisions if we determine that an edit would change the author's intended meaning or idea.

PREFACE

The city of Hattiesburg, Mississippi, has a distinctive and important history: a history that is tragic in some ways, but also inspiring and exciting in others. While much of Hattiesburg's history has been documented, many voices still need to be heard, many stories are waiting to be told, and many intricacies need to be revealed not only to complete, but also to complicate dominant narratives that often ignore the lived experiences of everyday people. This book is the culmination of an impressive project that two women have been pursuing over the past two years in order to enhance our historical knowledge of Hattiesburg. As the book highlights their own experiences as youth coming of age in Hattiesburg, it also contemplates and scrutinizes the accounts of their classmates, who contributed their own reminiscences.

This compilation touches on various themes, including segregation, civil rights, and daily life within the city's varied and vibrant African American communities. This project has brought together students and teachers from the Hattiesburg public schools, students and professors from the University of Southern Mississippi, and perhaps most importantly, community members like the editors, Mrs. Doris Gaines and Mrs. Carolyn Abrams, who lived this history, and willingly share their experiences and stories with us. Such approaches are critical to the researching and writing of local history. These types of projects also appeal to teachers who seek ways to connect their students with the local community, and provide them an opportunity to engage with issues that may be ongoing and require new solutions.

Hattiesburg's history features many contrasts. In the years following the Second World War, the city experienced a period of dramatic social, economic, and intellectual growth. Despite promising change, however, Hattiesburg continued to suffer under a system of racial inequality and segregation that dominated life throughout the South. In response to severe discrimination and the violence of White segregationists, Hattiesburg produced a vast network of important civil rights organizers. Local individuals worked tirelessly on voter registration efforts; the city served as one of the major headquarters during Freedom Summer in 1964; and it served as ground zero for the Mississippi Freedom Democratic Party (MFDP)—a political party that challenged the all-White Mississippi Democratic Party at the 1964 National Convention. Unfortunately, major Civil Rights successes also led to a series of violent backlashes. Some of these include the firebombing and murder of local activist and NAACP president Vernon Dahmer, and the false imprisonment and death of Korean War veteran and Civil Rights pioneer Clyde Kennard.

This is the period when Mrs. Gaines and Mrs. Abrams grew up, and their experiences as young people during such a tumultuous time feature in the memoir that follows. The book, titled *The Class of 1968: A Thread Through Time,* weaves together the autobiographical accounts of these women and their classmates who belonged to one of the last segregated high school classes at the all-Black L.J. Rowan High School. Their journey through Hattiesburg's segregated public-school system unites the book thematically, but the essays also cover several other topics, including church life, the effect of floods on the community, working conditions, and the Vietnam War. While it is fascinating to consider how the lives of these individuals intersected with such significant historical moments, one of the great dimensions of the book is its discussion of the everyday details of life for people within the community. Many of these autobiographical accounts emphasize seemingly unimportant details that more traditional sources often neglect, but these details demand our attention in order to understand the character of the community at this time.

This project, therefore, provides the people who experienced these historical events with the authority and space to tell their own stories, identifying what was meaningful to them. The editors and their associates have worked incredibly hard to keep the accounts of those who submitted memoirs as close to the original as possible, in order to preserve their authenticity. Only in a few instances, to help clarify meaning, was the text changed. In most cases, the team refrained from making any revisions or edits that might alter the author's intended meaning. Once again, this project ultimately documents the experiences of the local community and the details that matter to them. So, while some members of the Class of 1968 talk about the deaths of activists like Vernon Dahmer, Clyde Kennard, and Medgar Evers and how these affected the larger community, others also discuss their specific family traditions on holidays like Thanksgiving and Christmas; their favorite teachers; people who influenced them within the community; and even the trouble they may have gotten into at school. We hope you will get a flavor for this variety as you read the pages that follow.

One final note: For over two years, starting in late 2017, Dr. Thomas V. O'Brien, Professor of the History of Education at the University of Southern Mississippi, and I worked alongside Mrs. Gaines and Mrs. Abrams, meeting with them twice a month—usually on Friday afternoons—in the downtown Hattiesburg Public Library. In total, the four of us spent more than 120 hours—five full days!—in each other's' company. In many ways, the hours together have served as a microcosm of life itself—minutes packed with joy, debate, laughter, misunderstandings, anger, joking, disagreement, unintended (and sometimes well-intended) insults, compromise, and ultimately, resolution. Dr. O'Brien and I initially signed on, at Mrs. Gaines' request, to help guide the project. As our time with Mrs. Gaines and Mrs. Abrams lengthened, we got to know each other, and—despite differences of age, race, gender, region, and country of origin—to genuinely *like and appreciate* one another. The four of us grew ever more determined both to honor and help extend the reach of the stories and rich life experiences of the Class of 1968. Along the way, Dr. O'Brien and I had front-row seats that gave us the privilege to witness—with awe and excitement——the feel of history in the making. Throughout, we have both made two very special and life-long friends. And for all of this, we feel not only wiser, but also blessed.

—Olivia Moore

COMMENTARY

I had never planned to be a consultant on a second project that mined the local history of Hattiesburg. In early 2017, I was working with a group of Hattiesburg High School students who were interested in studying the history of their high school. They wanted to know more about how race factored into their schooling as well as into the schooling of their parents, grandparents, and others in the community. The work required them to interview former students and teachers—Black and White—from Eureka, Royal Street, Rowan, Blair and Hattiesburg High Schools. But in the summer of 2018, while the students and I were recruiting "informants" at the registration tables of the multi-class EUROHA reunion in the former cafeteria at Eureka, a fast-talking woman working one of the registers told me she needed my contact information before I left so I could assist her and a friend on a book they were putting together about the Rowan Class of 1968.

The person who had approached me was Mrs. Doris Townsend Gaines, the salutatorian of the Class of 1968. Later I learned that her "co-conspirator" was Mrs. Carolyn Hall Abrams, the valedictorian of that class. Doris wanted my help because as she put it, "I have never written a book before and you probably have, so you could offer us advice." Doris, Mr. Grady Gaines, and I met a few times in late summer at the Hattiesburg Public Library to discuss the project. Carolyn was away, but came into the fold by the Fall. She seemed a bit more reticent. At our first meeting, and after greetings, Carolyn posed a direct question: "What do you see as your role, and what do you plan to get from this project?" Her words had the tone and feel of a visit with a conscientious mother before a first date with her teenage daughter: "Young man, what are your intentions?"

On my drive home I realized that I was dealing with two wise women, both school smarts and street smarts. Together they had the spirit of "we will get it done, and get it done right." On a number of levels Doris and Carolyn reminded me of my mother, the daughter of Italian immigrants, who co-raised five children on eastern Long Island, taught public school for twenty-eight years, and was the hard-nosed representative of her teachers' union. But Carolyn and Doris were Southerners, Black women, Christian, who surely faced a world of White hostility of a much different nature than what my mother, a lapsed Catholic in the northeast, had faced.

As time passed, Doris, Carolyn and I met twice monthly, and were joined after a few months by Olivia Moore, a young Ph.D. student in the USM Department of History who is enthralled with local Hattiesburg history. Olivia is from England, her heart big, and she seems quintessentially Southern, but in a liberal way with a social justice focus, along the lines of civil rights workers Mary King and Casey Hayden, or even Viola Liuzzo (who was from Detroit). Olivia brought to our circle a fresh perspective and the keen eye of a sharp, youthful scholar. We were now a team of four. To quote Jim Henson, "There's not a word yet for old friends who've just met."

For the next two years the four of us—Doris, Carolyn, Olivia, and I—became "thick as thieves" working on revisions to the book, but also sharing stories and memories, moments in time, jokes, and honest confessions. The topics of race, place, integrity, and justice anchored our discussions. We were and continue to be an odd group- two Black, two White; two Southerners, a Yankee, and a Brit—and we celebrate our commonalities and differences at every encounter. What follows is an insider's look at Black people's experiences coming of age in Mississippi at the start of and during the height the modern Civil Rights movement, and near the end of legally-sanctioned Jim Crow. But it is not only the memories of Doris and Carolyn, but also the stories of their many classmates—a remarkable compilation at a remarkable time.

In the COVID-19 world, as we put the final editorial touches on the book, Carolyn, Doris, Olivia, and I no longer meet at the library; Carolyn has moved to Atlanta, Olivia to Tennessee, and we are all "sheltering in place." Nevertheless, we all insist on a weekly conference call on Friday afternoons to reach our goal of publication and to go further with our collective friendship. It is not known who first said that "truly great friends are hard to find, difficult to leave, and impossible to forget." But I do not think I'm stretching the truth when I say the four of us have come to feel this way. I am grateful for their friendship and for their generosity in sharing their memories and wisdom with me.

—Thomas V. O'Brien, Ph.D.

INTRODUCTION

Greetings to the Classes of 1968 everywhere!
    There is no greater agony than bearing an
    untold story inside you.
    —*Maya Angelou, I Know Why the Caged Bird Sings*

In the late summer of 2019, ten members of Rowan High School Class of 1968 traveled by car to visit the Mississippi Civil Rights Museum in Jackson, Mississippi. We had planned the trip several times, but the various aches and pains of our late sixty and early seventy-year-old bodies always gave us reasons to postpone our trip. Since opening in 2017, we had heard many wonderful things about the museum, but no mere words prepared us for the rush of nostalgia and memories we felt as we navigated our walkers, canes, and a wheelchair through the exhibits.

Shouts of recognition and excited laughter echoed all around the museum. We saw our friends, neighbors, and classmates exhibited all over the walls. We recalled having marched along the streets of our city as preteens and teens as we made our way to the Forrest County Courthouse. The father of one of our classmates narrated an exhibit relating to the military. There were many things that made us feel that we were a part of the exhibit, too. When many of the other visitors to the museum realized that we were personally familiar with many of the people and occurrences in the displays, they asked to pose with us in pictures. We could just close our eyes and see our childhood memories brought back to us in the photographs and archives on display.

We wept as we examined the Vernon Dahmer exhibit and thought back to that day. Many of the civil rights activists from Hattiesburg were a part of our daily lives and were not recognized as heroes and heroines at home. They were our parents, uncles, aunts, neighbors, pastors, friends, and other everyday people in the community doing their very best under the circumstances. When we were young, we were unaware of the depth of their sacrifices and the danger of threats that they risked day to day to make a better world for us.

As we surveyed the Ku Klux Klan robes and hoods on display at the museum, the same feelings of disgust, loathing, and fear continued to permeate our spirits—feelings that we thought were long forgotten or buried. Some of the same masked people employed our mothers as maids. Our mothers traveled by foot or bus every day to these individuals' homes to clean their houses, cook, and raise their children.

As we share our memories, it is our hope that you gain a unique perspective into the past in this multi-colored, patched quilt of America. The members of the Class of 1968 grew up in simpler times, yet were a part of the most pivotal years in American history. We hope that you gain insight and understanding while reminiscing with us as you read our story and journey with us along *"A Thread Through Time."*

Sincerely,
Doris Townsend Gaines
Editor and Creator

What A Wonderful World
(first recorded by Louis Armstrong in 1967)

I see trees of green
Red roses too
I see them bloom
For me and you
And I think to myself
What a wonderful world

I see skies of blue
And clouds of white
The bright blessed day
The dark sacred night
And I think to myself
What a wonderful world

The colors of the rainbow
So pretty in the sky
Are also on the faces
Of people going by
I see friends shaking hands
Saying, "How do you do?"
They're really saying "I love you"

I hear babies cry
I watch them grow
They'll learn much more

Than I'll never know
And I think to myself
What a wonderful world

Yes, I think to myself
What a wonderful world

CHAPTER 1

This Is Us

"Mmmmm... This tastes gooood..."

The thought bubble above reflects my earliest complete memory. Many flashes of early moments still swirl around in my head, but I want to begin my fiftieth-anniversary memoirs with my earliest complete memory. That tasty moment above is the most significant because it is my clearest, most coherent memory about my life growing up in Hattiesburg, Mississippi. I was a toddler sitting on the edge of a bed in the back bedroom of my Aunt Nita's house, sucking on a baby bottle that was filled with what tasted like sweet Pet Milk and bouncing my heels against the side of the bed in a steady rhythm as happy as I could be. This must have been 1951–52. My Mother, Alice Britton, has a sister who survives today. When I asked Aunt Rachel about this memory, she told me that women would feed their babies Pet Milk mixed with a little Karo Syrup or some other sweetener. There was no baby formula back then. At any rate, it tasted good!

Aunt Nita lived on Atlanta Street at 9th Street on the southeast corner. Standing on the front porch of her house, I could look west down 9th Street and see the Park where Eureka played its football games. I vividly recall so many times during my childhood standing in a front doorway or standing on a front porch looking at the outside world. The Park was surrounded by a high wooden fence in those days, and I recall standing on Aunt Nita's porch looking down 9th Street and wanting to go inside that fence to see what was going on. I learned in the fourth grade that my parents lived on Atlanta Street near Aunt Nita, so I was always at her house, and when I would see people headed to the Park to see Eureka play football, I wanted to go too.

My dad, W. D. Denard Sr., had his photography studio at 421 East 6th Street, on the corner of Mobile Street and East 6th Street across the street on the diagonal from Eureka school. As a very young child, I would stand in the front door of the studio, look to the left, and watch the goings on at Eureka. I distinctly remember seeing Eureka band members wearing black and orange uniforms. At other times, I would stare at "big children" going to and from school. School seemed to be where the action was, and I wanted to go.

So this is how it began: The earliest memories for me were on the north side of Hattiesburg on Atlanta Street and on East 6th Street. Eureka loomed large in my mind at both these sites. "School" seemed always to be in the picture as far back as I can remember, and it has had a powerful hold on my thinking up to today. On the pages that follow, I will share my memories of growing up in Hattiesburg and being driven by the strong desire to "go to school" because it always seemed *the* place to be.

These memoirs will reflect the important influence on me and on the L. J. Rowan Class of 1968 that can be traced to the strong, tight-knit culture that Black people of Hattiesburg built over the years. School was at the forefront of that culture. Culture, in terms of the ways of Black people in Hattiesburg, their values, standards, humor, the personalities, the struggle for justice, and striving for excellence in all areas of life, was the golden key to our success as a community of people. I will use the culture of our people to frame this recounting of my experiences and the meaning that those experiences hold for me today.

I want to apologize at the outset for the length of what appears here. The reason for the length is that I have a lot to say about something incredible that happened in the world that our ancestors made for us to come into, and it needs to be chronicled in a way that attempts to do justice to their significant accomplishment. This will be a thick description of the greatness of the culture of our people and the premier schools that particular culture produced. I will speak from the perspective of a son who grew up in the Black community on the South side of Hattiesburg who is both proud and, most importantly, grateful to the brilliant and courageous people who made up the community that nurtured and protected us during a turbulent, dangerous time in history. By their work and faith in God, who made them for greatness, they prepared us well for the larger world that we would face and ultimately deal with successfully. Perhaps someone will later speak in depth from the north side viewpoint, where the greatness of our schools began, and from the east-side viewpoint. What our people did in Hattiesburg in the communities on the north, south, and east sides of town is remarkable and is worthy of a full exposé.

—*Don Denard*

On February 18, 1950, a beautiful little girl was born to the parents of Ernest and Addie Barrett Sr. They named her Deborah Lucille Barrett. She was the middle child of five children, two older brothers, Ernest Jr. and Ronald (deceased); two younger sisters, Eunice and Denise.

My Father had a third-grade education and taught himself how to read. He met my Mother while he was in the army stationed at Camp Shelby. They were married on August 29, 1943. He was from a small town of Tarboro, North Carolina. He had an older sister and a twin sister. His twin's oldest son had twin boys, and my Father's youngest daughter, Denise, has twin girls. Twins are common in our family.

We always referred to our Father as "My Daddy." When we spoke about him, it sounded like he was not the Father of us all. Other children would ask, "Isn't he their daddy, too?" We would say yes and laugh.

My Mother was the third child of four and the only girl. They could sing gospel music and praise the Lord. She and her brothers made beautiful gospel records, and she used her gift to lift up the name of the Lord, because this was her ministry. She graduated from Eureka High School and worked for PACE Headstart for twenty-five years.

When I look back over my life, growing up in a household with both parents and four siblings, it was pretty terrific because I was truly blessed to have parents. I was very quiet and shy, and didn't like to talk very much. Yes, there were many trials and tribulations, but by the grace of God, He brought us through. I didn't know what poor was because there was love, and sacrifices were made to provide for the needs of five children.

—*Deborah L. Barrett Jackson*

 My parents were Grady Gaines and Mary Johnson Gaines. I am one of six siblings: five boys and one girl. I was born across Highway 42 Bypass in a neighborhood called the Gravelline. It was called that because it was traversed by railroad tracks, and the train hauled gravel from the gravel pit through the community to downtown Hattiesburg where it was sent to many different places.

—Grady L. Gaines

I am one of seven siblings. Three older brothers (my middle brother has died) and three younger sisters. Believe it or not, we were close and did well together. We were in a home with a "short giant." No debate with nothing said. We knew we were loved, although it was not through spoken words.

We attended school every day, I went to church morning, noon, and night, and Vacation Bible School three times each summer, because there were three churches in my area. Not saying all this was bad. I really believe that has made me who I am today.

—Dianne Hart Breland

My early years growing up in the segregated South in Hattiesburg with my two sisters (Martha Nell Johnson and Rosa Lynn Johnson "Skiter") were very memorable. We lived on East 6th Street, which was across Bouie Street known as the Gholah.

My Mom and Grandmother were big influences in my life when I was young. They were very proud, strong, and independent-thinking women. My Mother worked for a White family so my sisters and I stayed with my aunts or our grandparents until we were old enough to stay at home alone. However, I always loved to stay with my grandparents, my Dad's parents who lived on East 7th Street, which was located directly behind (formerly) Eureka High School. I grew up spending a lot of my time at their house especially when I was small. I remember when I was no more than three or four years old, we spent a lot of time in the backyard where they had a garden and raised chickens. I was always a little afraid of the chickens, although they let me walk and/or play outside and they kept a close eye on me. As I grew, I loved to watch the older kids at Eureka so much as they played during recess and practiced band that my Grandmother bought me a little stool to sit on while I was outside.

—*Mildred "Cookie" Johnson Watts*

The journey of Melvin Miller to L. J. Rowan High School began on November 24, 1950, when twins were born to John W. Miller and Willie B. Miller in Hattiesburg, Mississippi. The twins, Melvin Allen Miller and Mildred Alice Miller, joined the family that already included Lorma Reda Miller, born two years earlier.

John W. Miller was a plasterer by trade, and Willie B. Miller was a teacher at Eureka Elementary School. Our home was on Memphis Street, located in the northeast section of Hattiesburg, two blocks from Eureka School and three blocks from Mobile Street, the hub of Black business and commerce in the city. We lived in the segregated South, in a time where civil and human rights for Black people were almost nonexistent. The bitter legacy of slavery was still apparent as the South was controlled by Jim Crow laws supported by violence and intimidation intended to maintain racial segregation in its most strident form. The public educational systems for Black people in the South conformed to this norm.

—*Melvin Miller*

I, Eva Mae Lenyoun Crosby, did not have a nickname in school, but a lot of people called me Betty on my side of town. I lived in the east side of Hattiesburg and came to Hattiesburg in 1967, so I went to Rowan for one year. There were no ifs, ands, or buts after high school. I had to find a job and go to work.

The year was 1967, when a girl from a small town was about to move to the big city of Hattiesburg. Before this, I lived in the small town of Oma, Mississippi, where there was no running water, no gas, no electricity, but I survived. I rode the bus every day for about twenty-five miles to attend McCullough High School where I played basketball. L. J. Rowan was our rival ever since I can remember. I remember us riding from Monticello, Mississippi to Hattiesburg to play ball, and of course, Rowan always won.

I lived in a town where there was only one big store where we bought groceries and everything else we needed. We had to go to Monticello to go shopping, but most of my clothes were brought from Hattiesburg when my mom came to visit my Grandmother and me. I used to tell everybody that I came from Monticello because nobody really knew about the town of Oma.

—Eva Lenyoun Crosby

I am the fourth child of six siblings. I had four brothers and one sister. We were raised in a Christian home. Our Daddy, Earlie Hudnall, taught us how to respect adults, work, and be productive individuals. He also taught us to be honest and not to tell lies. Growing up in Hattiesburg, Mississippi, I lived on Royal Street, which has now changed to Martin Luther King Drive.

—Mattie Hudnall Ponder

My full name was Ethelyn Fairley and I lived in East Jerusalem Quarters (Flats). I grew up at the same address in Hattiesburg, on McKinley Street, from my formative years through graduation from high school.

My neighbors, both adults and children, were viewed as family. We were people of different backgrounds and varied occupations, etc. but demonstrated a true example of a "village." We knew in our hearts that everyone cared and looked out for each other. Church and education were strongly emphasized.

—Ethelyn Fairley Reid

 I was born on March 9, 1948, to Leroy and Alma Jean Peyton, the fourth of seven children. I attended school at Eureka through second grade but had to repeat the second grade due to illness.

—Lionel Peyton

I was born in May of 1951, to Leslie and Mattie McDonald Townsend. They met in Laurel, Mississippi, back in the thirties. They moved to Hattiesburg during the time when the cloverleaf at Highway 49 was being built. Daddy worked construction on that project, and Mama soon followed him to Hattiesburg. I was the second of two children, a boy having been stillborn two years prior to my birth. Before moving to Hattiesburg, my Mother was a teacher at the now-defunct Benson School in Jones County. I am told that when I was born weighing in at only four pounds, my Mother would carry me on a pillow since I was so tiny.

SCHOOL DAYS 1961-62
MARY BETHUNE

After moving to Hattiesburg, my Mother worked as a pediatric assistant in the office of Dr. Mary Clark. She also did domestic or "day" work at Dr. Clark's house. At both times, she wore the very familiar white uniform that was the norm for Black women who did any type of domestic work during those times.

My Daddy had a third- or fourth-grade education and worked as a laborer at both Hercules and Dixie Pine, the largest employers in the area in those days.

When I was a little older, Mama wanted to stay home so she opened her own kindergarten, Townsend's Kiddy Nook, at our house. She was also a gifted pianist and played for several churches. She touched many young lives by teaching school and piano lessons for many years.

—*Doris Townsend Gaines*

I was born in Jones County to Odessa and Emanuel Mc Donald, Senior. They moved to Forrest County when I was an infant. My family consisted of three brothers and two sisters. I was the fifth child out of six. My family had very strong work ethics. Working hard was an honorable way of life for the people in my community. Most of the people in the community were poor. We did not openly talk about our love for each other, but we showed it (we were not perfect). I have memories of my Mother taking an RC Cola and dividing it among my siblings. We were taught to share.

Education was extremely important in the African American community. My parents did not graduate from high school. However, they were committed to making sure that their children graduated. We had chores to do, but homework came first. My parents were not able to assist me with my homework. The hierarchy system was practiced in my family. It was understood that the older child would assist the younger child. I felt special because I was able to attend kindergarten before going to school. My parents had to pay for me to attend a privately owned kindergarten (there was no Head Start to attend at that time).

—*Willie Ruth McDonald Sanders*

My name is Tommy Hall Jr. I am recording this message for the Class of 1968. My two brothers, Marvin and James, and I were brought up in the projects, Robertson Place. We also had a sister, Diane.

—*Tommy Hall Jr.*

36

I am Patricia Berry Blake, the fourth of six children born to John and Audrey Berry, of Hattiesburg, Mississippi. Although I have made Hattiesburg home, I was born in Brookhaven, Mississippi.

One of the most pivotal memories of my childhood was my family's transition to the Hattiesburg community. In 1967, my Father was offered a job as assistant principal at Rowan High School. This move was both an exciting and scary time, since it took place during my senior year in high school. As anyone can imagine, it was hard to leave a place where I knew everyone. While the transition was best for our family, for me, building new connections in the community and in school where relationships had already been formed was challenging. At the time, my three older siblings (Mary Alice, Jean, and Bobby), had already transitioned out of the house to attend college. And the nine-year difference between my younger siblings (Daryl and Cheryl) left me feeling my life had been turned upside down.

—*Patricia Berry Blake*

Thelma Bacchus grew up at 615 McComb Street in East Jerusalem Quarters, the village, as an only child to J. B. and Marie Bacchus. Growing up in a Christian home, my parents demonstrated hard work, ethics, and unconditional love for family and friends. East Jerusalem Baptist Church was my home base where I participated in the choir, Sunday School, BTU [Baptist Training Union], and Vacation Bible School. My parents had the most influence in my life because they demonstrated the virtue of being kingdom-minded. God gives to you to share with others and you are abundantly blessed.

—*Thelma Marie Bacchus*

I, Mildred Alice Miller Short, was born Mildred Alice Miller on November 24, 1950, to Willie B. and John Wesley Miller Jr. in Hattiesburg, Mississippi. I am one of three children in my family including a twin brother, Melvin Allen Miller, and one older sister named Lorma Reda Miller. When we were three months old, my brother and I went to live with our grandparents in rural Claiborne County. Our grandparents nicknamed us Little Bit and Big Boy by which we still answer to now. At the age of four, we returned to Hattiesburg, Mississippi, and lived on Memphis Street, which is located on the east side of the city.

—Mildred Alice Miller Short

Fellow classmates, it has been over fifty years since our high school graduation!

The first information I would like to share is that I am one of five children—four girls and one boy (who was the youngest in the family). I was raised primarily by my great-Grandmother, Mrs. Elsie Kelly, affectionately known as Mamma, even though my Mother was ever-present in my life. Mamma was the head of the household, which included my great-grandfather, Rev. J. L. Kelly. I was also blessed to have another sister, Katherine "Bonnie" Berry. We were actually in the same grade, same homeroom, and graduated together in the Class of 1968. Born in the same month, even, only a few days apart.

I would like to spend a little time with you on my siblings. Of the five of us, my oldest sister, Beverly, and Dorothy Annette were the most humble. They didn't talk back and usually did what they were told. I can't begin to say that about the other three—me, Jeanette, and Joe Curtis. I stayed in trouble about getting the last word in. No matter how much of a warning I was given, I wouldn't give up. Beverly would tell me to "just be quiet," but it was only after I was "beat down" would I close my mouth. Eventually, I was able to fall in line—only getting off track every now and then.

—Patricia Ann Griffin

I was born December 1, 1950, in Hattiesburg to Hayes and Annie Boles. I was born and delivered in my home. The reason I was delivered at home is because at the time I was born, no Blacks were allowed in the hospitals in my hometown. Miss Vassie Patton, a midwife in my hometown, delivered me. I didn't find out the reason why I wasn't delivered in a hospital until later.

I grew up in a large family along with my three sisters and three brothers with my parents and Grandmother. I also had three cousins who lived with us in a three-bedroom house. Growing up with a large family suited me just fine. There was a lot of love in that house. My Father worked at Hercules while my Mother worked as a maid. My Grandmother sometimes worked where she ironed clothes for other people to make a living. My two male cousins worked at the Creosote Plant.

I remember growing up where there was always joy and laughter in that house. I lived on Barry Street, which was known as the 16th section part of town.

I really enjoyed myself growing up. Even though segregation was prevalent during my childhood, I was never made to think that I was a second-class individual. My Grandmother made sure of that. I remember she would always tell me that "no one on this earth is no better than you." I took that to heart, and I guess that's why I'm the person I am today. Even though my parents taught me things about life, it was my Grandmother who molded me. I loved that lady with all my heart.

—*Hayes Boles, Jr.*

My name is Vernette Wallis Andry, and I am the third child of ten born to Stafford and Dorothy Wallis at the hands of a midwife. I entered this world in August of 1950, and grew up on Highway 49 until I was twelve years old. During those years, I would go back and forth from Highway 49 to Houma, Louisiana, where my parents lived. I learned good values and morals at an early age because I attended Priest Creek and Mars Hill Churches with my Grandmother. There I received the foundation I stand on today, which is a relationship with Jesus Christ. When my siblings visited Highway 49, we were content with grass dolls and wooden horses made from broomsticks. We played jump rope, hide and seek, and marbles We once had a birthday party and the meal was black-eyed peas and root beer. Life was easy and simple, and we were content children. I had no idea what racism was and thought it was normal to enter Mr. Royce's house through the back door to clean up. My Grandmother, named Mama Dellie, would make most of my clothes but bought special outfits from a White man that drove around in a car. Discipline was rare, but when necessary, it was a peach tree switch with an explanation why. Lying would always bring the switch, and there was no knowledge of child abuse.

On May Avenue, I lived directly across the street from Mr. Clarence and Mrs. Lucy Mae Williams. Their son Randall Louis and I went to Rowan together and became lifelong friends. We enjoyed our own neighborhood, which was predominantly African American families.

My best friend was Mattie Hudnall, and we loved the football games and walking from her house to mine. Her dad impressed me by raising a really nice daughter alone. My oldest sister, Vera Wallis, impressed me because after she graduated high school, she went to college. I never had a summer job because I had six siblings to help my Mother with.

—*Vernette Wallis Andry*

My full name is Doris McNeill, but everyone calls me Dot T. I lived in the area of town called the Park. I am the second child of Ida Lee McNeil and the twelfth child of Floyd Jenkins. I remember when I was about three years old, my Mother gave us away to live with other family members. My sister Hazeline Smith lived with Mrs. Florence Davis. My sister Sandra McNeil Kemper went to live with Mrs. Pearl Bolton until they passed. My Father came from Laurel, Mississippi, for me to live with him and his family in Hattiesburg. After he passed, I went to live with my cousin. My siblings and I were passed around from house to house. I lived with Beatrice Bryant. I called her Big Mama. My sister Fredna Jenkins Hinkle taught me how to sew and do hair. It was a big part of my early years of life. Fredna made me want to always look good and dress well. What I learned from her helped me to dress my children.

—*Doris McNeill Collins*

I was born in June of 1950 in the community of Palmers Crossing delivered by a midwife not because my dad was unable to pay, but simply because of our skin color.

—*Claudia Polk Bivins*

My name is Hattie Ruth Williams Knight, and I am from the area of Hattiesburg known as the Mobile Street and East 6th Street area.

—*Hattie R. Williams Knight*

I am Barbara Thomas Ross, born in April of 1949, in Hattiesburg, Mississippi. My parents were the late Hezekiah and Annie Rose Thomas. I am the oldest of five siblings— the late Ray Charles, the late Lawrence Earl, Beverly Ann, and Robert Karl Thomas. We lived just off the great Mobile Street, down the street from Eureka School on East 6th Street. This is where I enjoyed my childhood years.

—*Barbara A. Thomas Ross*

My name is Kathryn (Bouie) Boyd, oldest of ten siblings. In the Bouie family, there was always something to do. Whether it was doing chores around the house or TV time, we always had fun.

—*Kathryn Bouie Boyd*

 My name is Juanita Mayes Walker also known as Tot. My Dad wanted to name me *Tockashema,* but my Mom said no. Whew! My nickname became *Tock,* and later it was transformed into *Tot* by my friends, but my family still calls me Tock. I was born in Hattiesburg, Mississippi, in 1950. I am the third child of six born to Annie and Trueheart Mayes (Herbert, Jonathan, Donnie, Beverly, and Ricky).

I spent my early years in the Kelly Settlement community attending Mary Magdalene Baptist Church. I was baptized in Vernon Dahmer's pond. Everything happened at the church—Sunday School, Baptist Training Union (BTU), Singing Union, Vacation Bible School, and all other meetings. I was there. When you live in the country, there's not too much else to do, but on some Sunday evenings, we did go swimming, play baseball, and have picnics at the old airport, which is now the Hub City Raceway.

—*Juanita Mayes Walker*

I am Rose Mary Montgomery Harrell, the fifth child of nine children.

—*Rose Mary Montgomery Harrell*

This is our celebration of years of growing up in Mississippi. I can only speak for myself as a child raised by my Mother and Grandmother after my Father's death. My sisters and I did not have a lot of material things, but we had what was needed—food, shelter, and love from our parents, teachers, neighborhood, church family, and friends. We thought we were the poorest family on our side of town, not realizing that we were very rich in spirit, and that mattered the most.

—*Margaret Hill Burger*

The story and special events of my life start on Willis Avenue in Hattiesburg, Mississippi. Things in life have a way of happening simultaneously like growing up as a child and going off to school. In the wake of my life reality, it was not just going to school, but also leaving school for work and coming home late at night to study and getting some rest. Then, it was a start of a new day.

—*James Chatman*

My name is Carolyn Ann Hall Abrams. I am a product of the Hattiesburg Public School System. I attended Eureka Elementary School, W. H. Jones Junior High School, and I graduated from Rowan High School in 1968. The school system was a lifeline for me. It was "my home away from home." My teachers, principals, and fellow students were family to me. They provided stability as I fought to walk steady on the path of life laid out for me. Both school and church nurtured me.

—*Carolyn Hall Abrams*

CHAPTER 2

Shining Stars:
A Preview of Our School Years

Teachers remind me of stars in the sky on a clear night. They give light, direction, and hope. All teachers impacted  our lives in one way or another. There were those who never taught us, but set examples for us to model after, and we admired them from afar. Without God and teachers, some students would have lost their way because there was no home foundation. Many students would not have eaten had it not been for the school cafeteria. Teachers were astute knowing which students needed that extra care, often using some of their own resources to help out.

Teachers who taught us were equipped with the gift of seeing potential in us. They nurtured us and provided the tools necessary for us to be the best we could be. All of us can look back and reflect on those teachers who went the extra mile. We are the sum total of all of their efforts.

Teachers didn't just show up for a paycheck. With their hard work and dedication, we saw through them a whole new world that was different from our own. We saw possibilities and hope that said "yes, we can."

The schools that I attended were Eureka Elementary School W.H. Jones Elementary and Junior High School and L.J. Rowan High School. There were teachers at each school who illuminated my path, and I had experiences that impacted me to this day. These teachers were my "shining stars."

To whom much is given, much is required. I am the sum total of every teacher who crossed my path, either directly or indirectly. There are many teachers who never taught me, but impacted my life. I could see in them the results of hard work and high standards. Growing up in the 60s with less opportunities for Blacks, teachers were revered. They gave us hope for a better life beyond our world or environment. By example, they showed us that we could too. It is very important how we live and the standards we set. Young lives are impressionable.

Just the other day, it was brought to my attention that my great nephew was struggling in two of his college classes. I immediately contacted him to find out about his situation. After listening to him, I gave encouragement, instruction, and guidance. My mind went back to those teachers who did the same for me. The journey continues. We are here on earth to use our talents and abilities to pour into the lives of others and make this world a better place. To God be the glory!

—Beverly Harris Abrams

CHAPTER 3

Our Early School Years

I grew up in the seven hundred block of East 7th Street, where everybody chastised everyone's children. I attended Eureka High School, which was about five blocks from our house. There was an elementary school in the next block named Lamar Elementary, formerly known as Fourth Ward, where White kids attended. We were not allowed to, so we had to walk about five blocks to Eureka. There was a sidewalk by the school, but if the kids were out for recess, we had to walk in the street.

—*Stella Brooks Clark*

At the corner of 7th and Bouie Streets, you would find a neighborhood school that we Negro children never set foot in. This school had electricity, water, gas, telephones, teachers, books, and a good playground. All we could do was go past it on our way to Eureka School. This school was just around the corner from my house. I would stand on the concrete sidewalk, the only one in the community, next to the school and look around a Negro neighborhood with a white-only school.

—*Ella Sue Jackson*

I remember having to walk to the bus stop on Mobile Street (corner of Alma Hall's parents' funeral home) to catch the bus to Rowan. At that time, there were only White bus drivers. We called our bus driver Roy Rogers, and sometimes the kids would give him a rough time. One of the reasons we called him Roy Rogers is how he would drive the bus. Sometimes he would go fast and stop all of a sudden like he was rocking or riding a horse.

—*Mildred Johnson Watts*

Mama lived not even a block from Eaton School, but my sisters had to go to a school that was six blocks away, which was Grace Love.

—*Eva Lenyoun Crosby*

I began school at DePriest School in Palmers' Crossing in 1956. In the 5th grade, I moved to Earl Travillion Attendance Center. After fifth grade, I transferred to Mary Bethune Elementary School. That was the beginning of my association with the Class of 1968. They became my friends, and a vital part of my life.

—*Claudia Polk Bivins*

Pre-Primer/Primer/Kindergarten

My siblings and I all attended Eureka Elementary School. I had Miss Mary Crawford (Primer), Mrs. Hardy, Mrs. Heard, Mrs. Henry, Mr. Pugh, and Mrs. Patrick. All these teachers taught us how to be well educated and how to conduct ourselves. We were taught to have morals and the importance of knowing how smart you are and how far your education would take you. I am so grateful to have had these teachers for my educational foundation.

—*Barbara Thomas Ross*

I started school in the pre-primer and the primer at the East 6th St. Community Center. I also had two cousins to start with me: Jason Parker and Samuel Showers. Mrs. Juanita Johnson was my first beautiful teacher. Most of the teachers lived close to us, and we had a good relationship with our teachers.

—*Benida Parker Johnson*

I started school in Hattiesburg in 1956 at 16th Section Elementary School (the name changed to Mary Bethune). I could have gone to school the year before (because of my birthday). I suffered a broken leg just before school started in 1955 and had to wear a cast. There was no way for me to get to school daily. My parents made me sit out the entire year. That turned out to be a blessing—I would not have been a part of the great Class of 1968. At that time, there was primer, first grade, second grade, etc. They ended primer; I went from primer to second grade.

My primer teacher was Mrs. Davis. She was a great teacher. From her, I learned that it was not okay to talk during class. On one occasion, Randall Williams and I were talking while she was teaching. She sneaked behind us and started pinching both of us. As she pinched us, she said, "Randall Williams and Willie Sanders, you will not talk in class anymore. Do you two understand me?" She pinched us for at least a minute. That would be considered battery today.

—*Willie Sanders*

In September 1955, I started school at Eureka Elementary/High School. My brother, Whitney, and I had to walk about five blocks to school. Sometimes we had a ride if it rained really bad. I started in the primer class and I really can't remember too much about that. My teacher was Miss Brown.

—*Carolyn Atkins*

In 1955, my Father remarried. My stepmother, Oristean Edison, was from Collins, Mississippi. We moved out of my grandmother's house on Manning Avenue because Daddy decided to tear the old green house down and build a new one. We moved to 204 Ruby Avenue while the house on Manning was being built and stayed there for a few years because my Dad built the new house "out of his pocket," meaning, he didn't get a mortgage. He was a professional photographer and had a good business, but building a house out of your pocket meant he paid cash for the labor and materials, so it took time. He and my stepmother worked hard and made a decent living. We lived a few blocks from Bethune at the corner of Ruby Avenue and Charles Street.

—*Don Denard*

When I attended elementary school at Eureka, it was still a high school. Mr. C. E. Roy was principal at that time and Mr. Patrick was the principal later as an elementary school. Since Eureka was overcrowded, we had to attend school at the E. 6th Street Community Center. My primer-grade teacher was Mrs. Juanita Johnson who also lived on East 7th Street across the street from my grandparents. She was the nicest teacher and very soft-spoken. She, like the rest of my teachers, knew my family because of my oldest sister, Martha Nell, who was four years ahead of me in school.

—*Mildred Johnson Watts*

My schooling began at Baker's Preschool under Mrs. Constance Baker. I remember singing "I Saw Mommy Kissing Santa Claus" on the Christmas program one year with me being dressed in pajamas and sitting on some steps. When Mrs. Baker shifted to teach in the public schools, I was sent to Happyland Kindergarten under Mrs. Mae Willie Mays. Her assistant was Mrs. Annette Woullard, the daughter-in-law of my pastor, Reverend R. W. Woullard Sr. Sometimes at night when my Mother had to travel to other churches with the church choir, Mrs. Woullard would babysit me. I had many babysitters in our neighborhood, and they all took real good care of me. Happyland was located on property adjacent to Sweet Pilgrim Baptist Church where Mrs. Mayes' husband, Rev. J. H. Mayes was the pastor.

My Daddy persuaded my Mother to open her own daycare in about 1955, which she named Townsend's Kiddy Nook. By four years old, I could read and write. That summer, I was sent to summer school held in Mrs. Lillie Burney's garage. Mrs. Burney was the principal at 16th Section (later renamed Mary Bethune Elementary School) and was a gifted teacher who instilled in me the love for learning. She and her husband, Mr. Burney, taught several of us our fundamentals, and there I mastered first-grade work. When school began in the fall, I skipped first grade and started second grade in Mrs. Teresa McGowen's room at Mary Bethune Elementary. Mrs. McGowen was a good teacher and fostered a love of learning in me that has lasted all my life.

—*Doris Townsend Gaines*

We attended Mrs. Mattie Robertson's kindergarten with Betty Bournes, Frances Davidson, Cherylyn Clark, and a few other classmates. After leaving kindergarten, I went to Eureka Elementary and Junior High School. Our first year was spent at the East 6th Street Community Center because there was not enough room for the primary classes to be held at Eureka.

—*Mildred Miller Short*

I was a big baby, all eleven pounds. All the adults would say how cute and fat I was. Children at Mrs. Mattie Robertson's Kindergarten did not think being fat was cute. Mrs. Mattie was a Black businesswoman. She and Mrs. Baker had a huge impact in the Black community. Black mothers had a place where they knew their children would be safe. Mrs. Robertson was a tall brown-skinned woman. She looked a little like Tyler Perry's Madea. Her house was her place of business. The living room was for the infants; the next room, toddlers. Outside, I saw children.

I would go to school with Willie Earl "Getway" White. The other children asked if he was my brother. Before I could answer, "He must be your brother. You are just as fat as him!"

"Do not mess with her. She is big Willie Earl's sister. They will mash you like a pancake."

"Hit her and run."

"She is too fat. She will not be able to catch you."

The children at the kindergarten were angels next to the kids at school.

Willie Earl White was a grade ahead of me at Eureka School. He took all the jokes about us being fat on the playground. In chapel, the teacher would have him say Humpty Dumpty. In the lunchroom, it was the same old question: "Are you Willie Earl's sister?"

"That's one of Mablen's big fat children."

Willie Earl and Shirley White's mother was named Mablen. In the fourth grade, Willie Earl went to W. H. Jones School. I had to face the music by myself. It was not always easy. I wanted to scream at the children because I was weak, lonely, and barely making it. Willie Earl was not there to protect me. He would never let them know that their words hurt us!

—*Ella Sue Jackson*

My earliest school memory was attending Miss Moore's Kindergarten on Deason Avenue.

—*Ethelyn Fairley Reid*

When I was five years old, I attended Happyland Kindergarten where I met my best friend for life. His name is Willie Darryl Brown, and to this day, he's still my best friend. We had some good times at Happyland and learned a lot.

—*Hayes Boles*

I entered primer with some skills (knowing how to count at least to one hundred, the alphabet, how to hop on one foot, how to sit in a chair for longer than ten minutes, and how to interact with other students).

I lived in the Newman Quarters. They were not called neighborhoods back in my day. There was a friendly rivalry among the "quarters." For example, Newman Quarters, East Jerusalem, Over Cross Town, Mobile Street, etc. I reflect on those memories with fondness. We did not have a bus in the Newman Quarters when I first entered school. I had to walk to and from school (no parents to pick you up in a car). Children had to learn how to cross the street, to look out for the train, and to obey older children. The school that I attended was called Third Ward (later changed to Grace Love Elementary School). My siblings and I were like the Pony Express mail delivery. We went to school rain, shine, sleet, or snow. We walked in groups so that we did not feel isolated. I recalled an occasional racial slur (but that was rare). I have a vivid memory of a large dog that would give us trouble.

When we arrived at school, we did not have breakfast waiting for us like the children today. If you did not eat at home, you had to wait to eat your lunch if you brought one from home.

To eat in the cafeteria or have milk with your lunch, you had to have money.

—*Willie Ruth McDonald Sanders*

Happy Land Kindergarten—Mrs. Mae Willie Mayes and Mrs. Annette Woullard gave me the best foundation for a good education that anyone could ever hope for. I still know every nursery rhyme I learned. I was valedictorian of my graduating class. I don't know what happened. LOL! I never could touch my toes without bending my knees, even at four years old. Mrs. Mayes had just had a concrete porch constructed and painted dark green. With some of the sand that was left at the site, I made sand pies on her new porch. I got the beat down of my young life.

—*Randall Williams*

I began school at Mary Bethune Elementary School. Because I was taught the basics at home, I skipped kindergarten.

—*Rose Mary Montgomery Harrell*

My first introduction to formal education was through various home-based kindergartens: Woullard, Baker, and I graduated from Owens.

—*Thelma Bacchus*

I attended Mattie Robertson's Kindergarten and then Kiddy Haven Kindergarten, which was run by the Owens Family. I attended 16th Section where I began school in the primer.

—*Tommy Hall Jr.*

As a young child, I couldn't wait to go to school. A lot had gone down in my family by the time I was two, including my parents' divorce and my Dad, sister, and me moving to my paternal Grandmother Alma's large green house on the South side of town. The address was 509 Manning Avenue, and it was located at the corner with Franklin Street. I remember much from the ages two to five, like taking a bath outside in a number 3 tub and this amazing one-armed ice man, whose name I don't know, coming through the neighborhood delivering ice for the pre-refrigerator iceboxes that people had in their homes. "You want a half a block or a whole block?" I also remember my grandmother being the first one in her neighborhood to get a television. It was a Philco, and neighbors would come over to watch shows like *Dragnet*. That ended when she got upset that some of the men would fall asleep and start snoring. The strongest memories of my young years, however, were involved with school, especially going to kindergarten. I spent a lot of time on the north side at the studio on East

6th Street and was therefore in a good place to be able to maintain my Eureka vigil. Eureka was a bustling place two times each day, at the start and end of school. Add to that the spectacle that was the bustling Black business district of Mobile Street, and you can see how a Black child's eyes and ears were filled with excitement and wonder all the time. There was also the usual smell of good food coming from places like Fat's Kitchen. Next thing I knew, I was old enough to go to Mrs. Mattie Robertson's kindergarten on New Orleans Street.

Now, that place was everything I had wanted in school. And I went to kindergarten every day *in style*—by taxi! Mr. Thomas Williams and Mr. Harvey Stewart would make the rounds picking up children on the south side of town and in the Quarters to take us to and from kindergarten every day. That alone was an adventure as we learned where the Mattie Robertson children on our side of town lived and were soon able to learn the route. I can remember Mr. Williams blowing his horn in front of my grandmother Alma's house and her calling out to him "just a minute" as she finished tying my shoes while I sat on the piano stool in the middle hallway of her house. I'd run out to the car with my lunch in my hands, greet my friends, take my seat for the ride to pick up other children, and then head across town.

Once at school, the first thing we did was to place our brown paper bag lunches on the table set aside for that, take our coats off if it was cold, and go into the classroom. Mrs. Robertson had this big house that served as the kindergarten. She would write lessons on the blackboard that we had to copy down on paper, and for me, this was *school.* I loved that as much as I loved playing with bricks at recess, pushing them along through the deep sand that she had all over the backyard. We would make streets, roads, and had a special technique for making hills in the sand roads. Most of the girls would stay inside during recess and play with sand that was in a large sandbox that sat a foot off the floor. They would stand on the floor and reach over into the elevated sandbox to play different sand games they made up, sometimes using empty drink bottles. But the boys were outside romping in the sand, even under the house.

Of course, Mrs. Robertson didn't play. Anyone not doing their lesson—let's just say there would be incoming fire! The house was just a few houses off 7th Street. One day, she let us know she was going to walk up to the store on 7th and that we should continue writing what she had put on the board. I finished my work and started looking at the world out the front window as I always did. I saw this boy across the street riding in his red pedal car on the sidewalk. I felt sad for that boy not being at school, but on the other hand, he sure was having fun riding that car up and down the sidewalk. And he had a red toy tractor that he would ride as well. I would see him from time to time and always wanted one of those pedal cars. When Mrs. Robertson came back from the store, she was not happy. Children had been "cuttin' up," and some didn't have their work done. Incoming!

One of my best memories at Mattie Robertson Kindergarten was the day we had a substitute teacher. That day, the bag lunches got all mixed up, and children were given lunch bags that were not theirs. Some children were upset. I had been given the wrong lunch bag, but when I looked in it, I saw something special. It had the customary bologna sandwich, but I noticed that the light bread was a bit greasy because the bologna had been cooked! Because my bologna was never cooked, I was happy with the mistake. I decided to eat the sandwich quickly, and Lawd, that was the best sandwich I had ever eaten in my life. It had the right amount of mayonnaise, and the bologna had that scorched spot in the middle, which meant it had buckled in the skillet while frying, had been split with a knife and turned over to cook the other side. I was so surprised at my good fortune that I ate quickly while some children were crying. I felt guilty, but I was not in charge.

At some point during these years, I was playing outside in front of my dad's studio and noticed a child playing across the street on the sidewalk beside Hall & Collins Funeral Home. The studio was in the Masonic Building on the corner of 6th Street and Mobile. The front of the Masonic Building faced Mobile Street, but Dad's studio faced 6th Street. Hall & Collins was on the opposite corner of 6th and Mobile facing Mobile Street. This little person was playing on the sidewalk on the Sixth Street side where I was, so I could see her very clearly. I couldn't have been more than four at the time, but I remember thinking that she was the most beautiful creature I had ever seen in my life. Her name was Alma Jean Hall, and we would become childhood friends. I don't remember Jean being at Mattie Robertson Kindergarten, but I imagine she attended. We would play together sometimes, and I recall feeling so sorry for her because they lived in a large apartment on the second floor of the funeral home. But she didn't seem afraid at all.

My time at Mattie Robertson's ended suddenly one day when we were playing inside, and my good friend Billy Joe Lang tossed and hit me in the forehead with a toy water pistol. It hurt bad and left a mark, so my Dad decided that evening to take me out of Mattie Robertson's. I was crushed, but he and my Grandmother thought things had gotten out of control and made the change to Mrs. Charlene Owens' Kindergarten on the South side of town where we lived. No more taxicab rides to school. My new school was on Rosa Avenue, only four blocks from where we lived on Manning Avenue. I don't remember how I got to school every day.

Mrs. Owens' was a wonderful place also and was filled with singing. This is where I first recall call and response singing, "No, you can't. Yes, I can." And we sang in rounds, where usually three or more groups of kids would sing a song, such as "Row, Row, Row Your Boat," in a staggered pattern. It was like controlled chaos and was fun. One of my earliest friends there was Lawrence Curb. We were five then and were learning a lot. One thing I learned from Curb one day had to do with traffic lights. Mrs. Owens was teaching us what the different-colored lights mean. She wanted to be sure we understood that red means stop and green means go. After saying this to us, she paused as if to let it sink in. That's when Curb spoke up, saying, "Miss Owens, the yellow light means be 'careful.'" She said, "That's right, Larry." I thought, *This boy is smart. He's helping the teacher!*

The time came for our school closing program when we were graduating from kindergarten. This was huge for us. We practiced a lot, and the biggest thrill of all was when we went to practice at Mary McLeod Bethune Elementary, where our program would be held. I was about to bust wide open with excitement because I knew about Bethune and so looked forward to going to "big school." Our main song was 'Sixteen Tons," a song about coal mining by Tennessee Ernie Ford. I still remember the lyrics and the props we used, which included little sand buckets and shovels. "I was born one morning when the sun didn't shine. I picked up my shovel, and I walked to the mine." The program was held on the stage in the old building at Bethune because the new building with the cafetorium and new classrooms had not yet been built.

—Don Denard

I lived near Mobile Street, on Atlanta Street, in the Evergreen. I first attended Mrs. Mattie Robertson's Kindergarten and then Eureka Elementary. Mrs. Willie B. Miller taught primer.

—Betty Bournes Hill

Elementary School Years

I started first grade at Eureka, after finishing at the 6th Street Community Center. It was very exciting to attend a big school two stories high. My grandmother would sit us down on her back porch steps and teach us to read from the Godchaux sugar package, and we could read when we started school. My grandmother would bring us lunch, and sometimes, I would bring a bologna sandwich to school and put it under my desk. The aroma would thrill you for hours before lunch. It does not smell like that now. (Laugh.)

—*Benida Parker Johnson*

My second-grade teacher was Mrs. Preston. She was a nice teacher. I remember winning a Math-Bee contest. Patricia Griffin, Mattie Hudnall, Margaret Hill, Don Denard, Lawrence Curb, and a girl who left and went to Washington, DC (Elizabeth Jones), were some of the people in that class. I also remember the straight, neat rows.

My third-grade teacher was Mrs. Williams. I believe she lived near Mobile Street. Don Denard and I were in her class. I believe we were her favorite students. She was kind to all her students, and I bet that all her students felt that they were very special—and of course, her favorite. She was a very good teacher, and we learned a lot.

There were a lot of fourth-grade students that year. To our joy and happiness, Mrs. Williams was our teacher again. That only lasted three to four months. Another teacher was hired; some of us had to go to the new teacher's class. I do remember her name. Because she was not a good teacher (in my humble opinion), I will not mention her name. My problem was that I wanted to be in Mrs. Williams' class, and not hers. That summer, a good friend of mine (Eugene Edwards) drowned. I often think about him and about the life he might have had. I participated in an operetta that year. Doris Townsend had the major role of a gypsy girl. Doris danced and sang several songs.

My fifth-grade teacher was Miss Simms. She was tall, strict, and authoritative. She had been in the military. Everything about her was perfect: her clothes, her nails, her hair, her speech, etc. She gave me a low mark in handwriting. I was angry about that. If you were to see my handwriting or penmanship today, you would agree that she was correct in her assessment.

My sixth-grade teacher was Mrs. Lee. Mrs. Inez Lee was my neighbor. She was an excellent teacher. However, when she wore red, watch out! I learned from Mrs. Lee that students *must* and *better* do their homework. She gave us an assignment to read chapter 5 in our history book. She began to ask us questions (individually). If you did not answer her question(s) correctly, she placed you in what was called the electric chair. She whipped you with a strap. She went in alphabetical order. She had whipped all the students from *A* to *R*. I had a chance to read some of the chapter. She asked me a question, and I answered it satisfactorily. She asked me another question—my answer was half right. She told me that I probably had not read the chapter. She asked me a question from the end of the chapter. I was clueless. She told me to sit down in that chair. She tore me up. After that experience from her class, I learned that it was imperative to do your homework (I did my homework from that day forward through graduate school). We also went on a field trip to Lincoln Beach in New Orleans that year.

—*Willie Sanders*

In first grade, my teacher was Mrs. Mattie Hardy, who taught all my sisters and brothers except one. I had five brother and six sisters, so that meant she knew more about my family than I wanted her to know.

In second grade, Miss (Skinny) Love was my teacher. She was really nice. She lived across the street from the school

In third grade, Miss (Bow-legged) Love was my teacher. She was really mean (that's what we all said at that time!). When we went out for recess, she would stand in the hall and not let us come back in to get water from the fountain. She stood in the hall with a "black fan belt" to hit you if you came back in before time.

Mrs. Ruby Henry was the fourth-grade teacher. She was a workhorse; Not only in the classroom but at her house. She lived on 5th Street around the corner from Mrs. Sandifer. After school, she would have a few of us go home with her to clean her house. I didn't mind because she always had something for us when we finished. I don't remember staying too long at her house after school.

Fifth grade was Mrs. Fielder. She was a very neat lady and she dressed nice every day. I remember we had to weigh in this class. I was ashamed because I was a fat child, and I always got mean comments from my fellow classmates. I think I weighed more than the other kids!

In sixth grade, Mrs. Johnson was my teacher. I can still see the "Siamese twins" that came to Hattiesburg every year for people to see. Mrs. Johnson would let us look out of the window to watch them go in and out of the house they lived in across the street from Eureka School. To tell the truth, I was afraid of them. I felt so sorry for them.

Mrs. Johnson loved to sing and dance. In our end-of-school program, all had to have an overnight bag because we had to perform the "sentimental journey" act.

My memories at Eureka were very limited. It's been so long ago. I know every May 1 was May Day. That's when we plaited the May pole and had a fun day.

—*Carolyn Atkins*

Starting school at Eureka was a bit frightening and exciting at the same time. From primary, first to sixth grade—all our teachers would tell us how important it was to stay in school and to get our education. I do, however, remember some students quit.

One memory I have attending Eureka is about stage fright. Our janitor, Mr. Mathews, was retiring and we were having a program to honor him. Janice Walton was asked to sing a song, "My Buddy." Well, something happened and she couldn't sing, so I was selected to replace her. Why? I didn't then and still don't now have a singing voice, but there I was. In rehearsal, Mrs. Juanita Johnson (teacher and school pianist) said I sounded good. On the day of the program, I don't know if anyone could hear me. I did, however, enjoy being a majorette (blue and gold), and our Thanksgiving Day parades.

—*Kathryn Bouie Boyd*

A few elementary teachers that I'll never forget were Mrs. Johnson (nice/sweet), Mrs. Crawford (always liked to use her trap/smoke/eat sauerkraut), and Mrs. Patrick. These teachers I remember all made such an impression in their own way. However, Mrs. Patrick was one of the persons that I'll never forget. She was firm, stern, and no-nonsense in and outside the classroom. Mrs. Patrick was so firm I definitely learned something about being disciplined and focused at school from her. I remember one time my sister "Skiter" *thought* she was playing "hooky" from school. Somehow my Mother found out and called the school. She talked to Mrs. Patrick regarding her absence from school without permission and where she may be. Mrs. Patrick *left* the school during the day, went down in "the Gholah," and found her. She whipped her and brought her back to school for the remainder of the day. After school Mrs. Patrick came to our house to talk with my Mother to tell her what happened and where she found my sister (I remember Mrs. Patrick sitting in a chair in our living room chewing gum as she talked; of course I was peeping / eavesdropping / not in the room). As a result, my sister got another whipping by our mom. Well, after witnessing the results of Mrs. Patrick's visit with my Mother up close and firsthand after that incident, she was definitely one of my most favorite teachers. I wasn't messing with her!

—*Mildred Johnson Watts*

My early teachers were caring and strong. They expected you to do your best at all times. They really demanded it or your mother was going to hear about it.

You knew what that meant. My Dad was a gentleman. He was the breadwinner.

We had good times at Grace Love School. Days like May Day, doing the May Pole, Halloween Fun Night, and don't forget Thanksgiving Day… Big day, parade, and big game day at Rowan.

—*Dianne Hart Breland*

My early years of elementary school were spent at Eureka. I mostly spent those days looking out the window at Ronnie Lindsay, because he was always well dressed and late for school.

—*Doris McNeill Collins*

By third grade, it was in my bones. Mrs. Marjorie Clark was my teacher. She was a very kind and patient instructor and had a daughter in my class, Cherylyn. Fourth grade was Mrs. Nareatha Naylor. I knew her before because she was a daughter of my pastor, Rev. R. W. Woullard Sr. Fifth grade brought a new teacher, Mrs. Dawson. I remember that she was young and fresh out of college, but a very good teacher too. Sixth grade was Mrs. Inez Lee. Mrs. Lee was a no-nonsense teacher who made us strive for the best.

I believe in third grade was when Patricia Griffin became my best friend. Later, Johnnie Bea Slay joined the group, and finally, at some point, we allowed Don Denard into our inner circle. We were and are still very good friends. Johnnie Bea Slay passed away in 2009, but remains in our hearts.

May Day was celebrated every year at Bethune Elementary School. It was a much-anticipated event. We'd practice plaiting the Maypole for weeks prior to the actual event. Everyone knew what his or her responsibilities were well in advance and usually it was the same every year. The girls wore pastel blouses and/or skirts; of course, that was before girls were allowed to wear pants at school. There was an in-and-out rhythm to the plaiting that resulted in the maypole looking woven from top to bottom. Invariably, someone would get confused on the actual day, even with all the smooth practices, and the maypole would have an imperfect weave somewhere. The day was similar to a Field Day with the Hokey Pokey, the Bunny Hop, and other dances going on at the same time.

At the end of each school year, we performed in an operetta. It was a mini-musical of sorts and the event was held in the cafetorium. One in particular I remember was *Jack and The Beanstalk*. In it, I was Gypsy Ann, a performer at a fair. I sang, "I am the famous Gypsy Ann; your fortune I can tell. I read your fortune in the stars and in your eyes as well." I was dressed in a neighbor's long skirt, a ruffled white blouse, and hoop earrings with a scarf tied backward around my head.

—*Doris Townsend Gaines*

Best teachers? In elementary school (Grace Love), my favorite teacher was Mrs. Lizzie Jackson. She was a teacher who emphasized my academics, with no inference of my family's socioeconomic status. I make note of this because I witnessed instances where some teachers were extremely critical and made inappropriate statements to students.

—*Ethelyn Fairley Reid*

I guess third grade started to shape my trust and opinions of human beings. In elementary school, we had school closing programs and there were always leading roles. I was always competitive as far as academics and sports. There were three boys who competed in my class for top honors and attention: Louis Payton, Samuel Hundly, and myself. The play was *Rink-Tom-Diddle-Diddle-Dee.* Louis Peyton got the leading male role, and Beverly Harris, the leading female role. I was disappointed, but I couldn't afford the costume anyway. When Louis Payton's folks told him they couldn't afford the costume, the role was up for grabs again. Samuel Hundly told Mrs. Sue Route, our teacher, that I had talked Payton out of playing the part and she believed him. She gave the part to Hundly. It was at that young age I started to distrust people. Hundly didn't tell the truth, and I remember it to this day.

—Grady Gaines

At six years old, I attended Mary Bethune Elementary where Mrs. Davis was my first-grade teacher. My first day at elementary school was very scary. I cried for my Mother all day. Soon I got over it. It was there that I met my next best friend. His name is Don Denard, and boy, did we have fun. We are still friends today.

—Hayes Boles Jr.

I attended Bay Springs School in the Kelly Settlement community. I had the same teacher, Mrs. Tate, first and second grade. She and Mrs. Earl were the only two teachers in the elementary department. I loved school, especially the school closing programs. My parents were very supportive, and I was kind of smart then. I can still smell the aroma of the rolls coming from the cafeteria.

—Juanita Mayes Walker

I attended Mary Bethune Elementary School, where Mrs. Lillie Burney was the principal. During my elementary school years, we had plenty of good teachers that stressed the importance of learning. Some of my favorite teachers were Mrs. Thelma Harris, Mrs. Benton, and Ms. Inez Lee.

Some of my childhood friends were Lucille and Louise Womback, Gloria Pigford, and Vernette Wallis. I had two special friends that were about seven years older than me, and they lived next door. They were like big sisters to me. Their names were Grace Marshall (Bell) and Gloria Marshall (Bush) As they were raised by a single parent, Grace and Gloria taught me many things, and they showed me lots of love. Both are now deceased, but the impact they made on my life will never be forgotten. These memories are still in my mind and heart, and I loved them dearly.

—Mattie Hudnall Ponder

SCHOOL DAYS 1960-61
EUREKA

Hope for true educational equality for Black students occurred in 1954, when a U.S. Supreme Court decision struck down segregation in public schools. Mississippi's response, however, was to press forward with its segregated dual system of education. This is the educational system that

I, along with my sister Mildred, enrolled in as first grad-ers in Mrs. Mattie Hardy's class at the all-Black Eureka Elementary School in 1957. We were very familiar with Eureka and the first-grade curriculum because our mother was on the faculty, and she had given us a head start, hav-ing been our teacher when we were in Eureka's primary school level the year before at the 6th Street Community Center. Our first-grade school year went so well that we were able to skip the second grade, and we were promoted directly to third grade.

At Eureka, Mr. C. E. Roy and Mr. Jesse Patrick served as our principals, and my elementary school teachers included Mrs. Mary Crawford, Miss Ruby Henry, Mr. Major Pugh, and Mrs. Wynemia Patrick.

Mrs. Patrick was special to Mildred and me because of her involvement in our sixth grade class trip to Lincoln Beach in New Orleans in 1962. My parents had steadfastly refused to allow us to go on this trip. One day after school, Mrs. Patrick walked the short distance from Eureka to our house and pleaded with our parents to let us go on the trip. After an hour-long discussion, our parents finally gave in to Mrs. Patrick, and we were able to travel with our classmates for a day of fun in New Orleans. We will forever be indebted to Mrs. Patrick for going the extra mile on our behalf.

—*Melvin Miller*

My mother, Mrs. Willie B. Miller, was our first teacher at Eureka Elementary and Junior High School. We partici-pated in the tonette band, glee club, Girl Scouts, May Day activities, and school closing programs. After our first-grade year, my brother and I were promoted from the first grade to the third grade. We did not attend the second grade. A new school was built named W. H. Jones Elementary and Junior High School and our school was named Eureka Elementary School. In the third grade, our teacher, who weighed less than one hundred and ten pounds, was named Miss Mary Crawford. She introduced us to many new classmates—Nelda Fenner, Gloriastene Brown, Ronald Lindsey, and Carolyn Hall. One day, Miss Crawford left the classroom and instructed the students to read a story in our readers while she was gone. When she returned to the classroom, she called us one by one to her desk and asked us to tell her the name of the game that the children were playing in the story. Carolyn Hall was the only student who knew the correct answer. Miss Crawford punished everyone in the class except her. She was the only one in the class who had read the story. In the fourth grade, I was in Mrs. Ruby Henry's classroom. The fourth- and fifth-grade students had to attend classes in the Masonic Temple located across the street from Eureka. We spent about seven

SCHOOL DAYS 1960·61
EUREKA

months in that building because our school was being remodeled to include a new cafeteria, auditorium, library, bathrooms, and classrooms. The former cafeteria was next door to the school and the auditorium was upstairs. In my fifth-grade year, there was a terrible flood in the spring of 1961. Several children drowned and we were out of school for weeks. I was a majorette in the fifth and sixth grades and marched in the Rowan High School Homecoming

Day Parade, which was held on Thanksgiving Day each year. I was always super excited because my brother and I usually celebrated our birthdays after the activities. There were many teachers at Eureka, most of them lived in our community. They were Mrs. Mattie Hardy, Mrs. Teresa Wilson, Miss Mary Love, Mrs. Juanita Johnson, Mrs. Willie B. Miller, Mrs. Florine Love, Miss Mary Crawford, Mrs. Ruby Henry, Miss Cora Jones, Mr. Major Pugh, Mrs. Teresa Fielder Mrs. Waynema Patrick, Mrs. Savanah Davis, Miss Elizabeth Batts, Mrs. Mary Johnson, Mrs. Marjorie Clark, and Mrs. Ruby Thomas. My principals were Mr. Clarence E. Roy and Mr. Jessie Patrick.

—Mildred Miller Short

I am sorry to admit that some of the teachers had their favorite students. I was a quiet student who obeyed the rules. Light-skinned students or students with long hair (girls) or curly hair (boys) were often the favorite students of some teachers. Not all teachers showed special preferences. These students were called teachers' pets. I have great and positive memories of my fourth-grade teacher. She would read Bible stories to us. The children of Israel crossing the Red Sea was so exciting. She would make it so interesting that we could barely wait for the next day. In today's society, it would not be politically correct to read a Bible story in a public school. My principal was also my math teacher. We called him Professor Bailey. He was a no-nonsense person.

—Willie Ruth McDonald Sanders

Mrs. Mattie Davis was a statuesque tall lady with a beautiful smile, but she ruled her class with just her thumb and her index finger. She would catch the meat on your upper arm and give you a pinch that could make you wet your pants. Once, Curtis Calbert and my brother Robert Giles talked me into playing hooky from school. We spent the entire day ducking and dodging cars. That was the longest school day of my life. Mrs. Davis questioned me the next day. I had not quite learned how to lie effectively and was afraid that Mrs. Davis was going to call Mama, but she didn't. That was the first and only time I played hooky from school.

One Saturday morning, Doris Townsend and I danced together on the Rick Darnell Platter Party show, the first Black local TV program at WDAM TV station. Doris said as much as she practiced, when the time came, her feet would not go the way she wanted them to go.

Mrs. Ora Lee Preston, the sweetest teacher of all. I can't recall my exciting moments that stand out, but this is when I really learned to read. I was so proud of myself.

Mrs. Marjorie Clark (church member). It was the best of times and the worst of times. This was when I began to grasp the concept of math and learned the times table. One morning, getting ready for school, I had just gotten a bath. It was a cold morning, and the space heaters were lit. This was before the introduction of the Dearborn heaters that did not get hot on the top. I had a bad habit of backing up to the heater. The towel I had wrapped around me fell to the floor. Instinctively, I stooped to pick up the towel. I was out of school for three days because I couldn't sit down. I still have the scar on my butt to this day. LOL!

Doris Townsend, Patricia Griffin, and Annie Sue Walker were best of friends. At recess one day, they were all playing, and Doris accidentally hit Annie Sue across the face with a switch; at least she said it was an accident. Annie Sue pushed Doris down and caused her to scratch her leg. Doris cried a lot. After returning to class, Doris just couldn't let it go. She stood up and yelled at Annie Sue, "You old fool!" Needless to say, the scratch she got from the fall did not compare to the whipping she got from Mrs. Clark. Remember that, Doris?

I was one of Mattie Townsend's favorite children, and being her future son-in-law, she included me in a lot of their activities. For its school closing program, Townsend Kindergarten performed a Tom Thumb's Wedding. I was Tom Thumb, the groom. Doris was the preacher, and Jennifer Lynn Jackson was the bride. That was the beginning of the end of Doris and my, instigated by our parents, predetermined future. Jennifer was a cute little girl with big hips. Need I say more? Doris and I remained dear friends. I think she had her sights set on someone else anyway so it was a non-contested divorce. Karma is a mother because Jennifer Lynn had the hots for her classmate Alvin Cook. LOL!

Mrs. Naretha Naylor—This was the year I learned to tell time, use the jelly stencil, and manual ink printer. Mrs. Naylor and Mrs. Lee were the music teachers for the school's music ensemble. I learned to play the tonette, a flute-like instrument (now called a recorder). I wanted to play the autoharp, but Doris and Cherylyn Clark were the ones chosen. If it sounds like *hating,* you are right and I'm not over it yet.

Mrs. Thelma Harris (church member)—Miss Dawson was our practice teacher in the fourth grade and taught the fifth grade the following year. She was nice and I wanted to be in her class. But of course, Doris and most of my former classmates were assigned to her. Mrs. Harris had a reputation for being a mean teacher, and she lived up to her reputation. I believe the reason I have arthritis in my knees today is because her discipline method was to sit you in a chair and whip you across the knees. Barring her tortuous technique of discipline, Mrs. Harris was a very good teacher. I learned a lot from her.

Mrs. Inez Lee (church member)—Finally, there was a God. Mr. Lucas was known for being the meanest teacher in the whole school, meaner than Mrs. Harris and Mrs. Burney, the principal, put together. No one wanted to be in his class. After much going to God, my prayers were answered. I was back with my crew, Doris and the rest of the gang.

We had two new students that year, and I never saw one of them again, Martha LaFitte; James Rambo left us after the eighth grade. They were very friendly and smart, and I enjoyed them as classmates.

Every teacher had some kind of strap they used for discipline. Mrs. Lee's technique was no lick wasted. She would hold you by the hand and whip you. If you moved around behind her, she would hit you with a lick behind her back. Once, Doris got a whipping, and Mrs. Lee was really pouring it on. Doris yelled out, "Ms. Lee, that hurts!" Mrs. Lee's response was, "Yes, I know. Miss Lee wants it to hurt." LOL!

Sixth grade revealed many maturing circumstances, two in particular. One was a schoolmate in Mr. Lucas' class, became pregnant, and one of the majorettes in the Thanksgiving Day Parade took off her skirt to her uniform to reveal only the underpants. Mrs. Lee dismissed her from the squad.

While still participating in the musical ensemble, I was introduced to the flutophone, which was just a fancier version of the tonette. I still never got to play the autoharp; you know who still had that job. But that's okay because when I got to Rowan, I led the seventh-grade tonette band onto the field during halftime at one of the home football games, another proud moment.

If it seems that Doris's name has popped up numerous times in my stories, Doris and I have been dear friends probably the longest of any of our classmates. So many of our childhood experiences have stayed with me over the years. Our parents were good friends and had planned our wedding before we were out of kindergarten. Her Mother, Miss Mattie, was one of my favorite older adults throughout my life.

We had many happy times at Mary Bethune. Every May 1st, we had our school-wide May Day festival, which included wrapping the May pole, but the main event was the operetta. Each grade, fourth through sixth, would put on a performance, which usually consisted of a dance routine.

Once a month Reverend Wise, a White minister, came to the school and conducted "chapel" services. One Bible verse I memorized is, "Go ye into all the world and preach the gospel to every creature" (Mark 16:15). I remember Martha LaFitte, Tommy Hall, and Belinda Ratliff could not attend chapel because they were Catholic.

—*Randall Williams*

While at Mary Bethune, my sister, Mattie Montgomery, wanted to be in the same grade as I, so she did not tell our Mother that she had to pay for a schoolbook. The teacher held her back, but we completed school together.

—*Rose Mary Montgomery Harrell*

When we were in the fourth grade, Eureka High was renovated and renamed Eureka Elementary—first through sixth grade—after which we attended W. H. Jones Junior High in the seventh through ninth grades.

—*Stella Brooks Clark*

I attended Grace Love Elementary with some fun-loving people that would remain with me from elementary through high school. If you attended Grace Love, you encountered the Ratliff family as stern yet loving teachers, marched in the marching group (which every elementary school had during the early fifties and sixties) and sang in the glee club under the direction of Miss Ruby Houze. My next adventure in education was at the newly built Lillie Burney Junior High School, where I would reunite with some kindergarten classmates and meet new ones.

Good years of marching in the band, singing in the choir, and participating in Future Homemakers of America (FHA). One bad experience was in my last year of junior high when my parents had to pay a monetary price for something the principal knew I did not commit (which he later admitted).

—*Thelma Bacchus*

I attended 16th Section, where I began school in the primer. The next year, it became Mary Bethune Elementary. At Mary Bethune, the teachers there would have classroom activities, study hall, and on Wednesdays, we had chapel. This White man would come to the school and preach and sing, preach the gospel and play the trumpet.

—*Tommy Hall Jr.*

I attended Sixteenth Section where I began school in the primer. The next year it became Mary Bethune Elementary. At Mary Bethune, the teachers there would have classroom activities, study hall, and on Wednesdays, we had chapel.

—*Vernette Wallis Andry*

Mary McLeod Bethune Elementary had been previously known as 16th Section School because it was in what was called Sixteenth Section. I would learn later that 16th Section communities were school districts, and somehow the people living in the immediate area could only occupy the houses through long-term leases. They couldn't actually own the property. There was also a 21st Section community nearby, which is where the junior high school would be located some years later. Bethune served grades 1–6.

The first grade in 1956 had some interesting features about school. First, we attended what were called split sessions. Half the students went to Mary Bethune from 8:00 a.m. to noon, and the other half attended from noon to 4:00 p.m. I was used to being at school all day, so that was a surprise. Second, the bell would ring to signal the start and end of school, but it would be rung by hand with some-one walking around outside the school physically ringing a handheld bell. Of course, I wanted that job even in the first grade. I started school a few days after the other children and remember being told by my teacher, Mrs. Davis, when I came into the classroom that I should go sit at Hayes Boles's table. Walking and looking confused, a boy called out "This is Hayes *Boles's* table" and put his finger on the table where he was seated. That was Hayes Boles, who was to become my lifelong friend and "partner in victory," play-ing classroom games throughout school. Trying to act like I knew where I was going, I responded, "I know it." But I didn't know Jack and was glad he had told me where to sit on my first day of Big School. That was the start of my career in Hattiesburg Public Schools.

Mrs. Davis was very nice. She always smiled. We learned well under her. I remember the book we were assigned to read at Hayes Boles's table, and I remember that other tables had different books. Everything went well with Mrs. Davis until you messed up in class or misbe-haved. That's when she would pull your ears or pinch you on your sides. We would play games, such as guessing what was in a box that she would rattle. I never won anything. We also had a rhythm band in which kids would play cym-bals, rhythm sticks, all kinds of little shakers while singing little songs. One day when Mrs. Davis was out of the room, Johnny Jackson and I decided we would use our pencils like they were cigars. We put the pencils into our mouths and leaned back on the rear legs of our chairs with our feet up on the table like we were big rich businessmen smoking in our easy chairs. Our heads were close together as we would take a long drag on our cigar/pencil, blow the smoke out at the same time, then put our pencil back in our mouths. Unbeknown to us, Mrs. Davis came up behind us, bumped our two heads together, and asked, "What are you doing?" We almost fell over backward. Children snickered. Johnny and I knew it was funny and wanted to laugh, but we didn't want to make her any madder than she was.

Here are the key memories from grades 2–6:

By this time, 1957, a new addition to Mary Bethune had been built with two wings of classrooms connected to a cafeteria-auditorium. In hindsight, the split session during the first grade was due to the school being overcrowded. the Black community was expanding with baby boomers galore.

In the second grade, Mrs. Preston was the absolute sweetest teacher I ever had. A great teacher, we wanted to do well for her, and we did. We were good learners. Her room was on one of the new wings and was organized with two groups of students split up evenly in rows on either side of the room facing each other. The reason this was important was because, when Mrs. Preston was out of the room, the two sides of the room would do battle throwing blackboard erasers, chalk, paper, whatever at each other. There were chalk boards on the walls behind the two groups of students. Sometimes, the chalk boards would have pock marks after the battles from where chalk had missed a child and hit the board. We had this girl in our class who looked like a grown woman, even in the second grade. All the boys liked this pretty girl, who would become a majorette, and she reigned supreme in that class. One day while Mrs.

Preston was out of the room, she told a boy to pull down his pants in front of the class just for our amusement. "Do it, John, do it," she told him. He grinned, grinned again, and he did it—down and up very quickly. We roared.

I started out in Mrs. Peters' class (Imagine the theme music from *Dragnet*). In the third grade, Mrs. Peters had a reputation for being hard, so coming from sweet Mrs. Preston's class, it was a bit scary. But fate intervened. The class was too large, so students from Mrs. Peters's class and another overcrowded third-grade class were moved to Mrs. Annie Mae Williams's new class. Mrs. Williams became the next absolute sweetest teacher I ever had and was a really great teacher. My friend and classmate Willie "Sonny" Sanders and I flourished in all our third-grade work, and we became tight friends who would visit each other to play on the weekends.

Sonny's house had a creek behind it and woods. We would walk the creek for a mile or more, catch, and cook crawfish on a hobo stove we made from a large vegetable can, and we had a fort that we called Northwest Passage. When we played at my house, it was all about money. By this time, 1958, the house was finished, and we all moved from Ruby Avenue back to Manning Avenue. My Dad was keen on safety, so he told Sonny and me that he would pay us a penny for every nail (left over from the building of the house) that we found in the yard. We found some nails, but not enough so we decided to look under the house. We had so many nails that we said a prayer under the house, asking God to let my Dad pay us for all those nails. He paid us something but not the more than $7 we expected.

Meanwhile, back to school memoirs.

In the fourth grade, we received an advanced education in our segregated schools. In the fourth grade, we had Mrs. Williams again and were thrilled. She assigned each of us to write our autobiography in class. Think about that, our fourth-grade assignment in segregated 1959 was to write a paper. Now, Sonny and I were both totally into our grandmothers who lived in the country, and we talked about them all the time. His mom's mother lived on a farm in Newton, Mississippi, and my stepmother's mother lived on a farm in Collins, Mississippi. We both loved going to spend time on those farms and, as nine-year-olds, talked about it constantly. So much so that we decided together that we would write in our autobiographies that we were born in Collins and Newton because we thought that sounded better, I guess. Go figure.

In class on the day we were to write the paper, I finished my autobiography and proudly took it up to Mrs. Williams and went back to my desk. She began to read it. I was watching her. She read the first line, "I was born in Collins, MS…" But then she began to frown. She looked up at me and said out loud, "Don, what do you mean you were born in Collins? Boy, I remember when you were born. Your mother and Father lived across the street from me. Your autobiography is supposed to be true." Oops. Upon hearing me get busted, I looked at Sonny and saw that he was feverishly erasing the first line in his autobiography.

Miss Lottie Sims was my fifth-grade teacher. Very tall, elegant, attractive, and dignified, she ushered in the importance of etiquette and personal hygiene to complement the first-class education that we were receiving in Hattiesburg. Good penmanship was a virtue to her, so we did writing drills: push-pull, push-pull curved slants drill, ovals connected to endless ovals, endless straight slants, etc. The coveted penmanship award in her class was to have your writing drills selected for placement on the bulletin board. I made it only a few times, but there were some people who made it onto the board all the time.

The personal hygiene focus was intense. She took a lot of time giving instruction on the need to brush our teeth each day, take a bath each day, wash our faces every morning, clip your fingernails, polish your shoes, even if you have to use old bacon grease from the can on the stove, etc. "If I only had one set of underwear, I would wash that underwear every night until I could get more. If I only had one set of clothes, I would wash them every night so that I would have clean clothes the next day. There is no excuse not to be clean every day at school." After a few weeks of this kind of intense instruction, she instituted the dreaded daily "health checkup" in which each day a different student would go to each person's desk first thing in the morning to perform the "health checkup," take notes on what was wrong, and then go in front of the class to give the report on the problems: "Don Denard: fingernails, shoes; John Doe: teeth, fingernails, breath; Sue Smith: hair, fingernails, etc." She would admonish us to clean up whatever problem we had so that we would not be part of the report the next day. If a child had a chronic problem (e.g., with dirty long fingernails being on the report day after day), she would call that child up to the front of the class and personally clip the child's nails. Toward the end of the year, the health checkup report would be short, and occasionally, there would be no report at all. My problem was usually dirty shoes from playing before school started, but I'd like to think that I left her class more refined.

The fifth grade is when we realized the significance our teachers placed on students being able to reflect their learning through performance. School closing programs were the culmination of the year, and each grade had a program with all classes in the grade participating. These tended to be high-quality variety shows that always included a musical play, group dance numbers, and other features such as voice or piano solos, depending on the talents in the classes. We also had tonette (a.k.a. recorder) concerts in elementary school.

There was also this White minister who would come to Bethune essentially to preach and give religious presentations using a felt board to illustrate certain human characters and animals in Bible stories. I think he also played an instrument and would perform.

Mrs. Inez Lee, my sixth-grade teacher in 1961, was the mathematician. And she had a keen focus on current events. And on history. And book reports. In other words, she was the complete teacher who had a major impact on me and everyone in her class. (She also kicked butt if we didn't do our work or got out of line behavior-wise.) This was our final year of elementary school, and it ended on a high note. A few new students joined us, like the cute and smart Martha LaFitte, and this only added to a very high level of student performance that came from people on our side of town like Doris Townsend, Johnnie Bea Slay, Jesse Dent, Patricia Griffin, Lester Hollingsworth, and the great James Rambo, with whom we have lost touch since the ninth grade.

There was a presidential election in 1960 won by John F. Kennedy. *Junior Scholastic* magazine had a lot of articles on Kennedy and his opponent, Richard Nixon, and I remember Mrs. Lee having their pictures on her classroom bulletin board. We had class discussions about the election and presidential politics, and all of us preferred Kennedy. Mrs. Lee also taught us Mississippi history. We had to memorize all eighty-two counties and know the county seats for each. One day, James Rambo and I were walking to school together going over the counties and county seats. I got stuck on Winston County, to which Rambo went, "Winston tastes good like a [bomp-bomp] Louisville should," parroting a popular commercial of the day for Winston cigarettes. As you can tell, I never again forgot the county seat for Winston County, Mississippi.

The sixth grade was also the year that we had a competition for the best presentation of a book report. I always felt that Jesse Dent was robbed when he did not get the nod for his highly scholarly presentation on a book about Ghandhi. Charles Knox won it because of the drama he put into his presentation on a book titled *Parents Just Don't Understand.* Both were really good. Dent is now a big-time college professor and expert on Russia.

I contracted pneumonia twice during the sixth grade and nearly lost the battle. Fever, lots of shots, it was hard. Dr. Frank Jones, of the Charles Smith-Frank Jones Clinic, was my doctor. Missing school was awful but gave me a chance to read some books, which was the best thing about it. I read some of the Mandingo books by Kyle Onstott that later became all the rage during the civil rights / Black Liberation Movement. When I came back to school, I saw Miss Sims from the fifth grade walking with another teacher at recess one day, and she asked where I had been. I told her I had been out sick, to which she said she had missed seeing me around and thought I looked a bit "peak-ed." I immediately thought I had to go look that word up. Pneumonia is my excuse for there not being a lot about athletics and me in these memoirs. Bethune Elementary formed its first basketball team during my sixth-grade year. The basketball court where the tryouts were held was right next to Mrs. Lee's classroom or my classroom. The tryouts consisted of shooting a free throw. It seemed every fifth- to sixth-grade boy in the school tried out, including me. The line of boys who were trying out stretched the entire length of the court, and the goal was right outside the window of Mrs. Lee's room. All the girls in her class were at the window watching. They could see every person who took a shot. If you missed, you had to walk toward the windows of Mrs. Lee's class into the nearby bathroom door and go through to the hallway to get back to your class. Yes, I shot an air ball and was seen by all the girls in my class walking toward them to the bathroom door in defeat.

Believe it or not, there is a lot more I could share about my elementary school years, such as us referring to the school name with the alliteration "Mary McLeod Methune" and the time Mrs. Lee sent Herbert Charles

Knox and me to the office of Principal Stegall to get the tape recorder and Charles asked him for the tape recorder using his newly found New Jersey accent. Charles had visited his older brother, Ello, in New Jersey that summer. Mr. Stegall couldn't understand him, looked at me, and asked, "What did he say?" Another memory is the annual May Day celebration on May 1st, wrapping the maypole, and other fun happenings. Much more could also be said about Mrs. Lenore, our dance teacher, and a sensuous dance routine she choreographed for a number of couples but ended up being one couple, this amazing girl named Cheetah and John Howard Wilborn who performed to the song "Temptation." "Cheetah" Lindsey (I don't remember her real first name) was another girl who, like Margaret Hill, looked like a grown woman in elementary school.

—*Don Denard*

I know all the kids that attended Eureka remember Cora Jones (ground patrol). She would march around wearing all black with a black strap in one hand and a cowbell in the other. If you were caught out after the bell rang, she would lash your hand across your back and your knees would buckle, but she got respect. Today she would get jail (laugh) Ha-ha-ha. I was glad to get away from her.

When I entered junior high school, the teachers in general had negative attitudes toward the students. I had an English teacher who often made this statement: "I have mine. You need to get yours." She would say this often to the class in a negative, sarcastic way. We were not encouraged to go to college or trade school. I was never advised by a counselor. The counselor catered to certain students. I learned early in life that one must know who you are and have some idea on what you want to do in life.

Most people do not like to talk about the "dirty little secret" that occurred in the Black school system. We discriminated according to hair, looks, skin color, and socioeconomic status. From Eureka, I went to Grace Love and started in the third grade. I met a new group of kids. I attended Grace Love up to the sixth grade. Mrs. Boykins had a concession stand, and she would let me help her sell candy at recess. I enjoyed that. My house and Thelma Bacchus's house were back to back. Thelma had a dog named Boro. She would come out at night and call that dog like it was the end of the world, and I asked her why, and she said there was mold on his food bowl. We had a fence between our yards so Thelma and I had a fight across the fence. How can that be? We laugh about that today. Kids do silly stuff (laugh).

—Benida Parker Johnson

Mrs. Lizzie Jackson, my second- and fourth-grade teacher, had an extremely positive influence on my life. She identified strong academic skills that I didn't think were significant and pushed me to focus. I would go see her when I encountered challenges in junior high and high school and kept in touch with her throughout my adult years until her passing.

—Ethelyn Fairley Reid

In 1958, Earl Travillion Attendance Center opened in Palmer's Crossing community, and all county schools consolidated into that one school. I think we all got along pretty well being bussed from all parts of Forrest County. Don't get me wrong, there were some fights and arguments, but there was also love. Mr. A. B. S. Todd was the principal and didn't spare the rod. I loved my school and all my teachers. I was blessed not to have any of the so-called mean teachers. I remember having prayer and pledging allegiance to the flag every morning. School closing and Christmas programs, as well as wrapping the May pole on May Day, were big events. We wore our little special clothes and had a good time. After seventh grade, it was time to move on again reluctantly.

I remember Mr. Tademy in the high school science class had snakes, frogs, lizards, and all kinds of nasty things including a fetus in jars. All the younger children were afraid of him and his classroom. Thank God a new school came on the scene!

—*Juanita Mayes Walker*

Transitioning to elementary school was smooth because I attended kindergarten. I had already been taught the basics at kindergarten and at home by my grandmother. What impressed me the most the first day of school was the long hallway.

Mr. C.E. Roy was principal. He was an educator when my mother was in school. It was personal. He knew me along with most of the other students. I remember seeing him in the hallway checking to make sure students were in their classrooms and everything was okay.

I only attended Eureka for two years. My shining star was Mrs. Juanita Johnson. I remember her being firm, but kind and gentle. She made learning fun. Being a young child, she seemed to be taller than everyone with long wavy hair. I was glad she was my teacher and I admired her. Besides, she lived down the street from my grandmother's house and knew our family. Back then, schools were connected to the community. You not only saw your teacher in school, but also in church and in the neighborhood. It was personal. Everyone looked out for one another.

I was excited my third year of school. There was a new school in my neighborhood, W.H. Jones Elementary and Junior High School. We were proud and excited in my neighborhood to have a brand-new school.

Going to school for the first time at W.H. Jones, everything smelled new and looked massive to me because not only were there elementary classes, but junior high as well. We even had a gym. Mr. S.E. Wilson, Sr. was principal of W.H. Jones. I remember him being no-nonsense and a strong disciplinarian. To me, he was approachable and well-respected.

I admired all of my teachers at W.H. Jones Elementary School. They were all special and unique in their own way. I saw them as a team working together for the common good. My shining stars at W.H. Jones Elementary School—Mrs. Sue Route; Mrs. Route was my third-grade teacher. She introduced us to cursive writing. We had to do it over and over again until we got it right. Mrs. Route instilled pride in doing your work. I reflected back on Mrs. Route when my children were learning cursive writing. I too would insist that they do it over and over again until we got it right. Mrs. Route was a friend of the family. She lived in the neighborhood. School and community were personal.

Mrs. Fannie Lou Knight—Mrs. Knight was my fifth-grade teacher. Her class was one of order. She was knowledgeable and motivated her students to do their best. Mrs. Knight also lived in the neighborhood and knew my family. It indeed took a village, people investing in you, and encouraging you to be the best you could be. Mrs. Knight died last year. Her death caused me to reflect on how much she impacted my life.

Mr. Otis Chambers—Mr. Chambers was my sixth-grade teacher. Besides being my teacher, he was the Sunday school superintendent at my church and lived up the street from me. Again, school and community were personal. Mr. Chambers always made sure you understood the subject matter. He was dedicated and made sure his classroom was conducive to learning. I remember not being able to solve a math problem, so my mother sent me to Mr. Chambers' house. He was always willing to help.

Mr. Chambers impacted my life beyond his classroom. By the time I was in high school, he was counselor of a scholarship program at Jackson State University. I was fortunate to qualify for four years of college with full scholarship. To God be the glory!

—*Beverly Harris Abrams*

I would like to give special thanks to my first-grade teacher, Mrs. Mattie Hardy, for promoting me and my twin brother from the first grade to the third grade. This allowed us to be a part of and graduate with the Class of 1968.

—*Mildred Miller Short*

I was excited to begin school. My two older sisters were already in school and I wanted to go also. Books fascinated me. I remember listening intently one night as my mother helped my older sister, Doris, with her reading lesson. My mother spelled a word, but Doris couldn't pronounce it. I remember shouting out, "recipe." I was about four years old at the time.

My elementary education took place at Eureka Elementary School. While I loved being in school, I was probably absent more than I was present for the first four years. I remember crying because I had to stay home from school for one reason or another. Sometimes my sister, Doris, would stay home and allow me to go in her place, when one of us was required to stay home.

My parents divorced when I was in the fourth grade. My world fell apart. I had missed so many days of school that year, I was ashamed to go back. So I quit school. My sister, Joyce, and I stayed home and watched the soap opera, "Young Doctor Malone" for the rest of the year. I was so ashamed of my parents' divorce that I also stopped going to church.

All the neighbors said that my forty-three year old mother had deserted us, and left my five siblings and me with our sixty-seven-year-old father who did the best he could to take care of us. I found myself essentially on my own. Some of our neighbors even said that we would never amount to anything.

One day, during the summer of my fourth-grade year, my neighbor, Miss Gertie Johnson, called me over to her house and told this ten-year-old dropout two things I will never forget. She said, "Carolyn, you need to go back to school and you need to go back to church."

I knew she was right, but I was afraid of what people would say. I prayed and asked God to give me the courage to go back to school, although I would have to repeat the fourth grade. When I went to register, I found out that I had been promoted to the fifth grade. My fourth-grade teacher, Mrs. Davis, who had died during the summer, had written on my report card, "Pass her on. She has potential." I thank God for Mrs. Davis. I never looked back.

The next thing I did was return to church. I reasoned that if I went back to church, people would stop staring at me and talking about me after four or five Sundays. God, again, answered my prayers. Church became my anchor.

I thank God for Miss Gert, who would not let me give up on myself.

I thank God for the teachers at Eureka who impacted my life, including Mrs. Crawford, Mrs. Johnson, Mrs. Miller, Mrs. Hall, and Mrs. Patrick. I am also grateful for the support of our principal, Mr. J. K. Patrick.

I am equally grateful for the love and support of the members of the Ebenezer Baptist Church. Mrs. Nancy Goins, Mrs. Mary Ann Kelly, Mrs. Eartha Jackson, Deacon Ollie Jackson, and Rev. C. E. Lewis and many other church members encouraged me to give God my best.

—*Carolyn Hall Abrams*

The Cafeteria or Cafetorium

Not only did we have good times, we had the best cooks in all the Hattiesburg Public School System: Mrs. Cole, Mrs. Berry, Mrs. Conner, and others. Twenty-five cents was pretty hard to come by for five days a week for five children. Because we lived only a block from the school, I went home for lunch most days. Sometimes, I would get a treat and eat in the lunchroom, as it was called then. We had real food in those days, not the quick, fast, in-a-hurry processed meals that are served today. The yeast rolls were my favorite. I remember when the milk containers went from the little glass bottles to the half-pint paper cartons. I loved the sweet taste of the milk back then; that's how homogenized milk got its name…sweet milk.

I remember when the old wooden frame building was torn down and in its place the cafetorium—cafeteria/auditorium was built. Along with that came two additional wings, which housed the first, second, and third grades. The campus had many pecan trees, and in the fall, some of us kids would pick pecans for our parents. From the new building, it was easy to get on top of the building to get to the tree branches that hung over the building. On Saturday, Mr. Stegall, the new principal, came to the school to do some work. He walked because he lived just a block or so away. He was upon us before we could hide. There were several of us, but I don't remember who the others were. We had to work in the lunchroom for a week, cleaning up, for our restitution. That was okay with me because I got to eat in the lunchroom for free.

—*Randall Williams*

One moment I will never forget about the fifth grade involved me trying to get out of the cafeteria one day. And while I'm at it, I should mention that the food served in the cafeterias throughout all grades was outstanding. On our side of town, the Cole sisters ran the cafeterias at Rowan/Royal Street and Mary Bethune. They lived next to each other on Dabbs Street in houses that looked just alike, and both of their husbands worked at Hercules. They seemed to do everything together, including preside over the production of school lunch cuisine. Those school-made rolls with butter were delicacies. Children who did not eat in the lunchroom for twenty-five cents would pay five cents to buy rolls and a bit more to buy milk for lunch. Some children would pay for their lunch for the entire week while children like the Denards would have to get their lunch money from their Daddy each day before leaving for school. Rarely ever did I spend my lunch money on snacks from the vending machines or at the store on the way to school as some kids did. I was not about to miss the great food that the cafeterias served.

Back to that day, I had a problem getting out of the cafeteria. I had finished lunch and was headed out to go back to Miss Sims' class. There were these heavy-duty, maroon-colored screened doors at the entrance that you went through to get into and out of the cafeteria. They would only open in one direction, which was toward the inside. I got confused in coming out and was trying to push the heavy screened door toward the outside, but it would not budge. A girl was coming into the cafeteria just as I was trying to come out. It was Patricia Griffin. She just stood there with her arms folded as I tried in vain to push the door out. I leaned into it as hard as I could with my hands and arms extended and was almost fully stretched out and grunting while pushing, but that door would not budge because I was pushing instead of pulling. After watching me struggle and finally give up, she easily opened the door toward me and said to me in contempt, "You ain't even strong." She walked past me into the cafeteria. I just tucked my tail and walked back to class.

—*Don Denard*

My first year at Eureka, the cafeteria was on the right side of the building you see today. The home economics class and the cafeteria were in the same building. The building faces New Orleans Street. The bathrooms were also in a building to themselves in back of the cafeteria or lunchroom to some of us.

A group of all Black ladies with no formal education preparing food, sanitation, or maintenance, were able to feed five to six hundred children a day. They were all just blessed by God with the wisdom to do the job. Business ladies, wives, church ladies, and mothers made the groups what they were. Mrs. C. E. Roy, Eartha Jackson, Velma Johnson, Martha Mae Short, Vonceil Woods, Patricia Presley, Mae Lee Brown, and Sebelle Reeves are some of the names and are just a small part of the big pie. Hats off to these ladies. You put joy in our day!

—*Ella Sue Jackson*

CHAPTER 4

Those Junior High School Years

My years at W.H. Jones Junior High School were bittersweet. My dad died when I was in the ninth grade. I went to school the next day because I didn't know what else to do. I believe I went on a class field trip. I still remember some teachers asking each other if it were true that my daddy had died the night before.

Whatever I needed emotionally that day, school provided it. Maybe I needed some stability. Maybe I just needed to feel safe. School provided me the comfort I needed. I guess I felt I was with family, although I don't remember telling anyone my daddy had died.

I excelled academically at W. H. Jones. I served as student council president and participated in the band, cheerleading, and other activities. I received many honors and awards during my junior high school years.

I especially remember our ninth-grade awards and recognition night. As a special project for home economics, we had to make a dress to put on display. Someone cut up my dress with scissors while the program was taking place. That night, I received the top awards and honors as I usually did. It was bittersweet because I was there by myself. No Mom. No Dad. No family. I would have given back every certificate and award just to have someone care enough to be there for me.

I said that school was bittersweet. Overall, I remember more good times than bad. I had good friends and teachers. Many of my classmates have remained lifelong friends: Carolyn Atkins, Beverly Harris, Alma Hall, Mildred Johnson, Shelley Stallworth, Gwendolyn Murphy, Cherylyn Clark, Mildred Miller, Melvin Miller, and Katherine Bouie.

I also had great teachers at W. H. Jones: Mrs. Ruby Wilson (with whom I still have a treasured relationship), Mrs. Rhoda Tademy, Mrs. Georgia Robinson Walton (who allowed me to remain in the gym during lunchtime when I had no lunch), Mr. David Conner, and Mrs. Juruthin Woullard. Mr. Samuel Wilson and Mr. Percy Gambrell were great principals. I was inspired by their leadership.

—Carolyn Hall Abrams

As it was at Bethune, the Black school population was booming on the South and east side of town in 1962. A new junior high school was under construction. But until it was finished, Royal Street High School served grades 7–12. At some point, the school was renamed L. J. Rowan. Children on the south and east sides of town in 1961–62 went to the seventh grade at Rowan. We would learn later from Mrs. Burger that Levi John Rowan had been a president of Alcorn College. So when we "passed" from the sixth grade at Bethune to the seventh grade, this meant we would go…to… Rowan! It's worth mentioning that children rarely flunked in the segregated schools of Hattiesburg, at least not on the South side. We had outstanding teachers who got the job done. Going to Rowan was the main thing I had lived for up to that point in my life. Rowan was a beacon, a lighthouse that drew children to it. It was where the action was, and I wanted to go. Finally getting to Rowan for the seventh grade in 1962 meant everything to me.

The best day of my life up to that point was the year I spent at Rowan in the seventh grade. The junior high school was finished in time for us to leave Rowan after the seventh grade. But that seventh-grade year at Rowan was magical. The assistant football coach and future head football coach at Rowan, the great Ed Steele, was our seventh grade homeroom teacher. His class was in Prof Hervey's Industrial Arts building away from the school. Mr. Steele taught us social studies in that classroom. We spent weeks debating the question, "Is life better in the country, or in the city?" You can guess which side of the question Sonny Sanders and I took given our fascination with our country Grandmothers. We changed classrooms for the different subjects in the seventh grade instead of staying in the same classroom all day as we did in elementary school, and we had lockers! Best of all, we got to go to chapel programs in the auditorium every Wednesday with all those big children and hear Mr. Burger preside before turning the program over to the homeroom that was sponsoring the chapel program that Wednesday. I could spend a lot of time detailing the year and the deeds of greatness on the part of the students and faculty that we experienced at Rowan in the seventh grade. It was in this year that I remember hearing, for the first time, the iconic phrase "To Mr. Burger, members of the faculty and student body." This was the opening whenever students addressed the assembled audience. What happened in the high school was pure magic for Black culture in Hattiesburg. There were talent shows in the auditorium with amazing talent on display. Marching band members formed jazz combos that would perform. We took band class from Jesse Otto Cook, an amazing clarinetist from Jackson State who was the band director. We learned to clap complex musical rhythms and would compete as teams. This helped us to be able to read complicated music in our later years. He wrote and arranged original music for the marching band. I particularly remember him writing number 1, number 2, and number 3, original tunes for the band. I can still recall the melody of these tunes to this day. Perhaps the highlight of the year was the end of year awards program in the auditorium. All those big children in the upper grades were featured and honored for their academic achievements, and they went on stage to get their awards. I was shocked when my name was announced as the winner of the seventh grade math award and I had to go on stage to receive my pin in front of all those "big children." The pin read "Mathematics Award—Seventh Grade—Rowan High School." I remember it having a yellow background. Where is it today?

There also were moments of pain and suffering in the seventh grade. We took biology from Mr. John Bucklen. He announced that anyone who won a ribbon at the science fair would get an A in his class and would not have to take the final exam. My project for the science fair was a hygrometer used to measure humidity. I won a blue ribbon for second place and walked confidently into Mr. Bucklen's class when the time came for the final exam, expecting to be exempted from the exam. But he told me I didn't note him as the sponsor of my project, so I was not exempt and had to take the final test. I was devastated. My homeroom teacher, Coach Steele, was my project sponsor, so I went ahead and took the test. Mr. Bucklen left the classroom during the test and left Doris Townsend and others who had placed in the science fair to "take names" of anyone cheating. I did well on the final exam and finished early. But Doris Townsend saw me responding "what?" when one of my friends asked me a question about something on the test, and she wrote my name down. She reported me to Mr. Bucklen when he came back to the class as someone who had been cheating. Mr. Bucklen came over to my desk, took my test paper, tore it up, and tossed it into the trash can. That was too much for me. I was hurt, had not been cheating, in my mind, and felt that Mr. Bucklen had actually cheated me. I started crying. The test wasn't over for the other students, so while sitting at my desk with nothing to do, I started fidgeting with my ballpoint pen through my tears. I took the ballpoint pen totally apart, undid the metal spring, and stretched it out still crying. At some point, the sharp end of the metal spring got stuck in the flesh of my hand and drew blood while I was still crying. Doris, Patricia Griffin, and Johnnie Bea Slay would say later that "he was so mad about having his test paper torn up that he *stabbed* himself in the hand." Words can't express how upset I was at those three. I thought they were my friends, but I was wrong—until later when I got an A in the class and promptly forgave them for their treachery.

Doris Townsend was involved in another of my unhappy moments that year. I had been her biggest fan and was upset when she came in second to the eighth grader who won Miss Rowana at the conclusion of the Miss Rowan-Miss Rowana pageant back in the fall of the '62–'63 school year. Rowan always had this huge pageant to select Miss Rowan. During the years when the school served grades 7–12, there was a Miss Rowana selected for grades 7–9 and a Miss Rowan for grades 10–12. Both were featured in the homecoming parade and during halftime of the homecoming football game, so it was a big deal. The pageant consisted of a fashion component, a hobbies and crafts competition, and the high point of it all, the talent competition. Doris was, and is, a great singer who sang a medley of "Around the World" and "Moon River" by Henry Mancini. She nailed the performance and got plenty of house that night in the packed Rowan auditorium. No way the eventual winner from the eighth grade outdid Doris. On behalf of the seventh grade, I felt that we were robbed! I must add that some of the older girls at Rowan were amazingly talented and beautiful. I thought Elaine Armstrong was something special and Linda Harrell.

As of September 1963, Rowan became a senior high school serving grades 10–12. The new Lillie Burney Junior High School, serving grades 7–9, opened and was named for one of the iconic and worthy figures in education in Hattiesburg, Mrs. Lillie Burney. Mrs. Burney lived on Rosa Avenue on the South side and, after retiring in the late fifties, was known for holding summer school in her very nice home. I passed her house every day on my way to Rowan and Burney. Her husband, Professor Burney, was also a noted figure in education. Mrs. Burney served as principal of Mary Bethune before Mr. Stegall arrived, and she was principal of 16th Section School before Bethune. She was noted as being the enforcer at the elementary school in the fifties. Those Bethune teachers who chose not to administer corporal punishment to their students directly would send them, quoting Stevie Wonder, "to tha—principal's office—down the hall." Mrs. Burney would lower the boom when you were "sent to her office." I remember one former student saying recently on Facebook that Mrs. Burney would "use a fan belt and dust would be flying out of those jeans." It's all true. I am a witness as Mrs. Burney was principal when I first started at Bethune. Mr. Stegall succeeded her when she retired sometime around the time I was in the fourth grade.

Mr. James Boykins was principal of the school named for Mrs. Burney when it opened in September 1963. He lived across the street from us on Manning Avenue (now Milton Barnes Avenue), which brings to mind something special about the Black neighborhood back in those days: We were all together in the segregated Black neighborhood, a.k.a. the briar patch. And it was all good, despite the fear motive of White supremacy to hold us down and keep us in a system of apartheid, separate and apart from the wider community so that we would not out-compete them. That fear was behind their strategy. In my neighborhood at the corner of Manning Avenue and Franklin Street, we had Mr. Boykins, principal of Lillie Burney, directly across the street; Mr. Nathaniel R. Burger, principal of Eureka then Royal Street or Rowan up the street on Manning in the next block; Mrs. Bryant, home economics teacher, in the same block at the corner of Manning and Ronie Street; and Jimmie James Jr., band director at Travillion and the future chair of the Department of Music at Jackson State University, the first Black person to earn a PhD from the University of Southern Mississippi in Hattiesburg, and the legendary voice of Jackson State's famous "Sonic Boom of the South," who lived on the same block as Mr. Burger and adjacent to Mrs. Bryant at the corner of Spencer Street and Manning Avenue. We had the best of the best in the segregated community. Other Black communities in Hattiesburg and all over the South had it like that also. And to our right on the other corner of Franklin, Mr. and Mrs. Smith had a horse, cows, and chickens.

—*Don Denard*

As I reminisce over my educational journey, I think back to the year 1964 when I entered the ninth-grade class at Lillie Burney Junior High School. It was then that I was first introduced to sewing in the Home Economics class. Our teacher Mrs. Ruby Draughn handed us a pattern. I had seen a pattern before, but did not know that the actual envelope contained pattern pieces, and that these pattern pieces would be used to create the picture that was on the envelope.

The entire class was required to make an apron, (not just a simple one with a sash that tied around the waist) but this apron had to include arm holes and pockets. This very pattern would be used to teach the basic steps in sewing clothes. Who knew that this would inspire me and my best friend Doris Townsend to make our next item which was a formal evening gown! It was then that I discovered that I actually enjoyed sewing which developed into a passion. In fact, I loved it so dearly that my great-grandmother Mrs. Elsie Kelly bought me my very own Touch & Sew sewing machine which included a cabinet! I was so excited but I have to admit, I would not have taken such a chance to spend this much money on a ninth grader, especially since she made very little money babysitting. As time passed, I began to sew for others. At this point, I had four regular paying customers and the money I made was used to help pay for transportation to get me back and forward to my night classes in college. As I entered high school, I began to dabble in designing clothes. I then decided that once I graduated high school I would pursue a career in designing clothes.

—*Patricia Griffin*

The school facilities at Lillie Burney were exceptionally nice, and we were eager to attend. This made it a bit easier to say goodbye to Rowan. Things were done differently from the start. Homerooms within the same grade were distinguished from each other by a letter chosen by the homeroom teacher. Instead of 8-1, 8-2, and 8-3, the numbers denoting the section of the grade were replaced by a letter. I was in Mr. John Bucklen's homeroom class (him again). Our class was 8-Q. In the ninth grade, I was in 9-L. I learned many years later that Mr. Bucklen was a member of Omega Psi Phi fraternity in college, as I was later at Jackson State. The Omegas are known as the Ques. (The small case form of the Greek letter Omega is *q*.) We didn't realize it at the time, but Mr. Bucklen chose 8-Q as a salute to his fraternity. And that's the way it was—teachers chose the letter that was affixed to their section of the grade based on their personal discretion. The way the school was set up felt new and innovative in all respects. It was a long, long walk to school from my house though.

It might sound as though Burney was nothing but athletics and band; however, we had a first rate faculty and

administration and performed at a high level academically. The curriculum was diverse, including all the usual
academic courses and new areas as well. Everyone in the
eighth grade took industrial arts from Mr. Bucklen. We had
mechanical drawing in his class, did leatherwork, and had
a kiln for making pottery items. The English department
was outstanding with Mr. Clark and Mrs. Magee. If I recall
correctly, Mr. Alphonso Clark was my ninth grade homeroom teacher (9-L). The biology teacher was the lovely Mrs.
Poole. All the boys had a schoolboy crush on her, especially
since her husband was far away in Alaska serving in the
military. Needless to say, she received total cooperation
in class from the boys and was loved by the girls as well.
Mr. Clark taught eighth grade English and had us presenting in front of the class on current events. James Rambo
would usually wow the class with his erudite presentations
on current topics like the harmful effects of aspirin. On
the other hand, Tommy Hall and I would sometimes present on Hattiesburg American articles on shootings at the
High Hat Club, to which Mr. Clark would say, "That's not
what I mean by current events. Look, Rambo gets up here
and speaks on topics about science and politics, and you
guys get up here talking about what happened at the club."
Then he would shake his head and call the next person up.
In ninth grade English, Mrs. Magee held forth with the
future in mind. One day, someone made a verbal grammat-
ical error in speaking. She immediately interrupted the student, saying to the class, "Hold it, hold it. If you make that
mistake somewhere when you get grown, someone will ask
'Who did you have for ninth-grade English?' You're not

going to embarrass *me*. You're going to get this before you leave my class." This illustrates better than anything else the sense of mission and destiny that our Black teachers had in Hattiesburg.

The new junior high school, Lillie Burney, had a tragedy during the summer just before the school opened that deserves a mention. James Tate, a promising basketball talent, had what appeared to be a heart attack while practicing with the team in the new gym. We were devastated to learn that he passed away in the building before the school was occupied.

In more bad news, my good friend, Wendell Fairley and I got into a fight during a pep rally in the gym in the ninth grade, and got expelled. This happened on a Friday, and we had a football game that night. Mr. Boykins was no-nonsense about it when he saw that I, his neighbor, was involved, wanting to demonstrate impartiality. His action was swift. We were immediately expelled, and neither of us could perform with the band, which was just awful because we had a good halftime show planned and a band that was small. We couldn't afford to lose two people. The lower brass section consisted of one trombone, one baritone, and a tuba. Liddie Earl Simpson had to hack it alone and gave it his all on trombone while I stood stupidly in the stands watching them perform. I think our feature song was "Walk on By" by Burt Bacharach. Our parents had to bring us to school that next Monday in order for us to be readmitted. When they let us back in, Wendell and I were so happy, we shook hands while looking each other in the eye then rushed off to class.

We had May Day activities, in which Randall Lewis Williams and I won all the field games it seemed—

three-legged race, wheelbarrow race—and Randall won the sack race. We also had our own prom with a band and everything. I remember Randall and me planning to wear gold cummerbunds and bowties. Ugh.

—*Don Denard*

I then attended Rowan for the seventh grade, and the next year, a school was built and named for Mrs. Lillie Burney, the principal of Mary Bethune. I attended Lillie Burney for the eighth and ninth grades.

—*Rose Mary Montgomery Harrell*

After completing elementary, I attended W. H. Jones Jr. High School. I can remember, as a teenager, we would have to walk to and from school in the worst weather you could imagine. But we survived the good and the bad. I enjoyed those years at W. H. Jones. Sometimes it would be so cold there would be icicles hanging on the corner of our house and on the school, especially after a hard rain. The fun part of walking home each afternoon was being surrounded by my best friends. The group would stop at the store, Papa Stoper, to buy snacks, play, and just have some good old fun. My group of friends consisted of Carolyn Atkins, Hattie Williams Knight, Joann Conner, and Sarah Ann Evans. These were the best friends any girl could ask for. Even my teachers made those years at W. J. Jones not so bad.

—*Barbara Thomas Ross*

 It is now 1962, and I'm on my way back across town to W. H. Jones in the seventh grade. We are full-blown teenagers now, and this is the time when the boys like to walk you home and carry your books. I have fond memories of Miss Bell and the NHA. I was a member, and we had to wear navy and white on our adventures. I loved for Mrs. Bell to make those good cinnamon candy apples, the best. I remember when the Mexicans came to Jones from Piney Woods and we sang "South of the Border." The most tragic event of my time at W. H. Jones was the assassination of President John F. Kennedy. A sad, sad day, but we made it to Rowan. Praise be to God.

—Bernita Parker Johnson

After Eureka, I went to W. H. Jones Jr. High School. I sang in the choir directed by Mrs. Ruby Wilson. For May Day, we danced to "Shotgun" by Jr. Walker and the All Stars. We had special guests from Piney Woods School. Some of my teachers were Mr. Percy Gambrell (history), Mr. David Connor (math), Professor Richard Hervey (shop), Martha Hall (English), Georgia Robertson (PE), and the principal was Samuel Wilson.

—Betty Bournes Hill

After finishing the sixth grade, we had to attend another school, W. H. Jones Elementary. We had no school buses at that time so again we had to walk from Front Street to Lula Avenue.

I remember when it was cold, we didn't wear pants so we wore them under our dresses and pulled them off and put them in our lockers until after school. When I said *we*, it was Hattie Ruth Williams, Barbara Ann Thomas, Evelyn Lewis, and myself.

Mrs. Tademy was my eighth-grade teacher. We had to learn the poem "O Captain, My Captain." After we all tried to recite the whole poem, none of us got it right. So Mrs. Tademy was kind of upset with us. She started reciting the poem herself. Alvin Gamble said out loud, "She oughta know it. She's older than the Captain." Good thing she didn't hear him!

Some of my teachers while attending W. H. Jones were Mrs. Tademy (English), Mrs. Ruby Wilson (music), Mrs. Maude Hudson (P. E.), Mr. Gambrell, Mr. David Conner (math), Mrs. Ruby Bell (home economics).

—Carolyn Atkins

The only prom I attended was the ninth-grade prom, and I had a great time. I wore one of my mother's old flowered dresses.

—Doris McNeill Collins

I was introduced to music at an early age because my Mother was the pianist at several local churches: Sweet Pilgrim on first and third Sundays and Antioch on second and fourth Sundays. Mr. Jesse O. Flowers was my piano teacher for many years. I never really enjoyed the piano, but as I look back, I wish I had studied harder. What I really enjoyed was singing. Gospel was my forte, but I sang other genres too.

At Mary Bethune, I was a member of the tonette band (now called a recorder) where I played both tonette and autoharp.

The summer between sixth and seventh grades, I taught a few of my friends how to read music, and by the time school began, many were proficient enough to join the beginner band at Rowan. Most of us played in the band through high school and many through college.

—*Doris Townsend Gaines*

I attended Rowan in the seventh grade. At that time, Rowan was 7-12. I had Mrs. Ariel Barnes, Mr. Bucklen, and four other teachers. One of the teachers was the worst teacher I ever had. I will not mention his or her name. We did not learn anything in that class. All we did was sit and talk all period long. One day I asked him or her to please teach us something. He or she did a wonderful job. I thought for sure we were going to learn something now. To my disappointment, the next day and the rest of the year, we learned nothing. I made a prophetic statement. I said this to myself, "If I become a teacher, I would not let my students just sit and do nothing. I would do my best to educate them."

In the eighth grade, I attended a brand-new school (Lillie Burney Jr. High School). We were excited about having a new facility and a lot of new teachers. I can only remember four of the teachers—Mrs. Perry (history), Mr. Clark (English), Mrs. Poole (science), and Coach Dedrick. I made all-star that year. A tragedy occurred at our school that year. Mary Tate's brother was a good basketball player.

We were looking forward to beating W. H. Jones that season. We arrived at school one morning and heard that he had died during basketball practice. Also, Linda McGlothan was the first queen at Lillie Burney. I also met my future wife that year (Willie Ruth McDonald). We have the same first name. That's what got my attention. We married eight years later. All the boys were in love with Mrs. Poole. She was gorgeous.

The ninth grade was somewhat uneventful. We lost again to W. H. Jones. I believe Robert Knight was our quarterback. Two things remain in my memory (I'll only discuss one). We had an industrial arts class taught by Mr. Bucklen. He taught us mechanical drawing for six weeks. Don Denard and I were racing to finish first. We finished about the same time. He took his drawing to Mr. Buckley first. He had no mistakes (100). Mr. Buckley began to grade mine next. The bell rang; he told me to put my drawing away. He told me he would grade my drawing first the next day. When I looked for my drawing the next day, it was missing. Someone had stolen my drawing; Mr. Bucklen made me do my drawing all over again. I was miffed; I was incensed.

—*Willie Sanders*

My seventh, eighth, and ninth grade years were spent at W. H. Jones Junior High School. We changed classes and had a different teacher for each class. I was unhappy because my brother and I were not in the same class. I found new friends and soon learned to feel comfortable with this schedule. I joined the band and played the flute for three years. The band directors were Mrs. Ruby Wilson and Mr. Sherill Holly. Our teachers were Mrs. Martha Hall, Mrs. Rhoda Tademy, Mrs. Georgia Mae Robinson Walton, Mr. Melvin Cooper, Mr. David Conner, Mr. Percy Gambrell, Mr. Sherill Holly, Mrs. Ruby Wilson, Mr. Winfred Hudson, Mr. Prentiss Jones, Mr. Eugene Jones, Mrs. Ruby Bell, and Mr. Earl Carr. Our principals were Mr. Samuel Earl Wilson and Mr. Percy Gambrell.

—*Mildred Miller Short*

On to junior high! I attended W. H. Jones Junior High. Going to junior high was like a shot of adrenaline. Such excitement. One year I was Miss W. H. Jones. There were basketball games, and footballers, and cheerleaders. I even joined the dramatics club under the direction of Mrs. Tademy, our English teacher. Everything was so upbeat. One of my worst days in junior high was having a fight with the school bully, Charlie (Dewdrop) Harris (RIP). There was a lot of pushing and shoving. From then on, Charlie wanted to date, but that was a big no-no! I also made new friends at W. H. Jones Jr. High.

—*Kathryn Bouie Boyd*

There were so many students who stayed in the Gholah who generally walked in groups, i.e., Carolyn Hall, Shelley Mae Stallworth. Many others walked to school as we got older. Attending W. H. Junior High School was indeed an experience and although I played in the band, I also focused on my academics. My friendships with Carolyn Hall, Beverly Harris, Shelley Stallworth, Linda Leggett (were best friends) and others continued during this time. All our junior high teachers were all something serious: Mr. Percy Gambrell, Maude and Winfred Hudson, Mrs. Bryant, Mrs. Tademy, Mrs. Ruby Wilson, etc. Mr. Gambrell made such an impression. I remember an instance when he told the class to line up for lunch, and if we were not in the same place in line when we returned to class, we would get his strap in our hand. I was leading the line when we went to the cafeteria. After lunch was over, I was talking to someone and the line was leaving the cafeteria so I could only catch the end of the line and was now last. Well, when we got back to the classroom, Mr. Gambrell came down the line, checking to see if anyone was out of order until he got to me, and he said, "*Mildred*, are you out of line?" I said "yes, sir," but I tried to explain. He was so tall, looking down at me. I vividly remember we called him "Lurch" from the Adams Family! He said to me "*Mildred*, open your hand" and began to give me my punishment for not following his instructions. I never forgot Mr. Gambrell after that, and neither did I ever get out of line again going to the cafeteria in his class. Mr. Gambrell was an excellent teacher, but I just would always see his "piercing eyes" looking down at me, saying **"M I L D R E D,"** to see if I was on track. I was so glad and said "thank God" when I finished his class. I always thought Mr. Gambrell had something against me, but looking back, I think many of his former students probably felt the same way about him! I never knew he would be waiting for me after I finished high school. You will understand what I mean by the end of my memoir.

—*Mildred Johnson Watts*

At Lillie Burney, I wasn't allowed to date or go anywhere by myself. When the school had any activities, my parent would chaperone all the dances. The kids at school called my Father "Moses on the March" because when you saw me and my sisters, you saw my Daddy. Some of the parents in the neighborhood would let their children go with us.

When school started in September of 1965, we had to walk to school. I didn't know I had an admirer, or today he'd be called a stalker, who watched me every morning walking to school. Wow! His name is Terry Jackson, a tenth grade student at Rowan High School. His classmate, Jackie Poole, told him about me. My admirer wanted to know who I was and what I looked like. He fell deeply in love with me that very first day he saw me, and I didn't even know he existed until he came to one of our dances at Lillie Burney. It was love at first sight for me too. We didn't see each other often because I was not dating and never had a boyfriend. It wasn't his classmate that brought us together; it was God's intervention at His appointed time for Terry and I to meet. He has kept us together for forty-eight years. Our love for each other has not changed; it has grown stronger.

—*Deborah Barrett Jackson*

For seventh grade, we went to Rowan Junior Senior High School. Coach Edward Steele was our sponsor and we changed classes that year. Our homeroom was out in the "shop" adjacent to the boys' woodworking shop. It was located outside the gymnasium and near the football field.

Coach Steele was said to be mean on the football field, but he was a kitten in class. He remained one of my favorite teachers and friend until his death.

I also competed for Miss Rowana, a part of the Miss Rowan pageant for the junior high students, where I won the cotitle that year. I sang a medley of "Moon River" and "Around the World in Eighty Days." Deborah Barrett (Jackson) was also a contestant for the seventh graders. We had to make an exhibit about ourselves in the library where I displayed the tonette, autoharp, my clarinet, a picture with me seated at the piano and other pictures, and a jewelry box made with mosaic tiles.

—*Doris Townsend Gaines*

In junior high (Lillie Burney), my favorite teacher was Mrs. Carrie Magee (English). She pushed me to do the work, not make excuses.

—*Ethelyn Fairley Reid*

After elementary, I attended L. J. Rowan Senior High for the seventh grade. During that time, a junior high school was not in my hometown. At Rowan, I really enjoyed myself.

After my seventh-grade year, they finally built a junior high school. It was called Lillie Burney. There I met my next dear friend. His name is Felder Tatum and like P-Wee and Don, we are still best friends. After junior high, I attended L. J. Rowen again for my sophomore through senior year; I graduated in 1968.

—*Hayes Boles Jr.*

In 1962, my Grandmother died and we moved to the city to live with my grandfather. Lillie Burney Junior High School (another brand-new school) was completed in 1963. So I attended another fresh and consolidated school where I got to meet all new people again. Only a few came from Earl Travillion, but I had already met Gloria Pigford, Betty Keys, Climmie Adams, and Gregory Walker. It wasn't long before I fell into a group of true friends: Hettie Marsh, Linda Russell, Mattie Harris, and Geraldine Shaw. We studied together and copied off each other's homework as much as possible. I remember Mrs. Rubye Draughn really taught us a lot in the home economics class. She couldn't help but laugh when some of those aprons and dresses came out lopsided. The cooking and sewing classes really helped and prepared me for life. Now the English and literature class was stressful to me. Mrs. Magee, with that story about the Ancient Mariner and the story with the Peggotty family, really rocked my nerves. It was probably because I didn't take time to really read the book. I understand now, but back then it was just confusing to me. I went to my first prom in the ninth grade. My date stood me up so my Dad took me in his pulpwood truck. I walked back home with someone else's date. I remember going to the teen center on Royal Street on Friday nights. It would be packed with teens doing the Boogaloo and slow-dancing. I finished the eighth and ninth grades at Lillie Burney; now time to move on again to another school.

—Juanita Mayes Walker

After "graduating" from the sixth grade at Eureka Elementary, my sister and I enrolled at W. H. Jones Junior High School. This was a step up as we now had lockers for our books, rotated classrooms and teachers, and "dressed out" in a T-shirt and shorts for our physical education class every day. This was "big boy" stuff to me. Mr. Samuel Earl Wilson was our principal, and the teachers were just as caring and dedicated as they were at Eureka. My teachers at W. H. Jones included Mrs. R. M. Tademy, Mrs. Rubye Wilson, Mr. Melvin Cooper, Mr. Percy Gambrell, Mrs. Virgie Gambrell, Mr. Otis Chambers, Coach Ralph Burns, Mr. Jones, Mr. Sherrill Holly, and Mr. David Conner.

—Melvin Miller

CHAPTER 5

High School

The tenth grade was a year of new faces, new teachers, and harder classes. Some of the teachers were Mr. Smith  (biology), Mrs. Johnson (English), Mr. Ellis (math), and Miss Weathersby (world history). I also met two very smart girls—Carolyn Hall and Beverly Harris. Out of all the tests and quizzes we had between grades 10 – 12, I only made higher scores than they did two or three times. I have to mention Miss Weathersby. We were excited about the Christmas holiday that was upon us. She wished us Merry Christmas and a Happy New Year. She said, "Before you all leave, I have an assignment that I want turned in on the first day of return to school." She gave us about five to ten pages of questions to do. These questions came from three chapters. I met Benida Parker that year.

The eleventh grade was good because that meant I only had one more year to go. I had the following teachers: Mrs. Burger (American history), Mrs. Nicholson (English), Mr. Pickett (chemistry), and Mr. Ellis (math). Mrs. Hudson tried to teach us how to square dance. A few of the students did well at square dancing; I was not one of them. I really enjoyed Mrs. Nicholson's English class. She had a sense of humor. I believe all her students enjoyed her class. We had weekly assembly programs (hymns, prayer, plays, etc.). I had a crush on Alma Jean Hall that year.

My senior year was full of excitement and nostalgia. I knew that would complete my schooling in Hattiesburg. I knew that college, marriage, children, and other things awaited me in the future. I had heard a lot about Mrs.

Chambers. Most students dreaded going to her class. I can truly say that I enjoyed her class of geography and civics. Her class was never boring. Here are some other teachers I had my senior year: Mr. Pickett (physics), Miss Sandifer (English), Mr. Ellis (math), and Mrs. Eastland (typing). I learned to type using a blind typewriter. I have used that skill all my life and even now. Mr. Pickett took the science club to NASA in Houston, Texas. What most students feared and dreaded about Mrs. Chambers's class was the end of year. If you owed her anything, she kept a record of it. If a student did not make up whatever she had you down for, you were not going to graduate. The seniors were trying to clear up all assignments and pay expenses. All the senior teachers were in the auditorium to check us off. Mrs. Chambers was at the end of the line. When my time came, she looked in her roll book. She looked and looked.

She said, "I don't see where you owe me. You must owe me something. Yes, you do owe me something. Willie, you mispronounced the word *corporation*. You must pronounce that word correctly." She told me to say the word.

I said, "*Cor*-po-ra-tion."

She said that was not correct. She enunciated the word for me: *cop*-po-ra-tion. To this day, I still disagree with her. To graduate and get out of school, I did not argue. I pronounced the word exactly as Mrs. Chambers had done. That year, I participated in a play; I went to the prom. Mr. Pickett gave us a problem to do for our final exam in physics. I was the first one in class to get it right. I got the problem right before Beverly and Carolyn.

—*Willie Sanders*

Now on to Rowan High School for bigger and better things! Although I still had to walk to Mobile Street, we now could ride the city bus to school. Some of us got on the bus at Hall's Funeral Home; others got on at Mrs. Lillie's newsstand. I was shy and I really didn't like Rowan. We had to meet the students that stayed on that side of town. Some of them weren't very nice. After a few months, it got better, thanks to God! Each year got a little better. Good enough for me to graduate with the Class of 1968— thanks be to God! I could not have a better group of classmates. Love you all!

—*Carolyn Atkins*

 On to high school: L. J. Rowan High. Those living on the Mobile Street side of town had to catch a city bus to Rowan. We had to walk from our homes to Mobile and Sixth Streets. For some of us, it seemed like a mile walk (more or less). We buddied up to make that walk so it wasn't so bad. Rain or shine, we were determined to get to school every day. I enjoyed Rowan, the teachers, students, and all the extracurricular activities at school. I enjoyed my applied chemistry class with Mr. Pickett and Mr. Albert Peyton. This was an after-school class, and those attending earned extra credit. Overall, my high school years at L. J. Rowan High were most important as I'm sure they were to all graduating seniors, Class of 1968.

—*Kathryn Bouie Boyd*

My most favorite memories of Rowan were so many outstanding teachers, football games, our band or trips, homecoming parades, prom, and competitions with other schools. Our school was so competitive. We had the very best teachers. They cared about us outside the classroom and wanted us to be the very best. They taught us about current world events and made sure we stayed current. Whether an administrator, teacher, or coach they all cared. Although we didn't have much, you just felt you were well off. There was so much love, enough to go around.

My other favorite memories were just being around my friends, i.e., I really liked being around Carolyn Hall (I think everyone did). She was so smart (still is) you knew you could have an intellectual conversation and fun at the same time. I can say the same about Beverly Harris, Doris, Denard, Melvin Miller, and others. Each one brought their own individuality to the conversation. Whether I was at band practice, Shelley Mae Stallworth was so inspirational. But all I can say is our class of 1968 was just a group of smart, talented, mature visionaries and I can go on and on. I hate to call just a few names. In my opinion, everyone had something special, even those who were relatively quiet and soft-spoken (i.e., Carolyn Atkins, Patricia Turner, Katherine Bouie, etc.). I just don't remember high levels of contentiousness among us (classmates) that you hear about in the schools today (i.e., fights, gangs, knives, guns, and police in the school, etc.). In my opinion, we were just competitive with one another and not mean-spirited or vindictive. When

I look back at the atmosphere of our class, I saw it more like family in many cases and sisterhood and/or brotherhood.

—*Mildred Johnson Watts*

I don't remember much about Mr. Graves, but I believe he was only there at Rowan one year. Mrs. Georgia Johnson was my English teacher. She was a very good teacher who expected the best from each of her students. She sent me to the counselor's office once because she believed that I was eating in her class. That was not the case, and for once, I stood my ground. I don't know if she ever realized that I would not have taken that position had I not thought that I was right. Miss Iva Sandifer was a good listener and a good giver of advice. Of course, Mrs. Marjorie Chambers was a teacher who was no-nonsense and had a way of imparting information that you could retain. I still read the newspaper from cover to cover from her teachings. She had a bulletin board on which she posted pictures of renowned people that she called the Rogue's Gallery. I digress—tenth, eleventh, and twelfth grades were back at Rowan. My tenth-grade homeroom teacher was a Mr. Graves, eleventh grade was Mrs. Georgia Johnson, twelfth grade was Mrs. Iva Sandifer. I also was a member of the band, science club, the Tri-Hi-Y, the journalism club, and was on the yearbook staff.

—*Doris Townsend Gaines*

During the years I attended Rowan High, I'd say the experience was like the average teenager during high school—some good, others not so good. My favorite memories were interacting with friends and participating in activities (clubs, choir). My most troubled memories were being picked on (bullied), and negative experiences of being in a lower socioeconomic status.

In general, there were some teachers, administrators, coaches, and students that stood out and had a positive influence and others that did not. The most significant benefit of attending a segregated school was experiencing a strong sense of Black identity. I learned early in life to acknowledge or appreciate successes in the Black community.

—Ethelyn Fairley Reid

While attending Rowan, which was an all-Black high school, it was a little different from junior high school and elementary school. At Rowan you could meet other students from the surrounding neighborhoods. The teachers and the administration were there to give you moral support in all areas of education. My most terrible memory of school was going into Mrs. Eloise Hopson's class and getting up in front of the class to give an oral report. I would be so nervous and afraid. You would say that I was a shy and timid person. Another teacher that you had to be on your p's and q's with was Mrs. Marjorie Chambers. You knew that you couldn't skip her class. She taught American history and government. I appreciated all the teachers and staff that were there for us; if not for them, we would not have succeeded. Another favorite subject was English taught by Miss Iva Sandifer.

—Hattie Williams Knight

 Some of the greatest memories I have are during my high school years. I met a lot of great people that I did not grow up with and developed lifelong relationships. Marjorie Chambers, Eloise Hopson, Iva Sandifer, Helen Nicholson, and so many others were ahead of the game. They knew what we were facing and exposed us to more than the norm.

—*Lionel Peyton*

The civil rights movement and the historical events of the past were very much on my mind as I prepared to enter Rowan High School in the fall of 1965. I was excited, yet a bit fearful of what would lie ahead. The world around me was changing, and I was confident that Rowan High School could prepare me for these challenges and any future opportunities they represented.

During my first year at Rowan, I took the college preparatory curriculum because my parents had instilled in my sisters and me the importance of going to college when we graduated from high school. For me, education represented a means to escape a life of poverty and possibly being relegated to just hanging out in the cafes and pool halls on Mobile Street. Not that I was any better than those persons who were currently in these situations. It's just I realized that doing my best at Rowan and entering college were essential steps in reaching my goals in life.

At Rowan, I took classes in English, French, math, chemistry, history, and other courses that would prepare me for college. I even enrolled in a typewriting class under Miss D.

I. Easterling. We were taught to type on "blind" typewriters, which had no lettering or numbering on the keys. We had to memorize the keyboard and not look down at the typewriter while typing. At that time, I did not really appreciate having to learn to type that way, but years later, this skill proved to be a tremendous asset for me in college and my professional career.

Our principal at Rowan was Professor Nathaniel R. Burger, who provided the kind of quiet, professional, and rock-solid leadership that commanded respect from students, faculty, and staff. Looking back, it is apparent to me that our teachers were competent and highly motivated. The building and grounds were always clean, and the school spirit at Rowan was always high. Our football team, the Mighty Rowan Tigers, was always championship caliber and the pride of the community. Professor Burger was an excellent school administrator, who had earned the admiration of the people of Hattiesburg, both Black and White. This was no easy task given the social unrest and turbulent times of the 1960s.

Professor Burger assembled a great faculty at Rowan. The teachers, in my opinion, were caring, gifted, and extraordinarily talented. "Prof" Samuel Ellis was our math teacher, and he was particularly good at getting us to really work hard in the classroom. He taught a new concept in math called sets. I was never really excited with the sets concept and once thought about not doing my homework assignments. But Prof Ellis had a no-nonsense approach to teaching math, and since he was also a coach on the football team, I did not wish to find out his method of discipline.

I took a public-speaking class under Mrs. Eloise Hopson, another no-nonsense teacher who insisted on us doing our best at all times. She was also smooth, eloquent, and dedicated to her craft. Her critiques of our oratorical presentations were detailed and exacting. I gave so many speeches that my hands eventually stopped trembling, and my self-confidence improved dramatically. Thanks to Mrs. Hopson's speech class, I even won a mock election for Mayor during our Hi-Y and Tri-Hi-Y regional meeting in Purvis, Mississippi, in 1968.

One of the most intriguing teachers was our biology teacher, Mr. Charles Smith, who wore a bow tie and kept it in a lab specimen jar when not wearing it. I marveled at Mr. Smith, who never opened the biology textbook as he taught us in class, but he knew from memory every page and paragraph in the book!

Another science teacher of note was Mr. Roscoe Pickett, who taught us chemistry and was the science club sponsor. Mr. Pickett's greatest contribution in my life was when he took the science club to Houston, Texas, to tour the NASA Space Center. Each student had to raise twenty dollars to cover the cost of the trip, so I joined several classmates— Walter Crosby, Willie "Pee Wee" Brown, and others—for four consecutive weekends to cut grass, rake yards, and do odd jobs to raise our part of the funds needed. We were successful, and about twenty students made the trip to Houston. To save money on hotel expenses, we stayed one night in New Orleans at Tulane University and one night in Houston at Texas Southern University. This also allowed us to visit two college campuses while we were seniors. In addition to NASA Space Center, we also visited the famous Astrodome and watched a professional baseball game. Mr. Pickett taught us to think big, work hard, and realize our dreams.

There were many other teachers who greatly influenced me at Rowan, including Mrs. Addie N. Burger, Mr. Richard Hervey, Coach Edward Steele, "Prof" James Harrison, Mrs. Helen Nicholson, Miss Iva E. Sandifer, Mrs. Marjorie Clark, Miss Fredna Bell, Mrs. Eleanor Harris, Mrs. D. I. Easterling, and Mrs. Jayne Sargent.

But the teacher who captured my undivided attention was Mrs. Marjorie Chambers, our twelfth-grade social studies teacher, affectionately and otherwise known as the Hawk. Mrs. Chambers was the most professional, most demanding, and most creative teacher that I have ever met. She was tall, smart (valedictorian of her high school and college classes) and took special interest in all her students. There was so much activity in her classroom each day—pop quizzes, oral reports, Weekly Reader assignments, daily current event questions, and special projects—that we were never bored or disinterested. Discipline in Mrs. Chambers's classroom was never a problem because no one wanted to be on the receiving end of one of her terse, intellectual, ego-deflating tongue-lashings, delivered with superb diction and enunciation as she reprimanded you in front of the entire class.

One final comment about Mrs. Chambers is that she was a master of student psychology. On our very first day in her class, she told us that although we were high school seniors, she would treat us as if we were first year college students and she expected as much from us. Consequently, we were eager to display our best decorum given our newfound status as "college freshmen."

—*Melvin Miller*

I loved being a student at Rowan High School. I looked forward to going to school every day. My years there were very affirming.

When I entered tenth grade, I knew my dream of graduating high school would become a reality. All I had to do was continue to work hard. I had wonderful teachers who supported and encouraged me. I was surrounded by other students who also wanted to achieve. In the twelfth grade, I was voted most competitive, while in reality, I just wanted to do and to be my best. These words of Langston Hughes became my mantra:

> Hold fast to dreams
> For if dreams die
> Life is a broken winged bird
> That cannot fly.
> Hold fast to dreams
> For when dreams go
> Life is a barren field
> Frozen with snow.

Extracurricular activities were very important to me. I joined every club that would allow me to join. I was proud  to serve as president of the student council and Tri-Hi-Y Club. I was a member of the debate team, journalism, science, and dramatics clubs. I held district and state offices for several organizations and was able to travel, compete, and meet students from other schools. I also developed valuable public speaking, leadership, and debate skills.

I had excellent teachers at Rowan:

Mr. Samuel Ellis taught us math, and he offered advanced math classes after school to help prepare us for college.

Mrs. Ira Sandifer taught us literature and poetry and insisted we learn about the classics.

Mrs. Eleanor Harris taught business skills and worked extra hard to teach me to type, with minimal success. I certainly appreciated her patience with me, and I enjoy her friendship today.

Mr. Roscoe Pickett was a teacher and mentor. He not only taught us physics, but he taught us life lessons as well. He offered an advanced science course after school for his students. Mr. Pickett also took a group of us on a senior trip to Houston, Texas, to the Astro Dome and Space Center.

Mr. Edward Steele was a football coach and math teacher. His math classes were easy and with college preparatory classes, we sometimes needed a break.

Mrs. Eloise Hopson was an exceptional teacher who taught speech, debate, and drama. She demanded our best and we delivered, not only at Rowan but also in district and state level competitions. I still cherish the speech and debate trophies I won under her tutelage.

Mrs. Helen Nicholson was one of the toughest teachers I had at Rowan. She taught English, and she demanded that her students use correct grammar in their speech and writing. I rejoiced the day I got my first exam paper back that had no red marks. I was so delighted to begin receiving

A's in her class instead of Bs. She taught us how to write essays and to be precise and concise when necessary. She really and truly helped prepare us for life.

Mrs. Marjorie Chambers taught us social studies and economics. She holds a special place in my heart as a teacher, a mentor, and a friend. Her role in my life is profiled in another section within this book. There were other outstanding teachers who touched my life at Rowan, including Mrs. Gloria Bryant, Mrs. Addie Burger, Mr. Leon Taylor, and Miss Clara Weathersby. As regards Mrs. Nicholson, Mrs. Hopson, Mrs. Bryant, Mrs. Burger, and Mrs. Chambers, our lives would later reconnect as fellow Methodists attending church events together.

I held fast to my dreams of completing high school and attending college. On graduation day, I was proud to be the valedictorian of my class. My dream of attending college became a reality when I received a full scholarship to Tougaloo College—the first in my family to complete high school and to attend college while paving the way for others. I would later go on to earn two master's degrees. I thank God that my dreams did not die.

—*Carolyn Hall Abrams*

 Arriving on Rowan's campus the first day of school was better than I had anticipated. The juniors and seniors were nice, even though it was initially difficult making friends. Being involved in extracurricular activities helped me meet other students. These activities included Tri-Hi-Y club, dramat-

ics club, debutante club, and the Rowan concert choir. The choir was my favorite outlet. I fondly remember my music teacher, Miss Fredna Bell, having to tolerate my nonsinging in her beautiful choir. I can recall her gritting her teeth when my soprano part was off-key. She was really nice about not singling me out. I shall never forget how much Mrs. Eloise Hopson (speech), Mrs. Addie Burger (social studies), and Mr. Roscoe Picket (friend of my father) took time to check on me to make sure I was okay throughout the year. I can recall, even today, how Mrs. Eloise Hopson called me to her classroom to give me some tips on giving a speech to an audience. She told me to not make eye contact with my audience, but to look a little over the audience heads. That is the technique that got a nervous girl through public speaking. It still remains a technique I use and I share with many of my own students and family members. Ginger Thomas, a student who had also moved to Hattiesburg, would always come to my library table during study hall to see if I needed help or just to carry on small talk.

One experience that will remain with me was a geography project assigned by Mrs. Marjorie Chambers. The assignment was to gather information on a country and explain the geographic location, culture, language, and economy in a group presentation. In addition to the assignment, I was the only female in my group. Among my group were Howard Lockett, Tommy Hall, and Clarence Breland. The group met regularly to gather information and to assign different parts of the presentation. It was a nightmare keeping the guys serious and on topic. I didn't know then what I know now about high blood pressure. In the end, all my stress led to a beautiful presentation. Each member pulled off their part and presented well enough for us to receive an A minus. Thanks, Mom and Dad, for your input as well!

As my senior year began to wind down, my thoughts turned to making preparations for college. Jackson State College was my first choice. I did not know a lot about Jackson but that Jackson is where I wanted to be. A negative comment made by a teacher stands out in my mind and troubles me even today. This teacher asked me where I was going to college. I responded saying in an exciting voice, "Jackson State College." The teacher's comment was, "You won't make it at Jackson State." This statement would become one of the driving forces in my desire to succeed. This negative statement also brought back my parents' confidence and love in me. They knew I would be successful at whatever college and career I chose.

—Patricia Berry Blake

During our senior year, one of my classes was with Miss Carter who taught math. We received the news of Martin Luther King's assassination the night before, and when we got to Miss Carter's class, everyone began crying so she could not have class. One after the other, we cried—the entire class. When Miss Carter entered the classroom, she did not say one word. The next day, she told us we would not graduate until we apologized to her. We were speechless and shocked, but we apologized to her before we could march down the aisle.

—Rose Mary Montgomery Harrell

Finally, the BIG one. L. J. Rowan High was filled with experiences I will forever cherish. Teachers that would change my educational experience for life. Miss Fredna Bell was an awesome choir director who taught me the technique of breathing and holding, which would later help me earn a scholarship to Jackson State University. Mrs. Marjorie Chambers was the *best* teacher (history repeats itself). She could use the outdated handed-down old books and bring us into the current news. Through her teaching, I gained an appreciation for news and the awareness of the politics of the world, country, state, county, and community we lived in. Mrs. Hopson and Miss Sandifer taught me the appreciation for literature and the fine arts.

Wow! We had some of the best coaches in football (the Big Eight champs) and basketball. Good days and years at Rowan. I participated in the choir, band (majorette), Tri-Hi-Y, Future Homemakers of America, debate team (which was not my strongest) and represented my class section for three years in the Miss Rowan Pageant. My senior year, I was crowned Miss Rowan 1968. What an honor I still cherish.

—Thelma Bacchus

My senior year at Rowan High School was very exciting. There were all kinds of extracurricular activities to do in the classroom and clubs to join on the campus. We had band, choir, football, basketball, track, FBLA,

NHA, advanced math class, Tri-Hi-Y, Hi-Y, Debate Team, trade and industrial arts, the yearbook staff, Miss Rowan Pageant, the applied chemistry club, cheerleader club, student council organization, science club, and journalism club. I joined the band and the Tri-Hi-Y, a club for girls only. Our sponsor was Mrs. Marjorie Chambers who took us to district and state conferences. We would excel in all areas of competition and always won first place in the talent competition with the help and expertise of Miss Fredna Bell, our music teacher and choir director. We had about sixteen sets of siblings in our class, including two sets of twins and numerous cousins, which are too many to list. It seems like everybody was related to somebody in the class.

Graduation time was very exciting because it was always held outside on the football field at Rowan High School. We would have baccalaureate services on Sunday morning that included a commencement sermon at 9:30 a.m. in the gymnasium and we would attend our own churches at 11:00 a.m. Our graduation was scheduled for Monday night on the football field. My twin brother and I (Melvin Allen Miller) experienced several disappointments on the days before our graduations. My grandparents and cousins had come to our house on Saturday to help us celebrate the occasion. Everyone was very excited. Late Saturday evening, my Mother and I went to Mt. Carmel Baptist Church to help work on the graduation program for the seniors who attended our church. I had about fifteen classmates graduating who attended church with me and my brother. While we were walking home, my Mother had a stroke and was rushed to the hospital. She was unconscious for about thirty to thirty-six hours. My family was very upset. My Grandmother said that my Mother would have wanted us to attend the graduation and be with our class. We rushed to the school on Sunday morning and our classmates were happy that we were there. On Monday morning, we put on our caps and gowns and went to visit my Mother in the hospital. She was very happy to see us. We graduated on Monday night, May 27, 1968, from L. J. Rowan High School with the Class of 1968.

—Mildred Miller Short

The 1961-62 school year was a milestone in my school career. I began junior high school. I was proud to be in the seventh grade. Students from Eureka Elementary joined us at W.H. Jones in making up the seventh-grade class.

Jones Junior High School was different from elementary school. We had a homeroom teacher and changed classes for each subject. Time management was important between classes. I remember not being able to get my locker opened in time to get my gym bag. Hearing the bell ring and still struggling with my combination lock was not a good feeling. Finally getting the locker opened I dashed off to class. Mrs. Georgia Robinson Walton, who is one of my shining stars, upon hearing my dilemma, excused my tardiness. Teachers who saw the sincerity of students and their efforts would work with them.

My shining stars at W.H. Jones Junior High School— Mrs. Rhoda Tademy; Mrs. Tademy was my English teacher. She was older and from a generation that believed in hard work. She instilled in her students the desire to work hard.

Besides English lessons, we would recite poem after poem. At this level we developed not only memory skills, but self-expression skills and confidence in public speaking as well.

Mr. Gambrell taught me social studies. He was a serious instructor who maintained order in his classroom and challenged his students to the highest level. Mr. Gambrell towered over us, being over 6-feet tall. His appearance got our attention, but he was kind. Mr. Gambrell impacted my life after high school. He had transitioned from teaching at the junior high level to college professor at Jackson State University. As I was a social studies and sociology major at Jackson State University, Mr. Gambrell not only taught me but oversaw my student teaching at Forest Hill High School in Jackson, Mississippi. Seeing him in my classroom to evaluate my performance only brought back memories of junior high, when he challenged me to be my best.

Mrs. Ruby Wilson taught me music appreciation. She was a serious teacher but with her "sunny" personality, learning was fun. Mrs. Wilson played for the classroom plays and oversaw musical productions. We were expected to fully participate. In one of her productions, we sang "Somewhere Over the Rainbow." I remember to this day the emotions this song evoked—Joy, hope, confidence, and inspiration. I was encouraged to say, "I can, too." Mrs. Wilson lived in the neighborhood and taught my sister and me piano lessons. School and community were personal.

Mr. David Lee Connor taught me math. He was a brilliant teacher with a laid-back demeanor. He taught fundamentals, application, and problem-solving techniques that all of his students could understand. Mr. Connor made math relevant to everyday life. His ease with students made math fun, and not intimidating. Mr. Connor lived in the neighborhood. Again, school and community was personal.

Mrs. Georgia Robinson Walton taught me physical education. This was the first time we had an organized class for physical activity, and we were given a grade. Class instruction, demonstration, and application were the foundations of the class. Mrs. Robinson Walton didn't just tell us to demonstrate a fundamental or technique. She showed us how. We were taught by example. She was patient with her students. I did not have a love for stunts, tumbling, and especially climbing the rope, but with her patience and instruction it was not intimidating.

Mrs. Juruthin Woullard. Junior high presented opportunities for participation in activities besides going to class. I was a member of the student council. Mrs. Woullard was our sponsor. We were taught leadership and organizational skills, in addition to representing the student body and making sure their voices were heard. Mrs. Woullard made sure we learned Parliamentary Procedure in order to conduct meetings that were orderly and productive. Her no-nonsense approach challenged us to be our best. When I see Mrs. Woullard, today I am reminded of the principles we learned that form the basis of society today: rules, law, and order.

In 1965 I transitioned to senior high school in the tenth grade at L.J. Rowan. All of my training and prior experiences had prepared me for the "big stage." Each level built the foundation for the next. All of my teachers in elementary and junior high school imparted in me knowledge and life lessons that propelled me to strive to be the best.

Since I stayed on the east side of town, I had to get to school on the bus for the first time of my school career. This meant getting up earlier to ensure I would not miss the bus. This was a layer of responsibility added to the life of senior high school.

I remember my first day of school. I was excited to be riding the bus. I remember getting off the bus and seeing the principal, Mr. N.R. Burger, standing outside to greet the students on the first day.

During my three years at Rowan, I remember Mr. Burger was always the same—professional, approachable, and encouraging. He set the example for hard work, dedication, and not to give up. He was an inspiration to his staff and students. Mr. Burger lived in the neighborhood. Again, school and community, it was personal. I salute all the teachers at Rowan. There were many who never taught me but formed a lasting impression because of their hard work and dedication.

Mrs. Helen Nicholson. Mrs. Nicholson taught me English. When you entered her classroom, you knew you were there for business. Make no mistake about it, her students received the grades they earned. I enjoyed her class because the bar was raised high for excellence. To some Mrs. Nicholson was intimidating but if you came to class and applied yourself, you had the best experience ever. She was professional, knowledgeable, and only wanted the best for her students. I often see Mrs. Nicholson today and remember how she inspired me to work hard and aim high. She is still classy, professional, but personal.

Mrs. Marjorie Chambers—Mrs. Chambers taught me social studies. Words to describe her are—scholarly, excellent, thorough, dedicated, and personal. Mrs. Chambers let you know early on what the course requirements were and what was expected. She did not lower the bar for students. Mrs. Chambers was wise enough to know that every student had different gifts and abilities. She challenged her students to be the best they could be. Students to this day will tell you that it did not go well for those who came to class unprepared. I admired Mrs. Chambers' drive for excellence. Her platform and subject-matter motivated me to pursue her field of study at Jackson State University. Under Mrs. Chambers's leadership, I was a member of the local chapter of Tri-Hi-Y and was assistant secretary of district Tri-Hi-Y during my senior year. I remember sitting in Mrs. Marjorie Chambers's room with someone watching through the glass wall to let us know she was coming back. Mrs. Chambers influenced my decision to attend Jackson State University and major in her field of study.

I remember Mrs. Ira Sandifer calling me "Mildred" because she had taught my Mother whose name was Mildred.

I remember Mr. Roscoe Pickett teaching us about life in his science class and taking us on a senior trip to Houston, Texas. A man of wisdom, he knew there was so much knowledge we lacked in facing the real world.

I also remember missing the school bus because of extracurricular activities and having to walk toward town (to connect with a bus to get home) with books stacked up to my chin.

I remember Mr. Charles Smith in tenth grade coming into the room shouting at everyone to be quiet and saying, "Harris, shut your—mouth."

Mrs. Eleanor Harris taught me typing. As with all of my shining stars, she raised the bar for excellence. Instruction, demonstration, and application were the blueprints for learning. We would work with those keys until we got it right. With Mrs. Harris' patience and dedication, some students would come in after class to practice. I recently saw Mrs. Harris at a funeral. She spoke as a neighbor. It was evident that besides the classroom, she was dedicated to her neighborhood and civic affairs. Neighborhood, school, and church. It was personal.

The skills I have acquired in Mrs. Harris's class helped me to excel in college, in my career, and beyond.

Mr. Roscoe Pickett taught me science. He was a unique teacher. Not only did he make sure we were knowledgeable in the subject matter, but he was a life coach as well. I remember he would often take time before class or at the end of class to teach us about life lessons, decisions, and consequences. Being young and sheltered, Mr. Pickett knew that there was a world and trappings that we had not yet experienced. Dedication and caring beyond the classroom made his star shine bright. Mr. Pickett was the advisor of the Science Club of which I was a member.

Mr. Pickett and his wife chaperoned a class trip to Houston, Texas in 1968. The trip was fun and educational, with Houston being the site of the Space Center. We also were able to attend a major league baseball game. Mr. Pickett's goal was for us to see that life was rewarding and fun as a result of hard work.

—Beverly Harris Abrams

We have now realized that L. J. Rowan Senior High School was one of the premier Black high schools in the state and in the nation. The school had the distinction of excelling academically and in athletics, sending students to some of the leading colleges and universities in the country where they performed with distinction. What we have learned from the many Euro reunions about how our graduates have fared in all professional fields, including athletics, is proof of the quality produced by our school.

In the tenth grade, the students from W. H. Jones and Lillie Burney came together for the first time. The result was a rich mix of talents and personalities who took some time to gel. There was a bit of competition among us at first. The students from "across town" were more urbane, cooler, it seemed, and they were sharp dressers, like the Mobile Street boys, and good dancers, like Larry and Glenda Brown. The competitive edge actually caused people to step up their game overall, and the enhanced performance by students showed up in the classroom, on the football, basketball, baseball, and track teams, and in the band and choir. Talent shows were exciting and always featured James Chatman playing boogie-woogie piano like a pro. Being in the band and going on band trips to places like Natchez, Greenwood, Canton, and Tupelo to support the football team was a highlight for me. Sometimes there might be a bit of drama, such as someone being put off the bus on the highway right outside of town for being caught with something problematic and Mr. Pickett having to come pick him up. Our band director, Mr. Harrison, was from Mississippi Valley State and had us going with a military style like Valley. Of course, we didn't get down like the Travillion marching band, but we were good. I remember us going to Jackson to play Jim Hill one year, and we cut their heads with our crispness and good sound.

When it came to girls, tenth grade was the start of something new. There were all these outstanding girls at Rowan, and my friends and I fell in love regularly. Didn't matter whether the girl knew it or not. Most times the girl didn't know it because you were too nervous to approach them for fear of rejection. You'd dial her number up to the last digit, think about it, then hang up out of fear. What would you say? Going to dances and house parties were some ways a boy got a chance to get to know a girl better if the girl went to the dance or party. Every girlfriend I had was, in my mind, "the one I'm gonna marry someday." I was convinced that I would, at different times, marry Erma Whitfield, Patricia Dowling, Patricia Turner (who broke my heart several times), Alice Adams, and by my senior year, I just knew that Jenna Young and I were made for each other. But Tee Tee, her Aunt, had other ideas about that. LOL!

My first class at Rowan in the tenth grade was algebra taught by a renaissance man in the form of Mr. Samuel Ellis. Renaissance in the sense that he represented the best of both worlds of greatness for which Rowan was known. He was a math wizard and an assistant coach for our championship football program. Having algebra for your first-period class and having Mr. Ellis meant you had to come prepared. During the first day of class, Tommy Hall asked the question, "Mr. Ellis, how many tests and quizzes will you give and when will you give them?" To which Mr. Ellis replied, "Nooo, son. I don't announce my tests and quizzes. My advice to you is 'Be ye ready at all times.'" Hall loved math, and he did us all a huge favor by asking the question. This let us know that we needed to be focused and serious like never before. Ever the renaissance man, Mr. Ellis also had an essential line of poetry on his bulletin board that stayed there all year:

> The moving finger writes and, having writ, moves on.
> Nor all your piety nor your wit shall lure it back to cancel out half a line of it.
> Nor all your tears shall wash out a single word of it.

It was so deep it was scary. I had never heard of Omar Khayyam, who wrote the poem above. That was our "welcome back to Rowan" party and an indication of the depth of the culture of our teachers and our people.

The other thing about Mr. Ellis was his penchant for proper behavior. Any misstep in his class would earn an invitation from him: "Come see me, son." That meant see him after school. When you got there, it was about placing your hands on his desk and, uhhh, meeting the wood. He would use a wooden pointer to administer stinging licks to the butt. When people would shrink away trying to avoid the licks, he would go, "Meet the wood, son. Meet the wood." It could be funny watching people get theirs while you're waiting your turn, and there would usually be several people from all his classes who had to come see him after school. I know from personal experience. Girls too. Doris was really funny when she had to go. She would be trying in vain to negotiate with him.

Mr. Ellis's teaching strategy (be ye ready, the moving finger writes) worked extremely well. One night at a basketball game, the scoreboard read 36–63 during a time-out as we were beating some visiting team badly. Doris stood up a few rows from me, looked over, and called out, "DENard!" She pointed to the scoreboard, saying, "Digits in reverse, digits in reverse." We had been studying algebra word problems in Mr. Ellis's class that dealt with forming equations to find two numbers whose digits were the reverse of each other. We were so focused on "be ye ready at all times" until we would pick up on algebraic situations while enjoying ourselves at games.

French class with Mrs. Nicholson was a joy at Rowan. We also had a French teacher named Mr. Jackson (Hall called him La Flippiaye) who was from Jackson State. Both teachers spoke the language perfectly and had our total attention. Cherlyn Clark did the best out of all of us with pronunciation in the dialogues we had to participate in because she wrote everything out phonetically, just the way it sounded and practiced until she got it right. I learned a lot from the way she worked it. She would do the same thing for Spanish in Señor Leon Taylor's class.

Mr. Roscoe Pickett was what would be called in sports today a beast. He taught chemistry and was a favorite. In class, Mr. Pickett demonstrated total mastery in teaching us the periodic table and all about molecules and how to balance equations. When a student accurately answered a question that he posed during class instruction, he would enthusiastically respond "Riiiiight!" Eliciting a "Riiight" from Mr. Pickett was a huge motivator. He was quiet, but you got the feeling that he was intense, and you didn't want to disappoint him because he had this look on his face that said things could get rough if you weren't careful. My Dad told me many years later that Mr. Pickett told him he stayed up late many nights in order to stay one step ahead of our class. Could have fooled me. He was on top of things.

Ms. Iva Sandifer was the woman who was the mother of our class and our class sponsor. Her English classes, instructional methods, and her graceful demeanor made some people take on the personas of the greats of literature. Randall had a lock on Paul Lawrence Dunbar's poetry. And Elester Hollingsworth became the poet laureate of our class based on his ability to render Shakespeare like no one else. When he would recite, Miss Sandifer would close her eyes and go to a special place mentally that only English teachers know. Elester was tight with James Rambo, and those two apparently decided years earlier that they would be the intellectuals of our class who were the most skilled at erudition and possessors of speech that was divine. Rambo left Hattiesburg before we graduated, so Lester was the bearer of the flame. At least, that's the sense I got when I would watch Miss Sandifer when he was reciting Shakespeare. He was awesome, and our section of her English classes excelled overall at pleasing Miss Sandifer, learning to write essays and earning good grades.

Mrs. Burger taught social studies in the eleventh grade. She was another in the line of sweetest teachers I ever had in my life. The girls would fawn over Mrs. Burger, and she would let them comb her hair. She also had the bad habit of letting Doris put their desks beside hers so that they could help her keep an eye on people who might be talking in class instead of listening. These girls would lean over toward Mrs. Burger and whisper, "Ms. Burger, look at DENard, look at Hall, look at whoever." Mrs. Burger is the one who sent Herbert Charles Knox and me to the principal's office one day when we got out of control. Hall had taken my book from under my desk, and Mrs. Burger had threatened anyone who came to class without their book. I continued to look for my book and wouldn't sit down when she instructed me to, so she tossed me out, and sent Charles packing based on his accumulated violations and the fact that he was laughing uncontrollably because I couldn't find my book and was desperate. In the principal's office, Mr. Burger gave us the lecture of a lifetime. It was scary. He told us one more incident and that would be it.

Mrs. Hopson taught speech. This is the point in my memoirs where I have a gripe. Mildred "Cookie" Johnson told me many years later about how they had special math sessions with Mr. Ellis and how things were in Mrs. Hopson's speech class. I never took speech in high school and wondered later how that happened. Mrs. Hopson was one of the legendary, gifted teachers at Rowan. But I finally figured out that, although I distinctly remember selecting college prep as my program at Rowan, I ended up in the general education program. My so-called friends—Doris,

Patricia, and Johnnie Bea—never found it odd and never mentioned to me that, although we did everything together in junior and high school, the exceptions were those special math sessions outside of school hours with Mr. Ellis and being in Mrs. Hopson's speech class. I was not in either setting but neither of them seemed to notice or care that I was missing out. I did fine in Mr. Ellis's class without the extra work, but I feel I missed a lot not being in Mrs. Hopson's class. I would hear some of the stories about what went on, how she would skillfully take it to students who didn't do what they needed to do, and how my "friends" took speech in the eleventh grade with seniors who were outstanding. I figured I would eventually be assigned to her speech class, but high school came and went, and I lost track of the fact that I never took speech from Mrs. Hopson until it was over. That's the main reason I took speech as an elective in college. Missing Mrs. Hopson is my one gripe about life at Rowan.

What I can offer as a memoir about Mrs. Hopson is what I recall hearing about an incident that happened with this one student who took her class. Someone told me about a conversation they overheard between two girls who were on the bus after school, laughing and talking about something that happened in Mrs. Hopson's class that day. Some boy had come to class unprepared to give a speech that had been assigned. According to the girls, this was someone who thought he was "smart" and quick on his feet, so he tried to fake his way through the exercise. At some point, Mrs. Hopson concluded that he was not prepared and angrily stopped him where he was. The story goes that people in the class felt bad for the young man because Mrs. Hopson didn't play and was fit to be tied. She was serious about her work as a teacher and had the expectation, after giving students a complete understanding of what they needed to do, that people would apply themselves, do their research, practice outside of class, ask for help if needed, and come to class ready to go. It was clear that this student was trying to fake his way through the assigned presentation and got caught red-handed by Mrs. Hopson. She reportedly read him the riot act in front of the class. The report was that students in the class were worried that the boy might have a nervous breakdown because he had to stand up there in the glare of criticism delivered in such terms that the two girls on the bus were talking about the masterpiece of verbal communication they experienced that day as Mrs. Hopson dressed down that student. They were like, "I bet nobody else will try that."

Mrs. Chambers, "the Hawk," was a force of nature. She scared people. Honestly, she scared everybody, including me. Former students were always dropping by to see her when they were home from college. We knew about that even before taking her class as seniors because we could see them in her class sometimes when we were walking down the hall. There was this full-length window to her classroom that allowed people walking in the hall to see inside the class. When we got into her class as seniors, her commanding voice let you know she meant business. Hall and Charles Knox were on their best behavior in Mrs. Chambers's civics and government class as were all of us. Hers was an approach to teaching that seemed to foretell the future that we would face. She was demanding while at the same time presenting subject matter and activities that held your interest. We studied the way that local, state, and federal government works, and she placed the information in a context that let us know that she was providing us insights that we needed to use in the future when that great getting up morning came. We studied how world affairs work and had this amazing unit on the United Nations that culminated in us convening a formal session of the UN Security Council discussing an issue of global importance and passing a resolution. As always, it was necessary for us to prepare thoroughly, and she wanted us to be able to present information and viewpoints in a way that was professional and convincing.

Two other examples are burned into my memory: the learning units on Money, Credit, and Banking and a mock gubernatorial campaign.

What is remarkable as I think about it now is the fact that she was innovating what is known today as experiential learning, before the concept came into common practice and before that was a term. When a student has a hands-on experience that requires the application of knowledge, this deepens understanding, builds skills, and takes the focus from being abstract to being practical. The way it worked in money, credit, and banking was that she taught us the mechanics of how financial institutions work. Savings and checking account deposits allowed banks to make loans because people leave a fairly steady level of funds in the bank

156

and don't all withdraw their money at the same. The banks can lend out some of these funds and drive business activity that produces jobs and more useful economic benefits to society. Once we got the gist of how this worked, she wanted us to develop a creative project to present in class that would showcase what we had learned about the topic. The fact that she put her own Black pride spin on everything she taught, we ended up with a project that unfolded as the grand opening of the First Negro National Bank. We had a number of speeches as part of the presentation that built up to a ribbon-cutting ceremony and more presentations. She inspired creativity and was happy to see students take to the work. When you could make the Hawk smile, you had done something.

The mock gubernatorial campaign was done by all periods, as usual. However, this learning unit was unusual because it took students outside of the classroom for some activities. The campaign was focused on real-life Mississippi politicians who were running for governor, John Bell Williams and someone by the name of Rubel Phillips. After studying how state government works and the important issues of the day, we launched into the campaign exercise that lasted a few weeks. We had to form two campaign committees, select the persons who would portray these two candidates, do research on the real-life candidates, conduct candidate debates, make campaign speeches on the issues, and hold question-and-answer sessions with the "voters." Some of Mrs. Chambers's periods ended up holding their events in the auditorium. I clearly remember Tommy Hall being John Bell Williams in the mock election campaign for his class period. In a display of realism, Hall came on stage with a crutch, limping, and with one of his arms under his suit coat because the real-life John Bell Williams had lost an arm. The fun began when he finished his campaign speech and took questions from the audience of voters. In his speech, he stated that the reason people should vote for him is because the government is supposed to serve the people, and he would do what the people wanted him to do as governor. Since majority rules, he would do what the majority wanted done. The first question he was asked came from a girl who wanted to know what he thought about Negroes demanding the same rights as other citizens. Hall stayed in character with the politics of the person he was portraying and responded, "If that's what the majority wants, that's what I want." The next questioner asked, what if the majority doesn't want Negroes to have their rights? His response, "If that's what the majority wants, then that's what I want." He stayed on that theme throughout. He couldn't help but give that knowing smile that said he was just playing politics and staying in character.

In my class, Charles Knox was Rubel Phillips, and I was John Bell Williams. My platform was not true to the real John Bell Williams. I turned my back on his views and supported equal rights for all. Mrs. Chambers liked for her students to be creative, so my campaign manager, Grady Gaines, and the committee decided that we needed to do something different with our campaign. We decided that, on the big day when we were to have the in-class debate between the candidates, we would have the campaign manager to give a short speech introducing the candidate then have the candidate enter the classroom accompanied by a small pep band playing "Go Mississippi." So I wrote up the music and drafted my old band buddy, Liddie Earl Simpson (trombone), Bobby Carpenter (tuba), and a student named William Harris, who was from the Quarters, on trumpet. They were having band class the same period that we had Mrs. Chambers. Rubel Phillips went first, giving his speech, to be followed by John Bell Williams. The problem was that the band had a bit of a problem getting the music right and wasn't ready, so poor campaign manager Grady had to stretch his introduction while I worked feverishly with the pep band going over the music with them in the band room. He told me that, while he was speaking, he would sneak a quick glance out into the hall through the large window in Mrs. Chambers' classroom to see if the candidate and the band were coming. If they weren't, he'd launch into something else about the candidate and the campaign. After what seemed an eternity, Grady finally saw us coming down the hall and began to wrap up the introduction. The band started to play "Go Mississippi" before we entered the classroom and continued to play for a bit while the candidate came into the room shaking hands as he passed the voters. Once they had played the eight bars of the song a few times, they stopped, got a rousing ovation from the class, and were able to leave going back to band class. We had kept this a secret, so everyone, including Mrs. Chambers, was shocked. After that, I gave my speech, then Charles Knox and I got into the debate.

What teachers like Mrs. Chambers and the entire Rowan faculty meant to generations of students cannot be overstated. When I got to college and later to grad school, I was ready.

—*Don Denard*

Some of the most memorable times of my life were at Rowan High School. The events that I loved most at school were talent shows and being a part of the marching band. The talent shows provided the opportunity for students to listen and see so many great outstanding performances such as singing, dancing, and playing a variety of instruments by our peers. I enjoyed participating in the talent shows. My talents were playing the piano and singing. These gifts came from God. Of course, I also enjoyed being a part of the marching band. The Class of 1968 was a community of learning, having fun, and developing lifelong friendships. Rowan High School was an extraordinary place that helped prepare me for the military, being a pilot, entrepreneur, and an elder in the church. This preparation aided me in my life-changing moment.

—*James Chatman*

The following names are just a few of my instructors and the subjects they taught. Miss Fredna Bell who taught chorus, always taught us to sing from our diaphragm. She said that this is the proper way to sing, and not from your throat. She did not want us singing like we were in a Baptist choir. When I decided to sing in the Baptist choir, they thought I was singing opera because I was taught properly. Mrs. Eleanor Harris was my typing teacher, and she would always say, "Keep your eyes on the text." Mrs. I. E. Sandifer taught English, and all she wanted us to do was read literature and recite poems. Miss Eloise Hopson, speech, oh my goodness. The first day in her class we were told to write an extemporaneous speech. I went to the counselor's office and told Mrs. Black that I needed to be put in another class. I wish I would have stayed in that class, because I missed an opportunity in speaking and writing. Mrs. Helen Nicholson, English, she would put two vocabulary words on the board every day for us to increase our vocabulary, and on Friday, we would have a test. It really helped increase my vocabulary. French, Mr. Jackson; home economics, Mrs. Rubye Draughn; Mrs. Marjorie Chambers, Economics, Civics, and Geography. Mrs. Chambers made sure that you knew the world map. Mrs. Thelma Harris, fifth grade, made sure we knew all eighty-two counties in Mississippi. We had to recite them, and she also made sure that we knew the preamble to the Constitution and the Gettysburg Address. I was in a band class and learned the basic scales. No, I did not play an instrument because Daddy could not afford one. He told me I needed to learn how to type because no one was going to hire me to play an instrument.

—*Mattie Hudnall Ponder*

In 1968, I, along with Doris Townsend and my other special friend Johnnie B. Slay, entered Dillard University. Due to the concerns of our mothers who wanted us to stay together, we were assigned adjoining rooms that were separated by a restroom. Our parents left with a sense of security knowing that we would still be together, and I was proud because I could still boss them around. With limited funds, I was only able to attend Dillard University for one year. Besides, I discovered that the major, Fashion Merchandising was unavailable. That year spent with my friends at Dillard I will always cherish because it afforded me the opportunity to feel what it was like to live away from home on my own in a dormitory.

 In 1969, I entered Mississippi Southern College (now University of Southern Mississippi) with the intention of pursuing Fashion Merchandising. Only a few years had passed since the university was integrated. One of the required classes in the home economics department was to learn about all the majors that were under the home economics umbrella. It was at that time that I learned how difficult it was for women to make a decent living in this chosen field, due largely to the fear that the money it would require to train women would be lost due to women being married off and having children. I then reviewed the course catalog and stumbled upon the word "dietetics"; I had heard the word before and learned that this major dealt with food and nutrition. I surmised, as long as there were sick people, nutrition would be vital to them getting well. Therefore, I declared a major in Institutional Management/Dietetics. Being the only Black person in all the required nutrition courses, I was definitely treated differently by the instructors. I was sent a packet of brochures by my counselor and the Dean of the School of Home Economics. These brochures were about nutrition programs at the Tuskegee Institute (now Tuskegee University) which was the closest place for Blacks to obtain this degree. In order for Blacks to become gainfully employed in this major they had to migrate north. This was an indicator that I was not welcome in the dietetic program at USM. It was an indirect

way of telling me that I should get the degree elsewhere. This made me even more determined to stay and get my degree in my hometown, Hattiesburg. I cried all the way home. Once I made it there my great-grandmother asked "What is wrong with you?" I tried as best as I could to explain the problem as I saw it. Although she did not have any formal education, she simply asked me to write the names of these instructors on a piece of tape. She placed these names that were listed on the tape in my shoe. Next, she told me to get down on my knees as she did the same and she prayed to God about this situation. After praying to God about the situation she then told me to return the brochures to the person who sent them to me. She asked that I humble myself and show kindness as I went into the office to hand back the brochures. The counselor was very apologetic. I told her that it was my goal to receive my degree from USM no matter how long it took. She promised to help me reach my goal. I eventually obtained my dietetics degree and completed an internship (which was hard back then because you were only allowed to apply to two places in the country). I received a direct appointment to the Veteran's Administration (VA) Hospital in Houston, TX and a second appointment at the Good Samaritan Hospital in Cincinnati, OH. I chose the VA. I was selected to become a member of the Home Economics Honorary Society, Kappa Omicron Phi.

—Patricia Griffin

A Special Teacher and Friend

I had been given my assignment years earlier when she said to me in her forthright manner: "Reverend Carolyn Hall Abrams, I want you to preach my funeral."

And I said, "Yes, ma'am."

On July 6, 2015, I preached the home-going celebration for Mrs. Marjorie Wilson Chambers and laid her to rest. It was an honor and a privilege to do so. It was the culmination of a fifty-year journey together that began when I entered Rowan High School as a tenth-grade student. Mrs. Chambers became my champion. I loved her, and she loved me. Her children referred to us as the "mutual admiration society."

We had spent a lot of time together in 2015 as she was preparing to transition from Dumas Avenue to her new home. We sang and we prayed. Sometimes I would read to her from her Bible or just sit in silence at her bedside as she slept. Even as cognition began to wane, she retained that air of grace and dignity that had always defined her.

One knew that she was special. She was Marjorie Chambers, and although incapacitated in many ways, she was still teaching lessons on faith and death and dying—never losing sight of Jesus.

She was a great teacher and she loved the Master Teacher. Over the years we spent countless hours talking about Jesus and the church. She sought my counsel, and I felt honored to listen and answer her questions. She loved the African Methodist Episcopal Church (AME), and she felt a kinship with my denomination, the United Methodist

Church. The truth is that she loved the Christian church regardless of denomination.

She was proud of her students who had become ministers. In fact, she honored us during a special event at her church, East Pine AME Church, where she presented plaques to each of us.

In high school, I considered Mrs. Chambers to be a teacher extraordinaire. I know I am not the only one who shared this sentiment. Not just my teacher, Mrs. Chambers was my friend and mentor who was determined that I would be treated fairly, academically.

She demanded the best from all her students and tried to prepare us for the real world. She did not pity her students because we were being educated in a segregated, unequal system. The reality she tried to instill in me and other students was that we would have to work twice as hard as a White person in order to have the same opportunity for success.

Mrs. Chambers taught social studies and economics. She also taught Black history before it was legislated. She required each of us to pass a Black history exam before we could graduate high school. Because of her foresight, I was inspired to learn more about Black history when I attended Tougaloo College. I subsequently majored in political science and Afro-American studies.

Mrs. Chambers continued to be a great support for me after high school and college. I will be forever grateful for the love and support she gave Robert and me following the death on our daughter, Veronica. She was there for us at a critical time in our lives.

I was blessed to be there for her during some of the trials of her life. When her husband, C. L. Chambers, was hospitalized, I was able to minister to him through prayer and visitation as he transitioned from life. I deemed it a privilege to minister to her beloved sister, Edna Delores Wilson, when she became ill. I preached her funeral on June 19, 2014. I was also honored to preach the funeral of Teresa Wilson, another beloved sister of Mrs. Chambers, in Atlanta on January 16, 2016.

It was a privilege to be of service to my friend and her family. I am so thankful that God allowed me to be able to give back to this family who had shared their loved one with me for more than fifty years.

—*Carolyn Hall Abrams*

During high school, there was a tight group that I was fortunate enough to be a part of that consisted of three girls and one guy: myself, Doris Townsend, the late Johnnie Bea Slay, and Don Denard. We were not a group that necessarily engaged in naughty things that would get us into trouble. Rather, the four of us were competitive when it came to our studies. I have to admit that I really felt inferior at times to these three folk as they were extremely smart— actually brilliant to me. Despite my heartfelt limitations, they put up with me and I was very competitive. We did have a few hang-ups that plagued each of us. Study always took place at Doris's house. The Townsends owned a car, and Doris was able to drop us off once study time ended. The main problem was that no one wanted to be first getting out of the car because the other three might talk about him or her. On one particular night, Don was the unlucky one. When he reached his house, which was right around the corner, he exited the car after saying his goodbyes. As we proceeded on, we discovered Don was still holding on to the car for nearly a block! He let us know that he was still hanging on just in case we were about to talk about him. This was so funny, and it makes me laugh even now.

—*Patricia Griffin*

As I was growing up, I had not just one special friend, but several. I consider special friends the following: Barbara Thomas Ross, Cherylyn Clark Cannon, Alma Jean Hall Henderson, Georgia Ann Adams Hunter, Alice Adams, Annie Stalling, Joanne Connor, Sarah Evans Rayborn, Wayne Nelson, Donnie Nelson, and Carolyn Atkins who is really like a sister. I can talk to her about anything that bothers me.

—*Hattie Williams Knight*

Football

 Tiger Field was on the corner of 9th Street and New Orleans Street. Today it's called Haston Knight Ballfield or 9th Street Ballpark. It had only one set of bleachers. Eureka was on one side, the bands in the middle, Oak Park on the other side. Hattiesburg and Laurel was a big game. Cornell "Big Train" Anderson played football for the Eureka Tigers. That was my brother. My Daddy would take the family to the park on Friday nights to see him show out. The first play of the quarter gave the ball to Cornell who ran fifty-five yards for a touchdown, giving Eureka the advantage over Oak Park. All you could hear was Daddy, "That's my boy! That's my boy!" I did not know what was going on. My eyes were on all the vehicles parked up and down 9th Street, that big Greyhound bus parked on the side street, and all the people. On top of the bleachers, I could see all down New Orleans Street, Mrs. Mattie Robinson Kindergarten, and the top of the school. Then I saw someone that made me very happy. Hot peanuts! Hot peanuts! Mr. Blue, the peanut man. This time his grandson was helping him out, running up and down the bleachers selling peanuts. It was Friday night. The bootlegger was doing as much business as Mr. Blue. Oh yeah, Eureka had a 6–0 win over Laurel. We were state champions that year!

—*Ella Jackson*

I started to play football in the seventh grade. Ralph Burns was the coach, and we had a very good team. Our biggest rival was Lillie Burney and that was really the only game that mattered. We were in the Tideland Conference. When we got to Rowan in tenth grade, I made some good friends from Lillie Burney. I continued to play football but used to get headaches. Mama took me to Dr. Smith, and he said I had high blood pressure. I continued to play, and by eleventh grade, the headaches were getting worse. This usually happened during football season. I later learned that during practice and games, we had to take salt tablets. They were in a gallon jug and we had to suck two or three at a time, and this kept my blood pressure high. I stopped playing in the eleventh grade.

—Grady Gaines

During the Royal Street High School years while I was at Bethune, I finally found my way inside the high wooden fence of the Park when I went with my Dad on Friday nights as he would "take pictures" at the Royal Street High football games. And I had a ringside seat being with him on the sidelines. I would carry his large camera case that had film in it. He had a Speed Graphic camera that used film cartridges that made one picture with each cartridge. So he had to be judicious in his shot selection and take with him enough cartridges to capture the essence of the game. I would carry the case and follow him as he moved along the sidelines with the action of the game so that he was in the right position to capture the plays on film. And I would sit on the camera case to watch the game until it was time to move. Of course, we had to be alert and ready to get out of the way in case the action came in our direction. There would be people all over the place, and Royal Street seemed always to win. We had Mr. Zoo Boyd and his crew refereeing and players like Marvin Woodson starring on the field. On the following Saturday mornings, Dad would have on display in the front windows of his studio the best shots from the game the night before. I remember Taft Reed and other football stars, such as Willie Townes, and their parents coming to the studio on Saturday morning after a win on Friday night and looking at the pictures in the display window outside then coming inside to see what other shots Dad had captured. And praise God, they would buy pictures.

—Don Denard

There were nine schools that Rowan played. The big rival was Oak Park from Laurel. Two of the scores were Rowan 38-Jim Hill 0, Rowan 7-Oak Park 0.

—Hattie Williams Knight

One day during the seventh grade year, we had a special program in the auditorium when Jackson State football stars, wide receiver Willie Richardson and quarterback Roy Hilton, came to Rowan to speak. They were fresh from defeating Florida A&M in the Orange Blossom Classic and were on a speaking tour of the state. My mouth was hanging open. Both of those players went on to the NFL. We took PE from the legendary Coach Bob "Big Nasty" Hill, who was on a roll, winning three straight Big 8 State championships as L. J. Rowan's head coach. Taking a shower after PE every day and bringing a "grip" to school was a major experience for us seventh graders. Coach Hill's mantra was "You *got* to get that showwwwer, T-Tony…eh?" When he would go "eh?" you had to reply "Eh, Coach." Nobody knew who T-Tony was, although we thought it was Curb, but we never asked. Rowan had a concrete stadium with locker rooms for the home and visitor teams underneath. Friday nights were legendary, and we were told that Big Nasty would lay some wood during halftime if needed.

In terms of school spirit, we immediately couldn't stand W. H. Jones Junior High on the north side because they became our rivals in sports. Jones beat the stew out of us in football the first couple of years because they were a well-established school and had good athletes and coaches. Students on the north side did not attend Rowan for the seventh grade because they already had a junior high school. So we suffered through the first few years in athletics. We would play high schools in the surrounding counties in order to fill out our schedule. More slaughter. My cousin Frank Denard and his friend Red Fluker attended Locker High School in Wiggins. They beat us 63–0 in the fall of 1963, our first year. Of course, Frank and Red were probably nineteen at the time, playing against young boys, as I told them. They laughed. But in 1964, we made it a lot tighter game. Our colors were black and gold, and our mascot was the hornet.

—*Don Denard*

The Band

I was in the choir and in the band at Lillie Burney. In band, I started on mellophone then switched to baritone horn. We had all new instruments. My role model for band was James Hall, whom I would stand behind in the band room at Rowan in the seventh grade and hear him playing baritone like a virtuoso. I wanted to play like that. Our band director at Burney was Mr. Sherril Holly, who was from a family of band directors in Jackson. We were so new to the point that our band uniforms didn't arrive until the second year. The first year, we wore black all-weather jackets, black pants, and gold ascots. It was okay. While we could play in parades, we weren't good enough to play on the field for halftime shows. Home games were played at Rowan. For the first few games, we would march on the field (which we did very well given a great drumline) and would march into a few different formations for our halftime shows. But to our utter dismay, we didn't play our horns on the field. Instead, Rowan's band would sit in the stands behind us and play while we stood there in formation. They really had a good band and sounded good, but it was awkward for us. We would move to another formation after they finished one song, and the same thing would happen in the next formation. Lawd! Wendell Fairley played trumpet. During that first halftime show with Rowan's band playing in the stands behind us, he couldn't take the humiliation and called out to us in the first formation that we should hold our horns up and pretend that we were playing. But no one thought that would fly, so we waved him off and said no. We eventually got uniforms in the ninth grade and finally played on the field during our halftime shows.

—Don Denard

My seventh, eight, and ninth-grade years were spent at W.H. Jones Junior High School. We changed classes and had a different teacher for each class. I was unhappy because my brother and I were not in the same class. I found new friends and soon learned to feel comfortable with this schedule. I joined the band and played the flute for three years. The band directors were Mrs. Ruby Wilson and Mr. Sherill Holly. Our teachers were Mrs. Martha Hall, Mrs. Rhoda Tademy, Mrs. Georgia Mae Robinson Walton, Mr. Melvin Cooper, Mr. David Conner, Mr. Percy Gambrell, Mr. Sherill Holly, Mrs. Ruby Wilson, Mr. Winfred Hudson, Mr. Prentiss Jones, Mr. Eugene Jones, Mrs. Ruby Bell, and Mr. Earl Carr. Our principals were Mr. Samuel Earl Wilson and Mr. Percy Gambrell.

—Mildred Miller Short

I began my love for music at a very young age by watching band practice. I loved the girls with the batons marching with the band. Since I was so young, I really didn't know that they were called majorettes. I would watch with excitement the girls twirling their batons. As a result, my Grandmother bought me a little wooden baton painted red, white, and blue, and I would march along the fence with the big girls as the band played, and she watched me from the porch. Many times my Grandfather would be working in the yard and my Grandmother would still watch me through the kitchen window. I just grew up watching the "big kids" during recess, looking through the fence as they played ball, plaited the Maypole, practiced band, etc. It was at this time that my Grandmother noticed my love for music at a very early age because when I would finish marching in the backyard, I would come inside and use her coffee table as a piano and sing. As a result, she started me taking piano lessons with Mrs. Olivia Hudson about age six. My Grandmother bought me my first used piano for $108.15 (including tax) from Roseberry Piano Company on East Front Street. I have a copy of the original sales contract today dated November 5, 1956. I took music lessons and played piano for many years. I remember some of Mrs. Hudson's students were Gwen Murphy, Linda Harrell, etc. I took lessons until I graduated from high school. I also played for Mount Bethel Church until I left for college in 1968.

When I finished elementary school at Eureka, I went on to attend W. H. Jones Junior High School; just like my elementary school, many of the teachers and experiences had a tremendous impact and helped me become the person I am today. When I started W. H. Jones, I decided I wanted to be in the band. This was my introduction to Mrs. Ruby Wilson (another sweet person) as the band director when we first got to W. H. Jones and many other students such as Shelley Mae Stallworth, Mildred "Little Bit" Miller, Melvin Miller, Charlie Harris, etc. It was here beginning with Mrs. Wilson trying different instruments, I finally decided on the trumpet. My neighborhood friend Shelley Stallworth had also just decided to play trumpet. Mrs. Wilson thought she was too little to play, but boy, she would be proven wrong. I knew my Mom couldn't afford to buy an instrument, and since my Grandmother had gotten the piano, I didn't ask about the trumpet. I won't forget my Mom finally got me a trumpet from the pawnshop on Pine Street. I was so happy; however, no one wanted you around when you started to practice so I would go to our backyard behind the garage. Junior high was fun learning to play the trumpet with Shelley Mae and my cousin Larry Knight. Since Larry played in a band with Eddie Lee Corley, he helped me a lot on learning my instrument. We would practice in the 9th Street ballpark (now named after his Father Hayston Knight). We liked to practice in my Aunt's backyard too, sitting on the back steps sometimes. She would be in the kitchen and tell us to take that "noise" to the ballpark. Shelley and I also practiced a lot together. Mr. Sherrill Holly became our band director later at W. H. Jones. He was so knowledgeable and patient with us because we were learning our instruments. Mr. Holly believed in us, and our band was pretty good I thought.

—*Mildred Johnson Watts*

Some of the band members in addition to Shelley Mae were Don Denard, Doris Townsend, Grady Gaines, Shirley White, Lawrence Curb, Johnnie B. Slay, Patricia Griffith, Randall Williams, and Patricia Berry. We had many experiences while playing in the band.

Specifically, I remember one trip to Sadie V. Thompson in Natchez, Mississippi, who was one of our biggest rivals; they locked us inside their fence trying to fight us, thank goodness we got out. Would you believe I married Mickey from Sadie V. Thompson High whom I met at JSU? He verified my statement and said, "Yes, that's what we used to do, close the gate and be ready for a good knockdown."

—*Mildred Johnson Watts*

 In my sophomore year of high school, I was a majorette and head majorette in my senior year, and a member of the school choir. High school was good. We had very good teachers who cared about their students. I didn't let negative talk affect my life.

Many days I didn't have lunch money to eat at school. I ran home to eat and back to school. When the band or choir travelled out of town, my parents didn't have money to give me, so Terry gave me money for food. I didn't worry my parents to give me what I needed because I knew they didn't have it to give.

—*Deborah Barrett Jackson*

I played basketball in the eighth and ninth grade for Georgia Mae Robinson. While at W. H. Jones, I played the cymbals in the band under the leadership of Prentiss Jones.

—*Doris McNeill Collins*

After the first year in Rowan's Beginner Band (Bb clarinet), I was named Most Outstanding Beginner. Note that we were in the Rowan Band too. I made lifelong friends in that band. There were majorettes, a flag corp, a drum major, and even an acrobat for a while. Some years the band had over a hundred participants. I think my greatest love though was for the classical band. I love to listen to concert music to this day.

For our eighth- and ninth-grade years, we attended the newly built Lillie Burney Junior High School on Ida Avenue built for seventh, eighth, and ninth graders on the South side of town and named for the Bethune school principal that I referred to earlier. Even in the eighth grade, we were still members of the Rowan High School Band. In the ninth grade, we moved to the junior high school band when a band director was hired. We were known across the district and state for our many superior ratings at band competitions. Our band directors were sought after, and many didn't stay very long: Mr. Hunt, Mr. Hess, Mr. Shirley, Mr. Holly, Mr. J. Marion Harrison, and Mr. Jesse Otto Cook. I was also a member of the library club and competed for Miss Lillie Burney where I was first runner-up.

In the tenth grade, I remained in the band and even tried to sing in the choir at the same time. Both rehearsals were after school, and I soon ran into a conflict with the schedules. I chose the band but always wanted to be a part of the choir.

—*Doris Townsend Gaines*

My time at Rowan also included membership in the Rowan High School Marching Band directed by Mr. James "Prof" Harrison. I played trombone, and my sister, Mildred, played flute. For me, joining the band was just a natural transition because I had played trombone in the W. H. Jones Junior High School band, and I played "tonette" at Eureka Elementary School. Being a member of the band at Rowan was also special because my sister, Mildred, and many other classmates—including Don Denard, Mildred "Cookie" Johnson, Doris Townsend, Patricia Griffin, Teleceno Carr, Willie "Pee Wee" Brown, Ronald "Big Time" Lindsey, Larry Strickland, Shelley Stallworth, Johnnie B. Slay, Randall Lewis Williams, Evelyn Boochie, Tilda Dent, Larry Bourne, Shirley White, Clarence "Flop" Breland, George Knight, Lawrence Curb, Cherylyn Clark, Margaret Dillard, Tommy Hall, Gregory Walker, and majorettes Margaret Hill, Bettye Lewis, Debra Barrett, and others—were also in the band. We looked good in our distinctive red-and-gray uniforms all decked out with red plumes on our hats and white spas on our shoes. We were proud to represent Rowan and support the Mighty Tiger Football Team.

Our band was always good, and we would earn "superior" ratings at the annual band festivals held at Jackson State. The band was also my ticket to travel all over the state and see towns and places that I would not otherwise have been able to visit. We learned discipline, teamwork, and leadership as band members. During my senior year, I was honored to serve as president of the band.

—*Melvin Miller*

I was a member of the marching and concert band. We had brand-new band suits and accessories to go with them. The band director was named Mr. James Harrison, a graduate of Mississippi Valley State University. Every Friday during football season, we would have pep rallies in the auditorium. The band, cheerleaders, and football team  would be on the stage. The visiting football teams would also be on the campus. They were fed before and after the football games by our Home Economics Department, because the White restaurants would not serve them. The band would play the latest soul hits, and the cheerleaders would lead us with their favorite cheers. Our school was a member of the Big Eight Conference. We played many other Big Eight schools from that conference—Jim Hill, Brinkley, Oak Park, Temple High, Threadgill High, Coleman High, Sadie Thompson High, and Harris High. Our coaches were Mr. Edward Steele, Mr. Winfred Hudson, and Mr. Samuel Ellis. We lost only one game our senior year, the Big Eight championship game against Coleman High. The band and football team traveled on chartered buses to out-of-town games. Sometime we would go to Jackson, Greenville, Greenwood, Natchez, and to Mobile, Alabama, to participate in the Mardi Gras parades. During concert season, we would travel to Moss Point and Jackson to participate in district and state band contests. We would always win usually with A superior rating. I would like to thank Mr. Doug Smith, our bus driver.

—Mildred Miller Short

CHAPTER 6

Life in the Community

Thanksgiving

Homecoming Day—the parade, big game, and turkey dinner with the family.

—Beverly Harris Abrams

I remember Bernita Parker and I were "Miss Home Economics," riding in the last Thanksgiving parade that started at W. H. Jones and went up Mobile Street, through downtown, and over to L. J. Rowan High School on Royal Street. Those parades were like the Black History Parade in those times. We looked forward to attending the parade and following it all the way over to L. J. Rowan where the big football game took place: Rowan and Oak Park School of Laurel, Mississippi.

—Carolyn Atkins

It was during my elementary years that I became very interested in bands while watching the Rowan High School Homecoming Parade. The parade was held every year on Thanksgiving Day at 9:00 a.m., followed by the homecoming football game at 1:00 p.m. The parade would start on Mobile Street, continue through downtown Hattiesburg, and end on Royal Street in front of Rowan, a distance of about three miles. I am proud to say that I marched as a band member in this parade from seventh through the twelfth grades. This experience was pure joy and excitement as we joined other bands, floats, cars, and organizations to celebrate Rowan's homecoming. The homecoming activities were a great source of pride and joy to all of us and helped form a tremendous bond between the school and community.

—*Melvin Miller*

I first wanted to become a majorette "twirling that baton," and I tried this for a very short period of time. I am reminiscent of those memories from when I was still small, marching along my Grandmother's fence. I also had memories of the older kids such as Emma Lou Boochie as head drum major, Pat as head majorette, Nancy Mobley and others marching in parades down Mobile Street. Since they were in high school, I guess I got some of my inspiration from them again still playing visions in my head. So when I was about fifth and sixth grades, I remember Mildred Miller "Little Bit," Shelley Stallworth and myself were majorettes at Eureka, wearing short blue-and-gold outfits with Tams. Well, it didn't last long for me because my Grandmother wanted my outfit too loose so it wouldn't fit me tight, so I lost interest in being a majorette.

—*Mildred Johnson Watts*

Our homecoming was always held on Thanksgiving Day. We would have a parade that began at 10:00 a.m. and started at the first Eureka ballpark and ended at the Rowan ballpark. There were bands, queens, majorettes, clubs, kindergarteners, Boy Scouts, and Girl Scouts all led by the reigning Miss Rowan in the parade. Miss Rowan was chosen at the annual pageant that was held each year at our school. The ball game usually started around 1:00 p.m.

after the parade. We would arrive back home about 4:30 p.m. to eat our Thanksgiving and birthday dinner.

—*Mildred Miller Short*

Homecoming was on Thanksgiving Day and was one of the best times of the school year. In the early years before the stadium at Rowan was built, Royal Street High would begin its homecoming parade on the South side of town at Cypress and Dabbs Street, work its way through downtown, and end at the Park where the homecoming game was played. Mr. Galloway's horses were at the front followed by Boy Scouts (which I was in), Cub Scouts, Junior Forest Rangers (which I was in), then floats, decorated cars, marching bands, and other units. The parade route reversed once the stadium was built starting on the north side at Seventh and Mobile and ending at Rowan where the game was played. In the seventh grade, we marched in the parade as a Tonette Band, which we weren't thrilled about because we didn't have that much volume. But we had on our red sweaters and gray pants and were marching.

—*Randall Williams*

Homecoming Day was a big event. You would have the parade from East 9th Street ballpark to Mobile Street, all the way to Royal Street (Rowan) for the big game. After the parade, you would change for the big game. After the game, there would be a dance either at Holy Rosary Center or at East 5th Street Community Center.

On Thanksgiving Day, we had our homecoming parade and football game. The parade started on Mobile Street and ended on Royal Street. After the football game, there was so much excitement in the air.

—*Mattie Hudnall Ponder*

At Mary Bethune, I also led the majorettes. We marched in every Rowan Homecoming parade and we even performed once at the 9th St. Ballpark for a halftime show with hula-hoops. The Royal Street stadium had not yet been built. The new stadium was eventually built behind Royal Street School. At that time, it was said to be state of the art. One year during the parade, I was picked up in a car after the parade went through downtown and rode over to Dabbs Street, where I returned to my unit in the parade. (My Mother thought I was too young and would be too tired to march the entire route.) I either rode or marched in every homecoming parade from about 1954 until graduation in 1968.

—*Doris Townsend Gaines*

Pictured (*l–r*): Doris Townsend, Victor (unknown last name), Cassandra Johnson on a float representing Happyland Kindergarten in Rowan's Homecoming Parade (around 1954).

Christmas

Our community was a close community; in fact, it was so close that I thought Santa Claus only came to the Gravelline. We didn't get a lot of toys for Christmas, but it was magic how the house smelled of fruit and candy during the holidays. I can still remember to this day how hurt I was when I saw Daddy coming out of the closet with what few toys were gotten and realized there wasn't a Santa Claus.

—Grady Gaines

Every Christmas was always great. We all had gifts on that day, and not one child was without a gift. We would have large baskets of apples, oranges, walnuts, large brazil nuts, and hard candy. Oh, so good! I can just smell that fresh fruit now as I write, and the smell of a fresh pine Christmas tree brings back so many memories. On Christmas Day, the weather was always very cold.

—Mattie Hudnall Ponder

Christmastime was surreal for me in my young years and still holds that special aura for me today. Hattiesburg was like a Christmas village where everybody decorated their houses and many their yards. The streets were lit up with lights, angels, Santa Clauses, and the like. The bus was our only mode of transportation, and it would run its route late for a few nights to allow people to get downtown to do their shopping. Just so happens that the bus route ran down Spencer Street where I lived. Mr. Mack, the driver, knew Mama, and most times he would let us off right at our doorstep. Everybody would be downtown walking from store to store. If you had a car or caught a ride, you parked in the Sears and Roebuck parking lot behind the store. Everybody would, at some point, walk through the Sears store and smell the popcorn and freshly cooked cashews at the candy counter. There were bin after bin of candies at Sears. You could just walk up there and gaze and let your imagination run wild and your mouth water. That would start things off. I don't know what Mama was buying, but I would follow her all over town. After a few hours, we would wait in front of the Ben Franklin store to catch the Dabbs Street bus for our return trip home. Wonderful memories! We always had a real Christmas tree, usually some kind of pine that Daddy would go to the woods and cut down. He would build a stand himself and the pine smell would permeate our house for weeks. We would place the string of big lights on it and sometimes have foil tinsel to hang from the branches. We had some kind of cotton-like "snow" too. I later found out that it contained asbestos. I remember once it was too big for the living room, and he set it up on our front porch. I can smell it now.

—*Doris Townsend Gaines*

The Nurses

Maybe you can help me… I ask for your help because I cannot remember Miss Voncile's last name (Harris). She worked at the Forrest County Health Department. In elementary school, she would come to the school to vaccinate the kids. We would line up by class in the hall to go to the lunchroom to get a shot. The school had two teachers named Love—Mrs. Bowlegged Love and Mrs. Skinny Love. That was the way we kids distinguished one from the other. Their jobs, along with Mrs. Cora Jones, was to keep us moving in line down the hall.

In the lunchroom were the nurses. Miss Voncile was the only Black nurse. She was loving and caring, and I wanted to be in the line she was working. She held our trust. Miss Voncile had compassion. The White nurses would just stick you and move you on. She would also come to visit our home and community. If Miss Voncile came to your house two or three times a month to see your mother, you could look for a new baby brother or sister soon.

In the summer, the nurses would be at the church. The line grew from Ebenezer Church to Bouie Street with children and adults of all ages. You had to keep eyes on your sister and brother. Sometimes they would run away just as it was time for their shot. The adults did not trust the White nurses due to newly learned information about the Tuskegee victims that were infected with syphilis. Having Miss Voncile there helped the adults to receive their treatment.

—*Ella Sue Jackson*

 I remember the nurses coming around to the schools to give us our immunizations. At that time, we were "colored." I guess we had so many different shades of people in our race.

There was only one doctor who would treat Black people. That was Dr. Graves. In his office, he had a White waiting room and a Colored waiting room. He'd treat all his White patients first, and then at the end of the day, he'd treat his Black patients. When we would have babies in the neighborhood, a nurse would come around with her little black bag. When she left, she'd leave a little baby boy or girl. My first experience with a Black doctor was with Dr. C. E. Smith. He went around to people's houses to treat them. He built a clinic on Katie Avenue.

The hospitals had one floor dedicated to Black people. There were four beds to each room. If there was no room, they'd put you in the hallway. when Blacks gave blood, they would give you a pink card because you were Black, or a white card if you were White. When you'd go to give blood, they'd give you a stack of pink cards for you to look through to see if there was anyone that you could donate blood to.

—*Tommy Hall Jr.*

My very first memory is being a young child, waiting at the health department downtown to receive a shot from the first Black nurse I had ever seen, Miss Voncile.

—*Ethelyn Fairley Reid*

Our Neighborhoods

Many people in the "village" of my childhood helped me complete school. Two people who encouraged and supported me in different ways were my cousins: sisters, Dorothy Goins Graham and Mary Goins Jackson.

Dorothy, or Dot as I called her, was my encourager and "life coach." Our families lived next door to each other, and whenever Dot came home to visit, she would call me to the fence that divided our yards and give me advice on how to conduct myself as a young lady. She taught me the "facts of life" and other things she thought a teenage girl needed to know. I don't think she realized how much our talks meant to me.

Dot was proud to see me graduate high school in 1968. As a graduation present, she invited me to visit her that summer in Puerto Rico where she lived. I did not go to Puerto Rico because I had fallen in love and did not want to leave my boyfriend, Robert Abrams. Dot reminds me, even today, that the invitation is still open. Robert and I hope to take her up on it soon.

I love Dorothy Goins Graham. I had the pleasure of performing the marriage ceremony of her daughter, Dottie, eighteen years ago. In 2017, I was honored to participate in the home-going service for her eldest son, Dexter. Our lives have been intertwined through joy and sorrow. Not only are we friends, but prayer partners as well, holding hands on this journey called life. She is eighty years old now, and she is still dispensing wisdom to all who will listen. I am so glad I listened to her then and continue to listen to her now.

> There is a saying that,
>> Angels live among us,
>> Sometimes they hide their wings.
>> But there is no disguising,
>> The peace and hope they bring.

One such angel was Mary Goins Jackson. From fourth grade to high school, I worked after school, on weekends, and during the summer to help support myself and stay in school. My main jobs were cleaning rooms in Miss Alma's boardinghouse and babysitting and cooking for Miss Shirley, a White woman, on Saturdays. From the ninth grade until leaving for college, I worked summers as a lifeguard and swimming instructor at the public pool for Blacks in Hattiesburg. Miss Alma paid me twenty-five cents a day, and Miss Shirley paid me three dollars for a day's work on Saturday. These jobs allowed me to stay in school.

A few weeks into my tenth-grade year, I found myself in a critical situation and I didn't know what to do. My money that I had saved from my summer job had run out. I didn't know how I would buy lunch and pay to ride the bus to school each day. For the second time in my life, I had to contemplate dropping out of school. The decision I faced was whether I had the courage to walk across town to Rowan each day as my classmates rode by on the school bus. (I felt I could handle not eating lunch; I'd already survived that ordeal at Eureka and W. H. Jones.) I didn't know if I could face the embarrassment of having my classmates know how bad off I really was. I didn't know if they would laugh at me or pity me. I feared either one.

I sat alone at home and prayed to God to help me. As I was crying and praying, I heard a knock on the front door and there stood my cousin, Mary Goins Jackson. My nickname was "Baby." She said, "Baby, I was wondering if I could hire you to do some cleaning and ironing for me each Saturday?" It was as if God had sent an angel to my door. Mary was my angel. God had answered my prayer and shown me a way to stay in school. With what she paid me, I was able to ride the school bus with my classmates.

My cousin, Mary, taught school and seemed to always have a smile on her face. During the time I worked for her and her husband, La Plause, I observed their interactions with each other and their children. Not only did she help me financially, but she and her family modeled a peaceful home life for me. Saturdays at Mary's house were special.

Mary is deceased now. She was truly my angel of hope here on earth, even if I did not see her wings. I know that God sent her to my house to help me. Now that she has her wings, what a tremendous blessing she must be to so many as she continues to spread hope!

—*Carolyn Hall Abrams*

A common sight in our neighborhood, Richard Carradine Jr., better known as "Doodie" by his family and friends, was my neighbor. Affectionately known as Doodie, he was what is today called "special." He was our schoolmate until the principal told him that he could no longer attend W. H. Jones School. I remember that day like it was yesterday. I was devastated, but Dooder didn't just sit around and feel sorry for himself; he began to sell newspapers full-time. Richard was one of, if not the only, longtime paperboys that worked for Miss Lillie McLaurin's news stand on Mobile Street. Rain or shine, Miss Lillie's Hattiesburg American paper was always on time. He had lots of loyal customers, both Black and White.

Richard's special spot was on the corner of Bouie and Pine Streets. Once he moved to the intersection of Highway 11 and 42, but he wasn't there long. He returned to his old corner. At ten to fifteen cents per paper, he sold from twenty-five to fifty or more papers each day.

Mr. Dan Bland was one of his regular customers and Richard would always save him a paper. Richard didn't talk much unless he really knew you. Mr. Dan would come by Richard's house to pick up his paper and joke around with Dooder. You could hear him laugh up and down the street.

I remember one night he was late coming home. His mother received a call from the police department who told her that he had been taken to an unfamiliar location and left there because someone thought he had a lot of money on him. They never found out who did such a dastardly thing. As a member of Ebenezer Baptist Church, he was active on the Usher Board and usually attended Sunday School and prayer meeting.

He sold papers there until he moved to Greenville, Mississippi, with his sister, Betty, when his health began to fail. Richard was a fixture in the community. Rest in peace, Dooder!

—*Carolyn Atkins*

I am reminded of the time that Doris Townsend came over to spend the night. Doris became my very best friend, a relationship that started in the second grade and continues to this day. She is beyond a friend but is more of a sister as if we came out of the same womb! Doris seemed to enjoy coming to our small house and "piling us" with us at Mamma's house. This is where my Mother lived at the time. It was the opposite for me.  I really enjoyed going to Doris's house because she was an only child, which meant I could sleep in a spacious bed, eat all the chicken I wanted, and look at TV. Wow! What a good thing.

Well, let me share this. When Doris came to the spend the night, Mamma treated her like a queen. She would tell Doris, "Baby, just come in here and lie down with Mamma while 'they' clean up the kitchen. You are nervous and need to be in here with me." Doris knew this was not true but went along with whatever Mamma said. Beverly and I would get upset, especially me. I would begin to complain because I knew there was nothing wrong with Doris. To rub it in, can you believe that Doris would get out of Mamma's bed and come into the kitchen and would have the nerve to sit down, would not lift a finger to help, and be smiling at us? I began to complain, and I asked her to go back in to Mamma. She would not! That made me fuss and I got loud with it. Mamma came into the kitchen to let Doris know to ignore that "crazy gal. She doesn't have good sense." Mamma gave me one more chance to shut my mouth, but I didn't. Even Beverly asked me to in a real low voice to just shut up. All of a sudden, Mamma said to Doris, "Baby, don't pay no attention to Trisha because she doesn't have good sense!" Without any warning, Mamma knocked me down. My lights went out. Guess where Doris went after seeing this—she hurried back to Mamma's bed! Thank God love prevailed between me and Doris.

—*Patricia Griffins*

The neighbors were considered your second parents. If you did something that you weren't supposed to do, you would get a whopping from the neighbors and another whopping when your parents came from work.

—*Hattie Williams Knight*

I loved my mama, Lillie Bell Hall, with all my heart, and it still hurts that she walked away from us when I was ten years old. Although she was the cause of my greatest hurt as a child, she is also responsible for the best that is in me. She gave me my Christian foundation before losing her own way. My mama taught me to pray. She is responsible for my abiding faith in God. I learned to serve from her examples of helping neighbors and feeding hobos who knocked on our door in need. She would always tell my siblings and me, "Never turn away a stranger. You may be entertaining angels unaware." I remember Mama singing, as the tears rolled down her face, "I know the Lord will make a way somehow; though you may not have a friend, He'll go with you until the end..." And I remember her talking about this Father I had up in heaven—wherever that was. I believed in Him because my mama believed in Him, and one day I came to know Him for myself. I thank God and I thank my mama for who I am today.

My daddy, James Hall, was one of the smartest people I have ever known. He was very patient and kind. He loved his children. He made toys for us to play with, including tom walkers, a telephone made from two cans and a string, and a see saw. He also made us a swing and built us a picnic table for our back yard. Although I never remember him attending church, he had a deep faith in God. He quoted many Bible passages and I never heard him use curse words.

My dad, who was seventy-seven when he died in 1965, was both a father and mother to us after he and my mother were divorced. To take care of us, he cooked, cleaned, ironed, sewed and did whatever it took. He worked until he couldn't. When he retired from cleaning streets, with a pushcart, for the City of Hattiesburg, he did yard work. He recovered from one stroke and went back to his yard work again because he had to "take care of my chaps." He did his best. He was a good friend. And he believed in me.

He was quite a storyteller, and sometimes I was the only one who would sit down and listen. He took me to visit some relatives in Hattiesburg where I remember walking with him through this long field while he told stories.

And I remember writing letters for him. He only got to the second reader in school, the second grade, but he taught me the first word I learned to spell: *compressibility*. "Do it like this, he said, "Com, c-o-m; press, p-r-e-s-s;i;bil,b-i-l;i;ty,t-y. Compressibility." I had no idea what it meant at the time.

The way he presented himself impressed me. When he had to go uptown on business, he'd always dress up. He always wore a hat. And he'd change his mode of speaking; he'd get real proper.

When he had a second stroke, he went to bed and couldn't get up. Over my dad's protest, I called Dr. Graves, but there was nothing he could do. Daddy told me he needed to talk to me and told me he was going. I said, "No, you're not dying." Then he said, "Yes, it's my time to go." I was holding his hand when he died. I was in the ninth grade.

—*Carolyn Hall Abrams*

Free Show

My siblings and I went to the movies at the Star Theater every Saturday morning and had corn dogs and mustard that were very, very good. In our later years, we went to the free show at the segregated Saenger Theater where we paid with six RC bottle caps. We entered through a side door and had the best seats in the house, the balcony.

—Randall Williams

 I attended the "free show" on Saturday mornings at the Saenger Theater in downtown Hattiesburg and the charge was six RC Cola bottle caps. The Negro section was upstairs in the balcony. We had to enter from the alley beside the theater. We saw cartoons like Wile E. Coyote and watched cowboy movies. All the kids walked from the Gravelline to the Saengar Theater and back. Sometimes it got to be very hot, but we were very young then.

—Grady Gaines

The Church

 The church played an important part in my life back then. If an adult saw you doing something wrong, they would correct you and call your parents before you got home. Neighbors helped raise the kids on our street and made us behave.

—Betty Bournes Hill

Generations of my family were a part of the True Light Baptist Church. I too, as a young child, became a part of the True Light family. Whether it was Star Light Band, GA Auxiliary, Junior Choir, secretary of the Sunday school, play productions, and working in the finance office, a strong spiritual foundation was set that enhanced every area of my life. Today, as I work in the finance office at the Mt. Olive Baptist Church, I remember the early training I received.

At True Light, there were many educators who used their training to teach and reinforce not only our spiritual but academic knowledge. If I was not at home, I was a school or church. My social life was church and school.

—Beverly Harris Abrams

I can't remember when I didn't go to church. My parents raised us up according to the scripture, "Train up a child in the way he should go; and when he is old, he will not depart from it" (Proverbs 22:6d). They did just what the scripture said. We were in church every Sunday morning: Sunday school, BTU [Baptist Training Union], and back for night service. We didn't own a car so my Father had to get someone on Dabbs Street to take his children to church. If he couldn't, we had to walk three miles to Friendship Baptist Church. We didn't cry or get mad, because this was a part of our life. At the end of Sunday morning service, I went home with the Otis family. They treated me as part of their family. Then we went back to night service.

My Father served as an usher; my Mother and Grandmother sang in the choir while we sat on the front row. We were not allowed to chew gum or talk during services. We had to get our water and use the restroom before service began. No walking was allowed during the church services.

I thank God for my parents who gave me a godly foundation. My mother's guidance and teachings have helped shape who I am today. Our parents loved their children. There were a few whippings, and we didn't disrespect or talk back to them. They never cursed their children, never smoked, nor did they drink. My Mother taught me early on to have respect for myself because no one else would. That statement I held on to through high school and my adult life. These same words I have given to my daughters and my granddaughters.

Before I met Terry, so many times I prayed to God that I would marry a husband that was much taller than me; I was five feet. He had to have curly hair. I asked for three children, a son and two daughters, and yes, the Lord gave me exactly what I asked for! Isn't God good?

I didn't have to kiss every frog in the pond to get my prince charming. All I had to do was go to God in prayer. What God has for you, it is for you. What God has joined together, no man can put asunder.

—*Deborah Barrett Jackson*

I grew up in the church with Pearl Bolton (Mama Bolton). She took us to Sunday School, regular service, BTU, and evening service. After church, just before BTU, I used to go dancing at Blalock Shop. That was the place to go after school and on Sunday afternoon.

—*Doris McNeill Collins*

I was raised up in the Antioch Baptist Church on Fredna Avenue. Many of my school friends also attended there. I was in the Junior Choir, Junior Usher Board, Sunshine Band, Young Women's Auxilliary, was secretary of the Sunday school, played piano sometimes for the Baptist Training Union and the Sunday school. Mrs. Mercy Bryant, Mrs. Davis, Mrs. Elnora Bryant, Miss Clara Weathersby, and others helped broaden my Christian education. Mrs. Claretha Knox was the Bible drill leader whom I would sometimes substitute for. "The B-i-b-l-e, yes that's the book for me. I stand up on the Word of God, the B-i-b-l-e!"

Some of my most memorable summer experiences were at Vacation Bible School. We would all go from church to church. The local churches would schedule theirs where everyone could come to each of the churches. The sessions lasted about four hours with Bible drills, lessons, arts, and crafts, music, etc. The programs were generic—not themed like today—and we all knew all the songs and chants like "Bring Them In" or "What's the Matter with the Bible School? (It's all Right!)" There were both adult and teenaged leaders and more than two hundred participants at each church. I attended Antioch Baptist Church, Sweet Pilgrim Baptist Church, Mt. Zion Baptist Church, and sometimes Friendship or Mt. Olive Baptist Church, all within walking distance. They would serve a snack before we went home: Purity soft ice cream, cookies, or sometimes hot dogs and the like. It was a rite of summer.

Does anybody else remember when Rev. Nathan Wheeler used to come around in his car with the loudspeaker on top and play gospel music?

—*Doris Townsend Gaines*

When my family moved to Hattiesburg in 1967, we joined St. Paul Methodist Church. After graduating from college, I became involved in the ministries of our church. It was at St. Paul where I learned from church members the struggles of African Americans in Forrest County. The rich history of these members: Mr. Richard Boyd, Mrs. Helen Curtis, Mrs. Alice Burns, and Mr. Hammond Smith, to name a few, was the guiding force that led me in wanting to know more about the civil rights movement in Hattiesburg.

Presently, I serve on my church historical committee, and we are involved in setting up a historical room in the basement of the church. A section of the wall displays the pastors and members who played an active role in the civil rights movement. I am very proud to be a part of this project because it gives me a sense of pride knowing that our history will be passed on to the next generation.

—*Patricia Berry Blake*

Summers

In the spring, my Daddy usually planted a garden on the lot next door. He had corn, okra, peas, butter beans, squash, and a whole plethora of vegetables. My job was to shell peas or beans, wash it all, and help Mama bag it up for the freezer. Sometimes Mama would buy a bushel of peaches and have some of the neighborhood teenagers come and peel peaches. She would then can them for the winter. After that, I could play and ride my bicycle. Everyone had to be in by the time the streetlights came on.

—*Doris Townsend Gaines*

My summer back then was spent shelling peas, butter beans, shucking corn, and whatever my Dad brought home. This would be our food for the winter months.

—*Dianne Hart Breland*

In the spring and summer, my Father planted a garden, which, back in the day, we called the field. In the field, he planted corn, okra, peas, butter beans, sweet potatoes, peanuts, and snap beans. When it was ready to be harvested, it was work to be done. In the summer, there was no playing. Our playing consisted of shelling peas and cutting corn. We had a Sears Cold Spot Deep Freezer, which is still working till this day. At the end of summer, the freezer was full of fresh vegetables for cooking during the winter months. He was teaching us work values, not to be lazy, and to be good providers for our children.

—*Mattie Hudnall Ponder*

As I grew older, we had to make some money to help out. There was a man that came around and we called him the rag man. The rag man paid you by the pound, and my Mama would tell us not to sell our good clothes. Later, I sold flower seeds from American Seed Co. and I also sold *Grit* magazines. I seldom sent them their money after the sale. I later had to pick cotton on Saturdays and got pretty good at it, but I hated it with a passion.

—*Grady Gaines*

All throughout my life, I relied on a seed of boldness that was planted as a young girl on her way to the Colored beach. At the beach, my greatest reality was experienced. I couldn't perceive why we couldn't stop in areas where people seemed to be having fun. My mother told me that these are White beaches and we have to go to the "Colored beach". My question was why were the White people lying in the sun? She replied, "To get *dark.*" "But they hate dark people" was my response. Seed planted, the realization that White people are inferior to dark people exploded in my DNA. I didn't know how to process it, but it was there and it made me know that I was special, unique. This was the catalyst that made me bold.

—*Claudia Polk Bivins*

The Floods

High water had hit the neighborhood before. Water would back out of the river and fill all the low spots. In 1961, we had a flood that devastated the Black community. We lived in the Goulah, on the corner of 9th and Fairley Streets in an apartment on the top floor. Our family had a pig named Big Bay that we raised to eat that had to be moved. The water was coming very fast. The Leaf River was in the back of us and the Bouie River was hitting us on the side. My Daddy put Big Bay in the empty apartment next door to us and locked him in good. It was time for the family to get moving. The adults were slow about leaving their home. It was night and hard to see. The neighborhood was on the move. Some of us went out on the city trash truck and some had to walk. My family went out in the car of the man next door—five adults and four children. As we went up 9th Street, some fast-moving water hit the car. We children screamed as the car floated over to the side of the street. The driver got control of the car, and we could see dry land. We all yelled for joy, children and adults.

The man's house we went to in Gomo Alley was a friend of my Daddy. We had been there about twelve minutes, and my Daddy came running in and said we had to keep moving and not to stop at the East Sixth Street Community Center but go on up the hill to St. Paul Methodist Church.

The next morning, I went to see where the water had stopped. Down at the rail crossing, you could see floodwater all around the community center. A very old man said he had never seen floodwater get up here.

I heard about three children in the neighborhood that had drowned. Someone said the name Ida Ruth Smith. I knew her and she went to Eureka School. She was just a grade ahead of me. Some Sunday mornings we would walk to Sunday school together. I had played at her house. Her Father was friends with my Daddy. Some people said that fast-moving water hit the boat she was in and turned it over. I thought maybe it was the same water that hit us on 9th Street. Ida Ruth was on 8th Street the night the boat capsized. My God! That could have been my family.

—*Ella Sue Jackson*

In 1962, we had a flood that affected most of the east side of Hattiesburg, Mississippi. What I remember is lying in bed that night with my sister Rose and our mother was watching the water on Pine Street, which rose at West Bros. Trucking Co. before it got in our backyard. After hours of watching the water, it was time to start moving things. My Mama was packing up clothes and cover in case we had to move. We were all afraid. By this time the water was getting higher and higher. I thought Mama was never going to leave the house. My brother had to put down two-by-fours from the porch to the street so she could get out. At this time, there were about eleven houses on our street. The Caradine's house was up higher than the rest of the houses on the street and, of course, our house was the lowest.

My brother Whitney was not at home at the time. He was in the "Goulah" with my Aunt. He came home wet from the waist down walking through the Central Shop to see about us. As he was coming, he said something had hit him in the side. He found out it was a dead pig, which was floating in the water. By the time he got back to my Aunt's house, the truck from Camp Shelby had come to pick up our Aunt Ora Lee and transported them to Eureka School. Later that night or early the next morning, they all had to be transported across town to Rowan High School because the water had made it to Mobile Street and 6th Street.

We went to our Aunt Honey's house on Tuscan Avenue. I think she housed about nine people at that time. It was tight, but by God's grace, we made it. We stayed about two weeks at her house. God has his way of bringing people together at his set time. My sister and brother would walk from Tuscan Avenue, hit the tracks, and go check out the house. When we got there, the water was up so high that all you could see was the roof of our house. It got about seven feet in our house. So that meant we lost everything. The things we didn't lose had to be thrown away because of all the mud and mold in the house. It was a mess, really a mess to clean up!

—*Carolyn Atkins*

I had a white dog whose name was Snowball. He died in the flood of 1961. I never wanted a dog again.

—*Betty Bournes Hill*

During one of the floods, my family had to leave our house in a boat with the National Guardsmen because of the flooding across Bouie Street. We stayed at Camp Shelby. I also remember Ida Ruth (majorette) and her cousin drowned. The entire school was so sad. I later served as a volunteer at Camp Shelby during the flood.

—*Mildred Johnson Watts*

In 1960, I witnessed my first flood across town and in the East Jerusalem and Newman Quarters neighborhoods. It was devastating.

—*Randall Williams*

Flooding was a problem in Hattiesburg on the north (Mobile Street) side and in the quarters. The year 1960 was a flood year, which seemed to come every five years. When this happened, people had to move out of the flooded areas and move into the schools on the South side or move in with relatives, which our family members did. This meant the schools closed. While it was fun living and playing with your cousins from the flood zones, no school was not a good thing for a child like me. Everyone in town had to get typhoid shots. That year, 1960, my Grandmother and I went to visit relatives on the coast in Biloxi while our schools were closed. I remember going to school one day with my cousin, Norman Cook, who was also in the fiffth grade. School in Biloxi was easy compared to Bethune. I was able to do all the classroom work despite not having had time to study what the other children had gone over.

Dad's studio on East 6th Street would flood also. This posed a huge problem due to him having a lot of expensive equipment for producing school day pictures. He decided to move the studio and all the equipment to our home. The civil authorities would help businesses move items of equipment out so that losses could be minimized. There was this one time when I was helping Dad get equipment moved out, and a White deputy sheriff with a boat was assisting us. At one point, the White deputy was rough-handling a piece of equipment Dad handed him to lower into the boat. Dad mentioned to him in what I could tell was a very diplomatic manner that this was a very expensive item, so please handle it with care. I was shocked when the deputy took out his gun, pointed it at the equipment, and told my Dad, "I'll put a hole in this thing if you say another word." Dad gestured that won't be necessary. We finished as quickly as we could with Dad and me doing everything. He told me years later that federal disaster relief funds and loans were made available to businesses affected by the floods so that they could restore their businesses, but the local authorities in Hattiesburg would not make these funds available to Black businesses. The studio remained at our 509 Manning Avenue home for a while, and I remember students graduating from Royal Street High coming there to have their graduation pictures made in our den and us all working to help him and my stepmother to develop, print, wash, dry, and prepare large school day picture orders that he had to get done. At one point, the enlarger for printing portraits was set up in my bedroom. The work had to be done at night when it was dark, and I would watch my Dad do his magic with the negatives and photographic paper until I fell asleep.

—*Don Denard*

The Country Club

As I got older, the hang out spot changed to the Country Club, on the other side of town. The country club was where the Blacks could go swim and hang out without getting into trouble. We would also have dances on Sunday afternoon. This was our hot spot.

I never would have known that Country Club Road was where I would meet my best friend, marry him, and have a life together. I met my husband, Perry Ross, at the swimming pool and the afternoon dances.

—*Barbara Thomas Ross*

I also spent many hours in the Country Club pool. It was so named because it was the old White country club with a golf course located in the Black community on Country Club Road. When they moved, they gave the pool and outbuildings to the city to be used by the Black community for recreation. Not long afterward, the pavilion was set on fire and only the pool was left. I learned to swim in that pool and spent many an afternoon paddling around and splashing water. A new pavilion has since been built in honor of Mr. Vernon Dahmer Sr., and it was renamed Vernon Dahmer Park, which is still in use.

—*Doris Townsend Gaines*

Mobile Street

I had been up and down Mobile Street on the bus with my Mother many times, but I had not seen it close up. The first time I went up the street was with my brother on our way to Eureka School. It was my first year of school.

Eureka had all grades from first through twelfth. My being on Mobile Street was like a country mouse in the city. We began on the corner of Mobile and Seventh Street. On the right side of the street was Mom Van's Café. Some of the best burgers in Hattiesburg were served at Mom Van's Café. Next to Mom Van's was a large house and some rent houses. My Daddy called them "shotgun" houses. He said you could look in the front door and see out the back door. It was a three-room house. A classmate lived there, Herman Jordan. Jackie and Maxine Bennett also lived in one of them.

I know some of you are looking for Mr. Fountain's store to be next, but this is 1955, before his time. Next was Big Queen's Rooming House. Miss Queen would sit on her front porch on a love seat—it was just the right size for her. She had rings on every finger and a big Cadillac out front on the street. Then Liberty Cab with drivers like Boot Mouth Howard, Thomas Williams, Herman Jordan Sr., and Tommy Hardy.

Ronald and Reginald Williams's parents were next door with Williams's Dry Cleaners. Dr. Smith had an office on the other side. Then Smith Drugstore. Mrs. Liz Revere worked the front counter. Mr. Cohen filled prescriptions in the back. Fat's Kitchen was next. Fat's was where the big kids would get a "fatburger" and fries for one dollar. I was looking to see Fats Domino in the place by the way the kids would be acting.

At the corner of Sixth and Mobile, Hall and Collins Funeral Home and across the street was the Help Yourself Grocery Store. Eureka was just around the corner. But there were more businesses down the street: Miss Mattie Anderson's Beauty School, the Green Door, the Blue Moon, the Star Theater, Hi-Class Cleaners, Mr. Solomon's Store, Williams Cab Company, Mr. Hicks Barber Shop, Miss Callie's Café, and Miss Lillie's Newspaper Stand.

—*Ella Sue Jackson*

I remember when we were very young children our parents would round up all my siblings and we would get dressed up on Wednesday nights and head to the Star Theater on Mobile Street. There we would watch our cowboy movie night. It was such a good time. We enjoyed our popcorn and drinks during the movie.

—*Linda Turner Harris*

Growing up on my side of town was the best. I remember us having a Black-owned grocery store, Bourn Grocery Store, Oscar Tyler Tower Cleaners, Smith Drugstore,

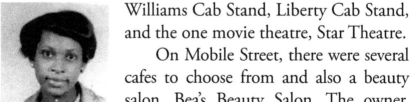
Williams Cab Stand, Liberty Cab Stand, and the one movie theatre, Star Theatre.

On Mobile Street, there were several cafes to choose from and also a beauty salon, Bea's Beauty Salon. The owner, Beatrice Ross, is also my mother-in-law.

There was also a high-end cleaner, Moe's Barber Shop, Gould's Shoe Shine on the corner of 7th and Mobile Streets, and a well-known café, the Bus Stop. Another popular place to all was Mrs. Lillie's newsstand. As a child, I couldn't wait to grow up so I could go to Smith Drugstore, where all the teens would go hang out.

—*Barbara Thomas Ross*

There were many Black-owned businesses and resources in our communities. The 6th Street Community Center was operated by Miss Lossie Glen. We would go to dances held there, make projects, play games, roller skate, and play basketball outside. We would go to the library next door with Mrs. Onell McCree to read and check out books. There were doctors and dentist offices, dry cleaners, grocery stores, shoe shops, funeral homes, beauty shops, barbershops, and a movie theater called the Star Theater. After school at W. H. Jones, I would go to Blalocks' or Poppa Stoppa's to buy snacks and play records on the jukebox. Sometimes I would go to Fat's Kitchen on Mobile Street and buy foot-long hot dogs and homemade cookies after leaving Eureka School. My favorite place to go would be Smith's Drug Store, which was also located on Mobile Street and was owned by Mr. Hammond Smith. On Sunday afternoons, Black children would come to the drugstore to socialize with each other and buy ice cream treats and drinks. Some walked for miles and were dressed in their best clothes. There were ballparks located in Pineview and on East 9th Street. We could swim, play tennis, and watch ball games.

—*Mildred Miller Short*

Mobile Street was the center of attraction and our business hub for all types of Black businesses. It contained Smith's Drugstore (where we would also get ice cream and the best milk shakes ever), Williams and Liberty cab stands, Dr. Smith's dentist office, Williams Cleaners, McBride's Café, Mrs. Lillie's paper stand, Hall's Funeral Home, the grocery store, the movie theater, and Mt. Carmel Church. We had everything on Mobile Street. There was a Farmers Feed market where I would go with my Grandmother to get groceries. I would always walk with my Grandmother; we would go up Mobile Street and sometimes we would walk on the train track.

—Mildred Johnson Watts

Greetings from the one and only daughter (Alma Jean Hall) of Thomas Jefferson and Lucy Rose Barnett Hall, who once lived at 600 Mobile Street. That address was also the establishment of Hall and Collins Funeral Home, owned by the uncle E.W. Hall and managed by his two nephews, Thomas J. and E.T. Hall. There were so many stories and topics to choose from to say a few words about Mobile Street until it was a real chore. That's because Mobile Street was not just a street, it was a collection of motivated, trained and dedicated entrepreneurs who owned successful businesses on both sides of the street from "GOMO ALLEY" to 7th Street. Consequently, there were many threads through time that made up its rich history.

Let's take a bird's eye view of some of the threads through the eyes of Alma Jean Hall of 600 Mobile Street which held the fabric of time together for the people of Hattiesburg, Mississippi. Besides her parents, she had three brothers: Thomas Jr., John Curtis and Alfred Leroy Hall. They were mischievous brothers at times. The boys would bring their friends into the funeral home, and scare them to tears. They would scare the hell out of their little sister when they felt like it. Also, the brothers were handsome and had many girlfriends. Their father would simply call all of the young ladies, "Honey Bunch," so he wouldn't confuse the names. However, the sister was a mere pawn with the girlfriends; actually, that was a good thing for her because she got plenty of attention, and even became life-long friends with some of them. Collectively, they had many friends because the corner that the building of their home sat on was like a mecca port of entry for the people of Hattiesburg. People had to pass by to go to Eureka school; Mr. Denard's photo shop; the shoe shop; Zee Baby's Cafe; the drug store; Dr. Smith's office; the cab stand; Mr. Fountain's Convenient Store; The Dawkin's Cafe; Dr. Fite's dentist office; Mr. Hagg's grocery store; the laundry mat and of course the church, Mt. Carmel. By the grace of God, all the businesses were Black-owned except one, Hagg's grocery store.

Besides businesses on Mobile Street, there was also the day life. If people wanted to be seen, they would stroll up and down the street, take a seat, or stand in front of one of the businesses and chat about whatever their minds told them to. Oh! If someone bought a new car, you better believe it was driven slowly with a hand polished high shine on it that looked like new money! The driver would grin and look to see who was watching. Ah, the pride was awesome for that driver. In reality, that thread was the talk of the town for at least a week. You see, during that era, the city was segregated and Black people amused themselves.

Since Eureka School sat right behind the funeral home of the Hall children, they knew most of the children who attended. Often after school ended, the children would stop by on their way home to jump rope, play hop scotch, play jacks, jump board or meet up at the community center for a good game of racket ball or skate with the Halls. Those were good clean games in that era, and children played outside. However, sometimes those games concluded with a good clean fist fight without the use of weapons! But by the next morning, most of the feuding was forgotten.

Another good memory was Thanksgiving. Many children were active in the band because a big parade took place. The majorettes and drum majors would do the high leg prance; the instruments were played with majestic tones and the decorated floats would follow. Oh how! Charlie Harris could beat the drums like a professional, so he thought. Poor baby only went to school to play the drums; eventually, he dropped out. Mobile Street was the starting point for the band. People would line up along both sides of the street to watch the activities. Then, some folk would walk along with the band all the way to Rowan High School, across town, because that's where the parade ended. Following the parade, there was the highly anticipated football game… Rowan vs somebody. At that time, the ambulance was stationed close to the field, in case one of the players got injured; he would be driven to the hospital. That's when football was a real physical game. Unfortunately, my brother Alfred was injured in one of those physical games and was knocked out. My momma was sitting in the stand. She saw her baby lying on the ground, not moving. Within the blink of an eye, momma was on the field and coach Hudson told her that she could not come on the field. Well, those words didn't mean anything to her and the coach knew it. Lucy Hall went to see about her baby. She took control of that situation, after saying a few choice words! (LOL) Those times were priceless.

Another thread was Mr. Denard, the photographer who made beautiful, lifelong pictures for the community. His studio was on the bottom level of the Masonic Temple across the street from our funeral home. He was an expert with a thriving business at the time. People would get dressed up to go to the studio to have photos taken. After they were processed, they would bring them on "the square," as my corner of Mobile Street was called, to be seen and praised to high heaven. You could just see all the pride in the eyes of the beholder. People were kind and sweet spirited in those days. Also, Mr. Denard's children would accompany him on occasion to the studio which was a good thing because some of them became lifelong friends.

At the end of the block on the opposite side of the street was Mt. Carmel Church. It was a beautiful church with Rev. Chandler as its pastor. I was baptized there with my loving cousins, Georgia Ann Adams Hunter (RIH) and her sister Alice Luvenia Adams Doss on the same Sunday.

My Moma told me that I had better join church that day. It was a good thing because I might not have been saved. Together my cousins and I played the piano for Sunday School with Lorma Miller (RIH). We attended so many services together: Sunday School, morning worship, BTU [Baptist Training Union] and sometimes night service. However, if I did not attend church, I couldn't go to the show or any other place, not even to the drug store for ice cream. By the way, I had a little job working at the drug store, selling ice cream or should I say, giving a lot of it away. But you know what? Dr. Smith (the owner) never said a word. He knew a lot of my friends couldn't afford a cone of ice cream. That's how wonderful and kind he was as a successful business man.

To go uptown, you either walked or rode the city bus. Right in front of the funeral home was a bus stop. Again, the Hall children and the people on the block saw the "Black people" get on the bus, pay the fare and move to the back of the bus. It was a normal thing to do back in the day. How sad! Also, there was the bus to take the "Black children" to Rowan High School; that bus was right across the street from the funeral home. One thing for sure, we knew we were Black!

Also, there was night life on Mobile Street. It was very entertaining some weekends. One young man stayed on the square too long; his mother found him; whipped his behind all the way home. You could hear him crying all the way home too! Then there was the big fight between Twister and two Butt sisters. Needless to say, Twister won the fight but not without being stabbed in the head with the tip of a metal umbrella…danger was lurking around. Every now and then, somebody got stabbed. Again, my Daddy had to get out of bed and take that person to the hospital in the ambulance. Besides danger, the people who strolled up and down Mobile Street for the most part were humble, caring, nurturing; focused with dreams of a better tomorrow. But Alma Jean would not forget how many came up to the square to get the latest news or gossip. The people would sit in a chair with her Father in front of the funeral home for hours just to chit chat, including Dr. Martin Luther King. Dr. King was helping to inform and form rallies in the Black churches of Hattiesburg to protest the inequality of Blacks. At that time, Jim Crow was getting ready to crumble. The time was up for civil unrest! Something had to be done. The Freedom Riders from the North started to embark on the "Burg" by bus loads of Whites and Blacks to protest the inequality. Unfortunately, one of my brothers moved to Chicago and returned on a freedom bus. He and the entire bus load of people were jailed. Because of this issue, my Father's phones were tapped; he was watched; he could not get loans to help grow the business. That action led to failure of the business. Consequently, a great thing came out of a bad situation. My parents and I moved to St. Louis, Missouri, where we still flourished by the graced of God. Praise the Lord!

On a personal note from Alma Jean, she had many close childhood friends that filled her heart with joy and admiration, even after she moved to St. Louis. Unfortunately, many passed on to glory, but the memories shall forever remain in her heart. Therefore, ending the story of 600

Mobile Street in the small mega city of Hattiesburg was simply and merely a thread through time where all of the stories and memories were not told.

Last by not least, the former Alma Jean Hall married and started her own family. Her two children (Roland, Alma J.) are grown with no grandchildren yet! They gave her three dogs (Sasha, Rocky, Nahla) who live with their parents. That made her and husband Charles Henderson empty nesters...what a blessing!

Today Alma Jean is content with her favorite pastime activities: traveling the world and watching her childhood hommie's daughter, Stacey Abrams, make national history in politics. When Stacey goes to the big house, I'm going too. I'm her Tt that her mother forgot to imprint in her memory as a child. Last but not least, I'm glad I grew up in Hattiesburg, Mississippi. The lessons I learned on and off the street made me the person I am; I like me!

—*Alma Jean Hall Henderson*

Working Conditions

Survival in the face of bigotry and injustice: Unlike many families today, most household had two-parent families. My Mother was a stay-at-home Mom until all of us kids were in school. Like most nonprofessional, working Black women, my Mother did domestic work. The White family that my Mother worked for lived in a big three-story white house on Bay Street. She was the downstairs housekeeper. The family dynamic was Mrs. Pauline C. Barrier, her son-in-law, Mr. Jack Butler, and his daughter, Polly. All adult White people were addressed as Mr. or Miss by any Black person, regardless of their age. Black adults were referred to as boy or girl and addressed only by their first name by White people of any age. In my mother's presence, Mr. Jack would address his daughter as Miss Polly. My Mother, being the assertive woman that she was well known to be, told Mr. Jack that if he was trying to give her a hint to address Polly as Miss Polly, he had another think coming.

Mr. Jack made Scrooge look like a missionary. He was tighter than Dick's hat band. The yard had very large oak and pecan trees. On Saturday morning, Willie Powe and I raked that great big yard. When we finished, that cheapskate gave us thirty-five cents each, twenty-five cents for raking and ten cents to come back on Monday to haul the leaves to the front for the trash truck. Willie refused to return, and had it not been the place my Mother worked, I wouldn't have either. My brother, Robert, had to come and help me.

My Father worked mostly in custodial services. He was the janitor for the Southeastern Life Insurance Building in downtown Hattiesburg. He was Clarence to everyone who worked there and they were mister and miss to him. The parking lot attendant was about just about two dollars above poor White trash, but my Daddy was Clarence and he was Mr. Pierce.

—Randall Williams

During the summers, I would come home to Hattiesburg from Jackson State University to work in order to help my parents with my clothes and school supplies. The less-than-minimum wage I earned was another factor in aspiring me to continue to pursue my college degree.

My first job was babysitting in my neighborhood on the weekends. During the week, I was a cashier at Stuckey's on Highway 49. This job did not last long after several loads of bus travelers surrounded my counter to check out. I became so nervous and overwhelmed that I could not count out their money fast enough to manage the crowd. Working with money was not my cup of tea.

My next summer job was housecleaning in a home on Hillendale Drive. Several times I would leave with sore knees from scrubbing baseboards. By the time the summer was over, I found out that maid work was not my calling either.

The summer of my junior year my neighbor got me on as a waitress at the Hattiesburg Country Club. I would soon learn that it was not just waiting tables but cleaning, peeling shrimp, shelling peas, and anything else that needed to be done before the opening of the dining room.

Hired help did not sit down or eat in the dining area. We worked and ate in an area I called the screened-in back porch. You ate with your food on your lap. It was not the good-smelling steaks either. We occasionally were given a hamburger and fries. I had the opportunity to work with two wonderful cooks, Mama (Mrs. Annie Bell Brown) and Miss Francis Whitsett. They made sure that I got something to eat and, from time to time, added a delicious dessert to my meal.

—Patricia Berry Blake

I remember when "my Daddy" was fired from his job at Dews Foundry because of a conflict between him and a young White guy. He came home with a big gash on his head and no job. Five children to feed and now with only one parent working. Williams Grocery Store in the neighborhood gave my Father groceries to feed his family. When I needed shoes, a close friend of my family had a clothing store, and she would let my Mother get what I needed. That's how I know the Lord was with us.

In the 1970s, when Terry Jr. was old enough for kindergarten, I went to work on my first job at Murray Envelope. I worked there for one month. Because I didn't own a car, I had to catch a ride with someone else to the job, but we were always late. The owner had us standing on the outside, cursing and talking to us like we were nothing. After working two days making military envelopes, my supervisor began to curse me for making a mistake on printing. When I left that day, I never returned.

As I was applying for jobs, the Lord sent me to J. C. Penney to put in my application. I was apprehensive, but I prayed that I would not have to take a math test and I'm not good at math. So I went to J. C. Penney, and to this day, I never had to take a math test because they could not find it. Glory to God! I worked there for seventeen years, the only Black person in the Catalog Department. I was there on time every day for work. I treated all my customers with respect and kindness, even when I wasn't treated the same. Some customers were rude, and I was called the N word by some. Since I wasn't treated that way by my parents or husband, and the Lord knew I couldn't handle all of this. He knew what I needed: Salvation!

—*Deborah Barrett Jackson*

My Daddy was a laborer at the now-defunct Hercules and later at Dixie Pine Products Company. I remember when sometimes they had to work overtime. He would let my Mother know that she needed to bring his supper. She'd make arrangements to have someone take her since we didn't have a car, and he'd be waiting at the gate. We would go across the street to someone's house and sit on the porch while he ate and talk to the wives of other men who had done the same thing until they finished eating. Dixie Pine was a small community of Black people, and my Mother once played piano at their community church so we knew just about everybody. Such pleasant thoughts!

—*Doris Townsend Gaines*

In March of 1972, I married my high school sweetheart, Ronald "Big Time" Lindsey. He was known as the "Life of the party" in high school and was the best dancer. He joined the U.S. Army and was stationed in Korea. Ronnie was able to take me to the VA[Veterans Administration] in Houston, TX to begin my internship in September 1972. His Korean assignment ended two weeks prior to my graduation in May of 1973. His next duty station was Fort Eustis, VA. I was able to begin working as a Registered Dietitian (RD). After ending his military career, we returned to Mississippi; he secured a job with the Shell Oil Refinery and I worked as a dietitian at the Singing River Hospital in Pascagoula, MS.

In 1977, due to employee unrest in food service at the VA Hospital in Jackson, MS the Equal Employment Opportunity Commission demanded that a Black dietitian be hired. Fortunately for me, I was hired after the Houston VA was contacted to fill this position. I joyfully accepted and served as the training dietitian. I only worked there for seven months as this was too much of a strain on me being separated from my husband.

During my short stay at VA Jackson, I gained good experience. I was also hired in a collateral capacity to serve as an Equal Employment Opportunity (EEO) Counselor. Each VA was required to appoint employees to serve in this capacity to process to EEO complaints of discrimination and help improve work relationships. I was returning to the Singing River Hospital. To my surprise, I was asked if I would like to continue working for the VA! It was my goal to work at the Biloxi/Gulfport VA. The director of the

Jackson VA contacted Biloxi after telling me that the VA needed someone like me. I was hired in 1977 as a clinical dietitian. Because of the extensive training I had received, I also continued as an EEO counselor collaterally. The only difference in these assignments was that this VA had two divisions plus four outpatient clinics located in Alabama and Florida. There was much unrest in this system and discrimination was rampant. I continued working as a dietitian until 1994. At that time the EEOC [Equal Employment Opportunity Commission] required that facilities with greater than a thousand employees hired an EEO manager. I was appointed and I realized that God had placed me there to do His will (which was to help bring peace and harmony). Under my leadership, a mediation program was developed between several local governmental agencies. Use of this program decreased the number of discrimination complaints filed and increased harmony within the organization. Programs of diversity, customer relations, and good customer service training were developed and implemented. Thanks to the success of the various programs developed by the EEO teams we were sought to conduct programs in several VA's in the country. Praise the Lord!

In 2006, I was the recipient of the EEO Manager of the Year Award. This prestigious award is given annually by the Secretary of the Department of Veteran Affairs, which is a presidential cabinet seat. A reception was held in my honor in Washington, DC where the award was presented. I served in this capacity for thirteen and a half years.

In 2007, I was placed in a new position—Chief of Workforce Development. It was my responsibility to ensure that mandatory training courses were conducted by the Workforce Development team. This team developed computer based programs that were sought by other VA facilities. A policy was developed by the same team that would enable employees to pursue their own educational goals. Up to that point, most of the educational funds were spent on nurses and doctors. This policy developed by the Workforce team was created to afford current employees educational assistance which would enable them to achieve their employment goals. Surprisingly, this policy was approved and any employee could apply for these funds. Fifty percent of the tuition and the materials (which included textbooks and/or computer training) were paid by the VA. When the policy was implemented the applications poured in. Many of these employees were already in school. The policy included those seeking certifications, Associate degrees, Bachelor degrees as well as PHD's. I find it difficult to come up with the words that best described how the approval of this policy had on me. We gladly shared this program with other VA hospitals around the country.

My employment at the VA afforded me the opportunity to serve in three different leadership capacities, each vital to the successful operation of the VA. I know beyond a doubt that I was placed there by God. He was the one who guided me and planted the right people to work beside me. I am so thankful and so appreciative, even for the opportunity to share with you, my dear classmates and others! After a thorough review of my forty years of working, I decided on January 3, 2011 to retire because my God given assignment was complete and it was time to make room for oth-

ers. I can truly say that my prayers had been answered and I accomplished all that God had set out for me to accomplish! With regard to my years of service at the VA, I know beyond a doubt that I left it better than I found it! I officially retired on February 1, 2011. To God be the GLORY!
—*Patricia Griffin*

CHAPTER 7

Civil Rights, War, Politics

Unlike many of the national civil rights figures whose contributions are widely recognized and need no introduction, the actions of the next three individuals discussed are often lesser-known. These local heroes, however, facilitated significant change for African Americans throughout Mississippi, and in the city of Hattiesburg more locally. Mr. Clyde Kennard is one of these unsung civil rights activists who attempted to desegregate Mississippi Southern College (now USM), in the mid-to-late 1950s. Segregationists went to great lengths to deny him admission to the university, resorting to two false arrests and imprisonment at Parchman Farms. Forced to do hard labor while seriously ill, Kennard later died on July 4, 1963. Scholars, activists, and others refer to the developments surrounding Kennard's attempt to desegregate USM as the "saddest story" of the modern civil rights movement. Despite his thwarted aspirations, Kennard never lost faith in the power of education to improve individuals and communities, and to better the quality of life for all. On May 11, 2018, during the Spring Commencement Exercises at USM, Mr. Clyde Kennard was awarded posthumously the Doctorate of Humane Letters.

Like Kennard, Mr. Vernon Dahmer was another Hattiesburg local who deserves recognition for his contribution to the civil rights struggle. Fighting against the entrenched system of segregation, Dahmer worked tirelessly to encourage local African Americans to register to vote, despite successful methods of prevention that existed throughout the Jim Crow South. On January 10, 1966, these actions resulted in Dahmer's murder as the Ku Klux Klan threw flaming jugs of gasoline into his home in Hattiesburg's Kelley Settlement. Dahmer died in the local hospital the next afternoon from smoke inhalation.

As the first Mississippi field secretary for the National Association for the Advancement of Colored People (NAACP) in Jackson, Mississippi, Mr. Medgar Evers was one of the most important civil rights leaders in the state. Like Dahmer, Evers was ultimately murdered by the Ku Klux Klan for working to register Blacks to vote and posing a serious threat to the system of segregation. Shortly after midnight on June 12, 1963, Evers was fatally shot while stepping out of his car after returning from work.

Clyde Kennard

Mr. Clyde Kennard is an unsung civil rights activist who in the mid- to late-1950s attempted multiple times to desegregate Mississippi Southern College (now University of Southern Mississippi). Segregationists went to great lengths to deny him admission, resorting to two false arrests and imprisonment at Parchman Farms. Forced to do hard labor while ill, Kennard later died on July 4, 1963. Scholars, activists, and others refer to the developments surrounding Kennard's attempt to desegregate USM as the "saddest story" of the modern civil rights movement. Despite his thwarted aspirations, Kennard never lost faith in the power of education to improve individuals and communities and to better the quality of life for all. In prison, even while ill, he taught fellow inmates to read and write. On May 11, 2018, during the 2018 Spring Commencement Exercises at the University of Southern Mississippi, Mr. Clyde Kennard was awarded posthumously the Doctorate of Humane Letters.

Mr. Clyde Kennard was a personal friend and neighbor of my family. My Mother and Aunt worked in his chicken house alongside him. My Mother kept it running as long as she could after he was falsely arrested. This was just devastating to us because we all knew what type person he was. I was privileged to have Mr. Clyde Kennard as my Sunday School and Club Meeting teacher. He went from house to house making sure we all had our homework done. He took us to our first Mardi Gras in New Orleans and on our first trip to the beach in Waveland, Mississippi. I learned later that was the only part of the beach Blacks could go in that area. Cassie Shears and Gloria Harrell shared in this adventure as well.

—*Juanita Mayes Walker*

Vernon Dahmer

Vernon F. Dahmer Sr. was killed on January 10, 1966, in a Ku Klux Klan terrorist raid on his home at Kelley Settlement in Hattiesburg, Mississippi. He was a voting rights organizer and was targeted by the Ku Klux Klan for liquidation prompting the Black Power movement.

—Excerpt from *Vernon Dahmer:
An Unsung Martyr of the civil rights Struggle*
by Abayomi Azikiwe

On January 10, 1966, Mr. Vernon Dahmer was murdered by the Ku Klux Klan at his home in rural Forrest County. The Klan firebombed his home, burning it to the ground. Gunshots were also fired. My Dad woke everyone up very early that morning after hearing the news on the radio and said, "They hit Dahmer last night," telling us what had happened. Mr. Dahmer died that afternoon. We knew the Dahmer family very well. My Mother and Mrs. Dahmer had attended Alcorn College together in the Bay Springs Community. In the summertime, on Sundays, we would visit the Dahmer Farm and play with their kids, eat red and yellow meat watermelons, and buy snacks and drinks from their store. He was killed for helping Black people to register to vote in his store. My family was afraid and very sad. My brother and I were in the tenth grade. Several years later, the murder trial of Vernon Dahmer was held in downtown Hattiesburg. Every day after school, my classmate named Shirley White and I would catch the city bus after school to downtown Hattiesburg, walk to the Forrest County Courthouse, and attend the trial for about two hours. What an amazing experience.

—*Mildred Miller Short*

When Vernon Dahmer's house was burned and he was killed, I remember my Dad being very upset because he knew him personally.

—*Juanita Mayes Walker*

Mr. Vernon Dahmer was a great civil rights leader as he made sure that Blacks had the right to vote. He lost his life to the hands of evil people, the Ku Klux Klan (KKK). Some other leaders in Hattiesburg included Dr. C.E. Smith, Rev. L. P. Ponder, and Rev. JC. Killingsworth. These are just a few that I remembered.

—*Mattie Hudnall Ponder*

It was also during this period that I became acutely aware of the civil rights struggles of Black people in America, particularly in Hattiesburg and the state of Mississippi. I began to take note and later participated in the mass meetings and street marches in support of voter registration and basic civil rights. I closely followed the Freedom Schools of 1964, the murder of the three civil rights workers in Philadelphia, Mississippi, that same year, and the fire-bombing and killing of civil rights leader Vernon Dahmer in 1966.

—*Melvin Miller*

Medgar Evers

The first Mississippi field secretary for the NAACP in Jackson, Mississippi, was one of the most important civil rights leaders in the state. Shortly after midnight on June 12, 1963, Medgar Evers was shot while stepping out of his car after returning from work.

I had attended Medgar Evers's funeral with my Father and witnessed the crowds of people who were there to show their respects. I thought this can happen to any Black man. There were people standing up to two blocks away; if you were not already in the church, you could not get in.

—*Ethelyn Fairley Reid*

The Rosa Parks Story and Hattiesburg

Born in Tuskegee, Alabama, in 1913, Rosa Parks is perhaps best known for refusing to give up her seat to a White passenger on a bus in Montgomery. While Parks' decision played an important role in initiating the Montgomery Bus Boycott, a mass protest to challenge the segregated public transit system that existed across the U.S. South, Parks also has a longer history of activism that dates back to the 1940s. During these years, Parks worked tirelessly on voter registration efforts, as well as investigating a series of sexual assaults against African American women in the state. She became the secretary of the Montgomery branch of the National Association for the Advancement of Colored People (NAACP) in 1943. Parks' commitment to the fight for equality was a source of inspiration for many individuals across America.

Following her death in 2005 at the age of ninety-two, Rosa Parks made history again as she became the first woman to lie in state at the Rotunda of the U.S. Capitol in Washington D.C. It is remarkable that one of Rowan's Class of 1968 students also played an important role in this story. Former graduate, Richard Turner, was part of the Flight Deck Crew that had the honor of transporting the civil rights leader's body from Montgomery to the nation's capital in November 2005. This Southwest Airlines aircraft was led by Chief Pilot Lou Freeman, the first African American Chief Pilot of any major airline, and included Rowan's Captain Richard Turner, First Officer Trevor Hinton, and Inflight supervisors Yolanda Gabriel, Rita Tubilleja, and Renee Gordon. It has been remarked that as the aircraft taxied out in Montgomery, it received a traditional water canon salute from the airport's fire department. This event was even featured in a news article by Southwest Airlines, in which Captain Turner made the poignant point in an interview that, "Fifty years ago, those same fire hoses were being used against Rosa Parks and now they're honoring Rosa Parks, so there's been some changes in the last fifty years."[1]

---

[1] Southwest, 11/13/2005. Available at: https://www.southwestaircommunity.com/t5/Southwest-Stories/Flashback-Fridays-Honoring-Rosa-Parks/ba-p/42953.

Living A Dream

When I was a young boy, visiting relatives in California, I was taken to the airport to watch planes take off and land. I became fascinated with planes and the vapor trails that followed the planes. After that, I always watched planes flying in the sky. In high school, a friend of mine in Hattiesburg showed me a catalog from Tennessee State University. In the catalog, I found out there was a degree in Technical Aeronautics. This degree included twenty hours of actual flying time as part of the curriculum. That's when I decided that's what I wanted to do, and that's where I wanted to go.

My first eleven years of school were in the segregated public schools in Hattiesburg, Mississippi. These schools were Eureka, W.H. Jones, and Rowan. In my senior year, myself and eleven other classmates attended Hattiesburg High School. This was historic because it was the first year of deseg-regation in high school. I was in ROTC during college, and received my officer's candidate school there. After receiving my degree in Technical Aeronautics, I was commissioned in the Air Force as a second Lieutenant. I attended pilot training school at Craig's Air Force Base in Selma, Alabama.

After six years, I received an honorable discharge to pursue a commercial pilot career. I separated from the Air Force as a Captain. I flew for Southwest Airlines for over twenty-seven years. I retired as Captain. The thing I am most proud of is flying Rosa Parks from Detroit to Montgomery for her funeral and then to lie in state at the Capital in Washington D.C.

—*Richard Turner*

Dr. Martin Luther King Jr.

The murders of Medgar Evers, Vernon Dahmer, the three civil rights workers, and Martin Luther King Jr. still hold vivid images in my mind. The hood-wearing cowards of the KKK were a group to be taken seriously. Their cross burnings, home and church bombings, and indiscriminate killing of Black people was a clear and present danger. I was seventeen years old when Dr. King came to speak at Mt. Zion Baptist Church. There were at least twenty armed men outside of the church for our safety. Dr. King was sneaked in and out of the city for his protection. It was a sad, sad day when he was assassinated. It felt as if the future of Black America had come to an abrupt ending. It was said that a White student in Hattiesburg High asked the question, "What does the death of Martin Luther King Jr. make his wife?"

"A black widow."

Very heartless, insensitive, and racially motivated.

—*Randall Williams*

I was among the privileged people who got to stay up late and hear Dr. Martin Luther King Jr. address the mass-meeting attendees at Mt. Zion Baptist Church a few weeks before his assassination. The tension was palpable in the building because of perceived threats to him that night. He was late getting there because we later heard that he had stopped nearby to rest and get a nap. I started to go home, which was just down the street since I felt that I would probably get another opportunity to see and hear him. However, I decided to stay and am so glad I did. He gave an inspiring speech that made me feel that I had a mission to accomplish. The morning after his death, we were called to assembly at Rowan, and the talented Clarence Lewis sang "Precious Lord" in his deep baritone voice. It was a moving and sobering experience for students and teachers alike. My thoughts at that time were that we would never overcome the bigotry and undeserved hatred that permeated our society.

—*Doris Townsend Gaines*

I was able to hear Dr. King's only speech in Hattiesburg at the Mt. Zion Baptist Church on Spencer Street. Even though we had to wait until after 10:00 p.m. for his arrival from Laurel—originally scheduled for 8:00 p.m.—it was well worth the wait. He was so intelligent and extremely inspiring; his speech provided insight into the significance of the civil rights movement and human rights. After Dr. Martin L. King's assassination, I was sad, but unfortunately, not surprised.

—*Ethelyn Fairley Reid*

 There was also a civil rights rally held at Mt. Zion Baptist Church, where Dr. Martin Luther King spoke. After hearing his speech, I had a different attitude concerning civil rights.

—*Mattie Hudnall Ponder*

In the early spring of 1968, Dr. Martin Luther King Jr. came to Hattiesburg to deliver a speech at Mt. Zion Baptist Church. My Father took us to hear him speak. The program began at 7:00 p.m. At 10:00 p.m., Dr. King had not shown up at the church and many of the people began to leave because we had to go to school and the adults had work the following day. We did not leave and about 12:00 a.m., Dr. King came to the church. Many of the people who had gone home began to come back. We saw him and heard him deliver a great speech. The next month on April 4, 1968, he was assassinated in Memphis, Tennessee, where he was leading protest marches to help sanitation workers. Everyone was very upset. The next day, we loaded the city buses that took us to school every day on the east side of town in front of Mrs. Lillie's newsstand, the Masonic Temple and Fairley and Jackson TV Repair Shop. We always had White bus drivers. That morning, we did not pay to get on the buses. The bus drivers drove us to the bus station near downtown Hattiesburg and left. They were afraid to be on the buses with us because there were riots happening all over the United States. We exited the buses and began walking to Rowan singing freedom songs. We arrived at school around 10:00 a.m. The principal and some of our teachers were waiting in the front of the school for us. They were glad that we had arrived safely. Many people were very upset, and some of us were glad that we had a chance to see Dr. King and hear his speech.

—*Mildred Miller Short*

The bus would pick us up at Miss Lilly's newspaper stand and carry us to Rowan School. Hattiesburg Mass Transit supplied the bus at a cost of a quarter there and back. A bus full of Black kids and a White driver. One bus from the "brickyard" and one from the Mobile Street area. The day after Dr. King's assassination, we needed a way to protest his death. As we considered the course to take, someone said don't pay the bus driver. We knew this would upset the driver. The young men on the bus encouraged us girls not to pay. As the driver drove up Mobile Street to downtown, his neck turned bright red and his face was as white as snow. At Main and Pine Streets, he abandoned the bus. We had to walk! As we walked up Pine Street, frightened White faces looked out from restaurants and doorways. At Pine and Hall Avenue, Mrs. Hudson and the girls' basketball team stopped their bus to pick us up. Coach asked what we were doing walking. We said the driver had abandoned us downtown, not saying one thing about our protest and not paying, and to this day, no one in authority has ever questioned me about that day.

—Ella Sue Jackson

When Dr. Martin Luther King came to Hattiesburg, we guarded him at the Holy Rosary. He took a nap in the sanctuary.

—Tommy Hall Jr.

The day Rev. King was killed was like no other. Who would do such a thing? You didn't know how to feel, *lost.* But as time goes on, you slowly find your way.

—Dianne Hart Breland

Dr. King's death was particularly eventful because it occurred during the height of the Civil Rights Movement, and the aftermath resulted in profound grief, anger, bitterness, and violence in many major cities across America.

At Rowan, the students were very angry. I recall that on the school bus ride home that day our voices were loud and filled with civil rights chants uttered by Dr. King. Several students put their hands through the windows and beat on the metal siding of the bus as a further way of venting their anger. I remember being quite upset myself, and I could not wait to get home and follow the news coverage of this horrific event. I watched every bit of the television in order to deal with my own feelings and emotions as well as absorb as much history as I could.

—*Melvin Miller*

 Oh, Captain, my Captain, our fearful trip is almost done. It is now 1965, and Stella Brooks and I were good friends then and we still love each other. High school was the best of all because that is the day (graduation) that we looked forward to. It has been fourteen years from the pre-primer to twelfth grade. I enjoyed all the years and meeting kids from all over the city. Mrs. Harris was my favorite teacher. I still love her. Evelyn Boochee and I marched together for graduation. Tragically, Dr. M. L. King was killed during our graduation time, but he blessed us with the spirit to live, love, forgive, and keep on running the race. Be blessed Class of 1968, live a good life for life is short but sacred.

—*Benida Parker Johnson*

President John F. Kennedy

I remember the somber and sad days that both President Kennedy and Dr. King were killed. There were tears, tears, and more tears. Hatred and racism were both exposed in the hearts of the children at our school.

—*Vernette Wallis Andry*

Mr. Conner was my eighth-grade math teacher, and on November 22, 1963, while I was sitting in his class, one of the teachers rushed in the room and told us that President John F. Kennedy had been shot and killed in Dallas, Texas. The classroom fell silent for a short period of time, then some of the students started crying. There was a sense of tremendous grief and despair in the room, not only for the death of President Kennedy, but also because we feared that this event would have dire consequences for the civil rights movement in America.

For the next several days, I stayed glued to our little black-and-white television set so as not to miss a single moment of the live coverage. In fact, my parents gave me permission to stay at home from school and watch President Kennedy's funeral because they knew my interest was genuine and sincere. From that point on, my curiosity about current events, especially as they related to Black people and the media, would be an integral part of my life.

It was also during this period that I became acutely aware of the civil rights struggles of Black people in America, particularly in Hattiesburg and the state of Mississippi. I began to take note and later participated in the mass meetings and street marches in support of voter registration and basic civil rights. I closely followed the Freedom Schools of 1964, the murder of the three civil rights workers in Philadelphia, Mississippi, that same year, and the firebombing and killing of civil rights leader, Vernon Dahmer, in 1966.

—*Melvin Miller*

I remember while we were in class, an announcement came across the loudspeaker stating that President John F. Kennedy had been assassinated and that he was deceased. It was a little chaotic. Students were crying, and it was like our hope was gone because he was working so hard to make sure Blacks had equal rights as Whites.

—*Mattie Hudnall Ponder*

When President John F. Kennedy was assassinated, I was very sad; I cried. At the time, I felt Black people had lost someone who really cared about us.

—*Ethelyn Fairley Reid*

I was very upset when President Kennedy was assassinated. I was in disbelief when Martin Luther King was assassinated. I listened to the television and heard what happened and was distraught.

—*Betty Bournes Hill*

When President John F. Kennedy was assassinated, Mr. James Boykins, principal of Lillie Burney, came over the intercom and made the announcement. There was a tense silence for several moments, and then many of the students began to weep and cry. I felt like there was no hope for the Black people in America. I remember the day of the funeral and watching it on the black-and-white tv. It was a sad time for this country, especially for our people.

—*Doris Townsend Gaines*

The year President Kennedy was killed was our first year at a new school, Lillie Burney Junior High. The word of his death came over the loudspeaker. Shocked, not knowing what to do or think, we finished the school day. On the walk home, all we saw was sadness. Upon arriving home, I saw the same sadness. Mom said they, "They have killed a good man."

—*Dianne Hart Breland*

One of the key incidents that sticks out in my memory was the time when Martin Luther King came to Hattiesburg and we all marched hand in hand together. When John F. Kennedy was killed, I can remember his son standing beside his mother and he saluted his dad.

—*Eva Lenyoun Crosby*

During our time, there were two unforgettable nationwide tragedies: the assassination of President John F. Kennedy and the civil rights leader, Dr. Martin Luther King Jr. For Black America, it was devastating. A President who demonstrated a concern for all mankind and then "the drum major for peace," Dr. King, the voice for Black America and oppressed people everywhere. A feeling of hopelessness was felt in America.

—*Thelma M. Bacchus*

We experienced one of the greatest transitions in the country's history that included the Civil Rights Movement and the integration of our public schools. Historical moments such as the assassination of Medgar Evers, Vernon Dahmer, John F. Kennedy, Robert F. Kennedy, and Martin Luther King Jr. occurred during our formative years and influenced our lives immensely. I would like to think that these great sacrifices were made for all of us that live in this continuously growing and changing democracy.

—Lionel Peyton

In the eighth grade, one of my classmates, Shelley Stallworth, told me that President John F. Kennedy had been assassinated. This happened on November 22, 1963, in Dallas, Texas. Everyone in the school was very upset and sad.

—Mildred Miller Short

I was in the eighth grade when John F. Kennedy was assassinated. We were stunned into silence when our principal, Mr. James Boykins, came over the public address system and reported the event. It took about thirty seconds for his words to sink in, and then you could hear some classmates sobbing.

—Doris Townsend Gaines

O Captain! My Captain!
(Walt Whitman)

O Captain! my Captain! our fearful trip is done,
The ship has weather'd every rack, the prize we sought is won,
The port is near, the bells I hear, the people all exulting,
While follow eyes the steady keel, the vessel grim and daring;
But O heart! heart! heart!
O the bleeding drops of red,
Where on the deck my Captain lies,
Fallen cold and dead.

O Captain! my Captain! rise up and hear the bells;
Rise up—for you the flag is flung—for you the bugle trills,
For you bouquets and ribbon'd wreaths—for you the shores
a-crowding,
For you they call, the swaying mass, their eager faces turning;
Here Captain! dear father!
This arm beneath your head!
It is some dream that on the deck,
You've fallen cold and dead.

My Captain does not answer, his lips are pale and still,
My Father does not feel my arm, he has no pulse nor will,
The ship is anchor'd safe and sound, its voyage closed and
done,
From fearful trip the victor ship comes in with object won;
Exult O shores, and ring O bells!
But I with mournful tread,
Walk the deck my Captain lies,
Fallen cold and dead.

The Vietnam War

The Vietnam War was a major concern because most of the young men eighteen years and older were sent off to war. We would see them, and the next day, they were shipped off. We had no knowledge of where they were or when or if they would return home. That made my Mother more determined that all her children would be registered voters.

—*Rose Mary Montgomery Harrell*

The Vietnam War made death real to me. In my youth, dying was something that old people had to deal with. The death of Larry Knight and Oliver Myers made death not just for old people, but for all ages. Oliver Myers was the first out of the Class of 1968 to die. He was killed in basic training.

—*Ella Sue Jackson*

The Vietnam War was another major event in my life. Boys were being drafted at the age of eighteen, while others who were younger volunteered to serve in different branches of the Armed Forces. Our classmate Oliver Myers was killed a few months after he enlisted.

—*Mildred Miller Short*

 My thoughts on Vietnam were not good. I didn't want to go and felt like the United States had no reason being there. I just couldn't see going to Vietnam helping others obtain freedom when we were still being treated as second-class citizens in our own country.

—*Hayes Boles Jr.*

During the Vietnam War, I had one brother that enlisted in the Marines, Earlie Hudnall Jr. He was sent to Vietnam and made it back home safe and sound—thank you, Jesus—because so many did not return. I also had two brothers that served in the military after graduating from high school, Jerry Hudnall, USN, and Walter Hudnall, USAF. My brother Earnest had a bad knee, so he missed military service.

—*Mattie Hudnall Ponder*

I did not understand much about the Vietnam War before history class during my senior year of high school. Afterward I started observing the politics of war and specific people in society who were directly affected by going to war versus people who made the overall decisions about war.

—*Ethelyn Fairley Reid*

My brother Leon Wallis went to the military after high school and served two terms in Vietnam. Watching the war on TV made me terrified for my brother. My neighbor was killed in Vietnam, and his body was laid out in his mother's living room, draped with a flag. What a sad time.

—*Vernette Wallis Andry*

The Hattiesburg Movement

Because my father, J. C. Fairley, was heavily involved in the civil rights movement as president of the local NAACP chapter, the only attitude discussed and desired at the time was integration. Segregation was not acceptable, by any means. My family's attitudes were to do whatever was necessary to move civil rights issues in a forward direction. I'm not big on second-guessing but desegregation and integration did what it needed to do for the Black community, at the time. I feel it is now up to us to do whatever is wanted if we say we desire anything different.

—Ethelyn Fairley Reid

The Class of 1968 returned to Rowan for the tenth grade in 1965 at the height of the civil rights movement. It is interesting to note the accomplishments of the Black community in Hattiesburg while fighting for the basic rights guaranteed by the U.S. Constitution, but denied to us. Any look back at our history would naturally take into account the unique political scenario in which Rowan existed and marvel at its ability to perform deeds of greatness.

By the time we came back to Rowan in 1965, many of the Class of 1968 were experienced civil rights workers having participated in what is now termed voting registration mobilization. We participated in mass meetings, Freedom Schools during the famous Freedom Summer of 1964, picketing for employment opportunities, boycotts, and protest marches in downtown Hattiesburg demanding voting rights for our parents and neighbors. I knew of young students who would sneak and participate in civil rights activities, knowing that their parents were afraid that they would get involved and meet with the same tragedy as other young people in Mississippi. I remember my Dad telling us about Mack Charles Parker, who was killed in Poplarville, a town where I had gone with him to take pictures of a black high school homecoming parade. But the Black community, overall, was resolute in their determination to fight for justice. One of my strongest memories about our culture was the goal that my grandmother Alma and other elders set for me and my friends: "I want to be able to send you anywhere and not have to worry about you being able to handle yourself." That was the call. And their standard was clear: "Ninety-nine percent won't do." So this was the context for our final years at Rowan. We had our families and community setting the expectations, and we had our teachers and administrators providing the means for us to achieve those expectations. These people were serious!

—*Don Denard*

Hattiesburg was a hotbed of activity during the civil rights years. There were marches almost daily, boycotts, fevered voter registration, mass meetings, freedom schools, and much more. We realized what we hoped would be accomplished and everyone was actively involved. However, in our early teens, most of our activities were supervised by our parents or other adults. There was nothing that we did independently. In junior high, we played in the clarinet choir made up of a section of the band just for clarinets.

Johnnie Bea Slay played the largest clarinet, the bass clarinet; Patricia Griffin played the Eb alto, with the rest of us playing Bb clarinets. Cherylyn Clark and Margaret Dillard both also played the Bb clarinet. One Saturday, as we were preparing for our spring concert, we agreed to walk to Cherylyn's house across town on East 6th Street to rehearse. Most of us met up and walked downtown and thought we would stop for a Coke. We entered the Standard Drugstore on Main Street where we knew we would find a lunch counter. As we all sat down on the stools, we noticed that people were staring at us, but we paid it no mind. Black people sitting at lunch counters was still new to some people. When no one asked for our orders, we began to squirm but stayed until the waitress said, "We don't serve Nigras here, and if you don't leave, I'll call the police." We walked with dignity out of the drugstore, but when we cleared the door, we ran all the way down Mobile Street to Cherylyn's house looking back, fearing that we would be pursued by the police. My heart was beating sooo hard that I could hardly talk because the last thing on our minds was to try to integrate the lunch counter. We were just some hot and tired teenagers looking for a Coke to cool down and refresh ourselves. Soon after, they closed that lunch counter just to keep from serving Black people!

—*Doris Townsend Gaines*

Doris Townsend pictured here while taking notes and tallying for officers of the Mississippi Freedom Democratic Party in 1964 during a meeting at Mt. Zion Baptist Church.

(from the Herbert Randall Collection archived at USM) By permission of Herbert Randall.)

Lillie Dwight (pictured during 1964 Freedom Summer at Freedom School, 1964) from the Herbert Randall Collection by permission of Herbert Randall.

More than a decade has passed since my Class of 1968 graduated from Rowan High School. Many encounters in my life have hit very hard and have been life-changing moments. Life has taught me that you sometimes need to get out of your comfort zone. Once in a while, great unusual things occur. This was the case in the 60's. Spirit of change was moving across the South and the nation in the 60's. There were cries for equal justice under the law, end to segregation in school systems and public facilities, and for full participation in the political system by all Americans, especially African Americans. Leaders of the Civil Rights Movement were calling for all hands on deck to raise the alarm for equality and justice across the country, not just in the South. Thousands of young, old, Whites, Blacks, rich, and poor people answered the call. No one could imagine in Hattiesburg, Mississippi, that hundreds of young Black teenagers would also answer that call. There was something that lit a flame in the souls of Black young people in Hattiesburg, including the Class of 1968. My sister, Alice Dwight, my brothers, James and Benton, and I were among those young people that felt the need to answer that call.

The driving force for so many was not to be left on the sideline but engage in the action. One could feel these events would live in history and become history changing occurrences. For my sisters, brothers and me, it was exciting just to wake up in the morning and walk down the street to Mt. Zion Baptist Church to attend Freedom School with family and friends to learn. There were a lot of interesting and learning experiences taking place all the time. I know that drama class was always exciting and fun for me. I just loved drama. Alice loved the debate class and all the issues of history and current events. Things began to move from just exciting and fun activities to more serious issues for me as I became involved in voter registration and going door to door. It was during these experiences that I saw the hate of many whites that were in opposition to African Americans voting. Don't be fooled. This was only the beginning! Things were changing from lighthearted activities to life-threatening challenges that would completely alter my sister Alice's life and my life forever. Alice, Margaret, my brothers (James and Benton), and I woke up about 7:30 a.m. on a pretty summer day. We got our breakfast and walked to freedom school. Our parents were leaving for work. This day started as just another day with us rushing out to Mt. Zion Freedom School. About mid-morning, leaders asked for volunteers to travel to Jackson, Mississippi for a peaceful protest march at the state capitol. The march was for the right for all American citizens to have the right to vote, specifically African Americans. Alice and I volunteered to go. The trip in the van to Jackson was fun and relaxing. Not being aware of the violence and brutality that was to come, we enjoyed a pleasurable trip. We never realized that this experience would change our lives forever, and we would never be the same again.

Once we arrived in Jackson, we departed the van and began to engage with other protestors in the march. After we had marched about one block, the police approached us. The police asked Alice and me if we wanted to turn around and go back or did we want to get in that garbage truck and go to jail. Alice and I made the decision to go to jail. We were not transported to a jail but to the Jackson Fairground. As this journey moved to the Fairground, it evolved into brutalization that cannot be imagined. People were being beaten to the point that blood was flowing from their heads and bodies. The floor became covered with blood. The nightmare continued until we were released from their custody. Recalling all the details would just be too lengthy and painful at this time. My sister, Alice, died this past July and we were very close. We shared a special bond. It is against this background that I share my most memorable moment as part of the Class of 1968. Pinpointing critical moments in life is sometimes easy, but it is also the everyday challenges that define who we are.

Challenges of life act as a factor in altering one's life. Encounters not only change lives, they also give some insight into one's character. You learned things about yourself that you did not know. Against the backdrop of the sixties, the Class of '68 achieved outstanding accomplishments; we became educators, lawyers, airplane pilots, and community leaders as well as political leaders.

—Lillie Dwight

I came to Hattiesburg when there were a lot of stores we couldn't go to. Restaurants that you had to go to the back door just to get a burger, but White people were sitting inside getting whatever they wanted to eat. There was a special place we had to sit in order to go to the movie. I remember when I first came to Hattiesburg, they were talking about Black Christmas where no Blacks would go into stores and buy anything for Christmas. I belonged to the East Jerusalem Baptist Church at that time. I can remember the church having meetings. At that time, all churches were having meetings discussing things that went on in the city. The churches were the meeting place at that time.

—Eva Lenyoun Fairley

I attended Freedom School at True Light Baptist Church. Rev. W. D. Ridgeway was a forward-thinking pastor who told us early on that Negroes would someday live on Main Street. I attended mass meetings and learned about ways to protest the wrongs of society so that we could receive our equal rights.

—Lionel Peyton

I attended Freedom School at the Mt. Zion Baptist Church on Spencer Street, just down the street from my house. We studied a variety of subjects, and this was my first exposure to a foreign language, French. We had a morning that started with breakfast and I believe we were served lunch too. I also took a dance class at Hawthorne Headstart Center, taught by a group of White volunteers. In the afternoons, we went into some of the black neighborhoods with some older youth to "canvass" for potential new voters, encouraging people to register and vote. When we got a favorable response, we would arrange transportation downtown to the courthouse for the potential voter to register.

—Doris Townsend Gaines

During the Civil Rights Movement, we attended mass meetings, which were held at St. Paul United Methodist Church located on E. 5th Street and Mt. Zion Baptist Church on Spencer Street. Our Freedom School was located on Mobile Street.

—*Hattie Williams Knight*

I remember attending mass meetings at Bentley Chapel, Mt. Zion, and St. James Churches during the civil rights struggle. I can remember crossing our arms, singing "We Shall Overcome" at the meetings, then being afraid to walk home. I went to jail for picketing a store on Country Club Road. I learned a lot about segregation and a lot about integration. We knew we wanted to be treated better than our parents and forefathers, and with God's help, we did make a difference.

—*Juanita Mayes Walker*

Freedom Summer and the Vietnam War were two major events that touched me personally during the sixties while I was in school. Freedom Summer began in 1964 and brought about a great change in Hattiesburg, Mississippi. There were many priests, ministers, movie stars, and college students from other cities in the north living here. I participated in sit-ins, marches, boycotts, and mass meetings held at different churches throughout the city. My father, Mr. John W. Miller, would often drive us to these events. There were laws and signs that stated "White Only" and "Colored Only" written on public water fountains, doctor offices, city buses, and restaurants. Volunteers from the north established Freedom Schools and libraries at several local Black churches. I would often visit the library to read books in the summer located by True Light Baptist Church. I would like to thank the many volunteers who helped me experience these events. I still attend and participate in the civil rights events today.

—*Mildred Miller Short*

One racial experience I will never forget while attending college is during the Jackson State shootings. I remember sitting in Alexander Hall with a few friends when the National Guard marched on campus and started shooting rounds of bullets into our residence hall. It took a while before we realized this was real. We ran to hide under beds and closets. By the next day, we saw a terrible scene. We realized we were very blessed that night as we observed not only many bullet holes that covered our dormitory walls, but also the realization that many lives could have been lost as a result of this incident.

That is why Jackson State campus is closed in the center of the campus today. That event would shape our lives. It also changed the appearance and security of the campus to its present existence.

—*Patricia Berry Blake*

After the Civil Rights Bill was passed, I was determined to exercise my rights as a citizen. I went to Kress 5 & 10 Store, not even being thirsty. I ordered a fifteen cents plus one cent tax orange soda with ice. I watched the lady loosely as she drafted my drink so I could be sure she didn't put something in it. To my surprise, she was very cordial. My nerves settled, and I enjoyed my soda.

—*Randall Williams*

I was a part of the first Freedom March in January 1964. It was a cold, rainy day. My sister and I went, and after the break, my sister went home, but I stayed until the end. Most of the young people were from Palmers Crossing.

—*Stella Brooks Clark*

The year 1968 was heaven on one hand and hell on the other. Our senior year is known for being the year that Dr. Martin Luther King Jr. was assassinated in Memphis after speaking in Hattiesburg at Mt. Zion Baptist Church weeks earlier. Our city, like others in the country, erupted in turmoil but not the violence that other cities saw and no deaths. We did lose Mr. Vernon Dahmer out in the Kelly Settlement whose home was firebombed by the Klan a few years earlier, and there were some notable beatings of White civil rights workers, like this one Jewish rabbi who worked on voter registration in Hattiesburg. But overall, Hattiesburg had quite a vigorous struggle for civil rights that somehow avoided a lot of killings and beatings. Of course, we had "the Spirit" that stood guard and protected our leaders. There was material damage, like the Klan throwing bricks through the window of NAACP President Dr. Charles Smith's house just a block from Rowan. And our leaders, Mr. Fairley, Reverend Charles Killingsworth, and Father Peter Quinn, had their share of threats. But God's grace seems to have been with us. Hattiesburg is known as the birthplace of Freedom Summer and has been noted in the scholarship that has been published on the movement.

—*Don Denard*

Jackson State also helped me gain a renewed insight of the loss of lives and suffering of African Americans in our country. We often tell our girls as well as grandson, Landon, that one way to bring about change is to vote in your local, state, and national elections. My reflection of integration during my early school years brings several things to mind. One being that of our textbooks. Most of our textbooks were used books, but it did not slow down the nightly homework. Many of our high school assignments were from the school's encyclopedias, magazines, and newspapers.

Second, the doctor visits and the state health department for our school vaccinations or immunization had a back door "colored" entrance.

I can recall in the sixties my family traveling on a summer vacation and stopping to eat at a restaurant in Shreveport, Louisiana, and having to endure raw eggs being thrown at the back car window. This was an unexpected and frightening experience for me and my siblings.

—*Patricia Berry Blake*

Desegregation

My memory of the public school integration process, per "freedom of choice," was that the process initially began with elementary schools, then on to the junior high schools, and finally the high school. My younger brothers attended White elementary and junior high schools prior to my enrollment at the all-White high school. The option was only available to me as a senior. I enrolled at Hattiesburg High School. I remember the buildings or campus layout was big and expansive. There was a period of time that I dreaded every day—trying to be on time for choir class. I had an arduous trek trying to get past crowds of students, with only a ten-minute time-frame to make it from bookkeeping class that was held in the last trailer on one side of campus to the choir room on the opposite end of campus, especially when it was raining. Initially, it was a very big challenge, but after a short while, I wasn't late for choir and probably got the best cardio workout ever.

In high school, my favorite teacher was Mr. Julian Bond (history). I was assigned to his class during the second half of my senior year. Having just returned to Hattiesburg after serving as a Marine Corps Officer in Vietnam, Mr. Bond shared extensive history and experiences of the Vietnam conflict, along with personal photos. Following the assassination of Dr. King, he immediately amended the class syllabus to study Dr. King's life history and philosophy. The final class assignment was a required analysis and presentation, with group discussion, of circumstances that led to Dr. King's assassination. As the only Black student in class, this was my first time to be involved in a group discussion with White students regarding Black-White relations.

The worst teacher I experienced was Mrs. Steadman in English at Hattiesburg High. She was blatantly racist toward all Black students. In my class, she had the Black students sit together on one side of the classroom with an empty row between us and the White students. Close to the end of the first quarter, several Black students realized she was systematically trying to unfairly flunk us. We requested a meeting with the principal, Mr. Patrick, requesting to change teachers, and provided detailed examples of her unfair treatment. Even though Mr. Patrick had communicated to Black students early on that he had an open-door policy for any of our concerns, we really did not know what to expect. We quickly learned that he had our backs because Mrs. Steadman's behavior immediately changed. Even though it was evident with her attitude that she still hated us, our previous grades were reviewed and assessed fairly, and we experienced no additional grading issues throughout the remaining school year.

The benefits of the school where I was exposed to many positive encounters or opportunities interacting with White students, I may never have experienced, if at all, until later in life. Not being accepted by students or teachers initially was the expected challenge. Surprisingly, other than a few lone wolves, like Mrs. Steadman, the majority of teachers were extremely supportive. The consensus, we found during ongoing discussions with each other, was our frustration with having to prove ourselves. In time, after White students saw that we were as normal as they were, it was not a very big problem. The blatant racists were always the same, or the covert racists just ignored us. In general, the initial bad experiences of the first months of enrollment changed dramatically.

Because all Black students at Hattiesburg High were treated the same, our status was not a factor. As a group, we were not included in any formal or informal social events or gatherings, and I was already used to this. I found myself in a position of focusing only on academics, and as such, did very well in my classes.

Overall, I feel integration had both positive and negative results. It broke down a lot of barriers for Blacks, but also diminished a strong sense of "self-identity" in our neighborhoods. I'd say Black-White relations pre-integration were extremely disjointed, had very few elements in common. In other ways, they were also polarizing, similar to what is happening today.

—*Ethelyn Fairley Reid*

I don't think integration was necessarily a good thing for the Black students in its early stages. The relationship between the school and Black family became nonexistent. Seasoned Black teachers were replaced by or made subordinate to less experienced White teachers. Many of them moved to other states rather than succumb to the degradation imposed on them. Our Black teachers were nothing short of second parents. Black students in predominantly White schools were like foster children that no one wanted.

—*Randall Williams*

I don't know if there were benefits in attending a segregated or all—Black school because, at that time, we did not have anything to compare it to. We got our lesson and attended school in order to do our best. I never witnessed integration until I got to college at William Carey, but I could not see any difference. They picked their classes and we picked ours.

—*Eva Lenyoun Crosby*

1954: *Brown v. Board of Education* is decided by U.S. Supreme Court, ruling "separate but equal" schools segregating Black students and White students to be unconstitutional.

(Maurice and Annette Holmes, circa 1954, Detroit, Michigan)

1964: The State attempts to avoid integration of schools by establishing a "Freedom of Choice" plan, by which parents could select the school their children would attend. Black parents who attempted to enroll their children in the White schools suffered various economic and physical reprisals. This ploy to avoid school integration continued through 1969, when the U.S. Supreme Court ruled in *Alexander v. Holmes County Board of Education* that desegregation had to commence immediately.

(*(Left to right)* Maurice Holmes, Annette Holmes Sowell, Sheila Holmes Osgood, friend, Gwendolyn Holmes Mason, circa 1958, Grenada, Miss)

After moving to Laurel, Mississippi in 1964, choosing which school we would attend was *not* a choice made by me or my siblings, but by our parents, Rev. Casey Holmes Jr. and Mrs. Arnessa Wilson Holmes. During the "Freedom of Choice" era, we initially attended all-Black Nora Davis Elementary, Idella Washington Junior High and Oak Park High Schools. In the summer of 1966, we attended Summer Enrichment Programs in Edwards, Mississippi and Mary Holmes Junior College. These seven-week-long camps were designed to "bring African American children, whose parents had 'chosen' for them to attend all-White schools, up to speed before school started." We were tutored by college students from all across the United States. We were introduced to horseback riding; taught to swim; taken on field trips to the Natchez

Trace, Vicksburg, Mississippi, Biloxi, Mississippi, to see the beaches and the Light House, and the Petrified Forrest in Flora, Mississippi, all to expose and enlighten us. We were shown how to "behave" in department stores when the salespeople followed you around and watched your every move to make sure you were not stealing.

"Nigger, nigger, nigger, go home, nigger" were the hateful words hurled at us as we enrolled in school. Enrollment for the Black families daring to cross the racial divide was scheduled so that each family would be there alone, as they walked through a gauntlet of angry White people, while police officers stood with their arms folded. That was September 1966. I, Annette, was a junior at R.H. Watkins and proudly graduated in1968. My friend, Linda Williams and I were the only two Black seniors to graduate that year from Watkins, which was no small feat, considering the obstacles placed in our paths. My brother Maurice and sister Gwen attended Stewart M. Jones Junior High. They were two of eleven Black students enrolled and each was strategically assigned to classes where they would always be the lone Black face in class. At the end of each school day, they gathered, with the other walking students, in the school parking lot, braving the incessant taunts, teasing, and vile remarks of their "classmates" and make a beeline back home, literally "across the tracks." Daily we heard snide, degrading comments from the white kids. One would say, "I smell a gar." "A cigar?", another would ask. "No, a niggar.", yet another would yell as they doubled over with unbridled, raucous laughter. Another chant would ensue, "Don't touch me." "That black might rub off on me." "Is your blood red?" "Don't use that water fountain. A niggar just drank from it.

One phase of our history was being ushered out, where students cared about one another and teachers instilled knowledge, self-worth, and respect while other students were initiated into a school system where you were often ignored by teachers, harassed by your peers, treated as though you were invisible and failure was expected. We are proud to celebrate with you, class of 1968, fifty years of a rich legacy where success was expected and definitely achieved!

—*Ann Holmes Sowell—Class of 1968*
W. H. Watkins H. S.—Laurel, MS

After graduation, I had my first encounter with going to school with Whites. I attended William Carey College my freshman year of college and found out what I knew all the time: Whites are no smarter than Blacks.

—*Hayes Boles Jr.*

My final three years, grades 10 through 12, were spent back at L. J. Rowan. My senior year was the year of "Freedom of Choice" in the Hattiesburg Public School District. Although many students chose to attend Hattiesburg High, most made the choice to remain at Rowan. We still consider the students that graduated from Hattiesburg High as part of the Class of 1968. They chose to make positive changes for our city.

There were about two hundred plus students in our class. Our senior year saw the introduction of White teachers at Rowan and across the city. That was a huge change for us.

—*Rose Mary Montgomery Harrell*

I remember how difficult it was for my little brother Roy to be bussed to a school in Brooklyn. I think that was the beginning of integrated school in Hattiesburg. Although difficult, it was necessary for the good of both Blacks and Whites. The learning environment was much better in the former all-White schools with more books and better desks. One of my greatest regrets growing up in HB was the divorce of my parents, which caused me to move to New Orleans, leaving my school and friends behind. However, change is good and sometimes necessary. I have had a great life after adjusting to that change.

—*Vernette Wallis Andry*

I never understood how people could take public entities and make them private. This puzzle made it easy for me to be one of the first seniors to integrate the White schools of Hattiesburg. It wasn't about mixing with people who hated you, it was about taking control of the dark lie of separating the races. There is but one race according to the word of God (Genesis 1:26-28). So the manmade races no longer faze me. Therefore, how can believers hate, kill, steal, or destroy. God is love. Hatred is of the devil. My experience at S.H. Blair High School was an adventure; exercising my right to take advantage of public education in a place White folks deemed private. Being able to return to the Rowan campus and receive the love of community, extended by the Tigers of 1968 was my saving grace. The understanding of the move was always one of acceptance, not rejection. I sacrificed a lot my senior year. I remember the smile of one White classmate: Lisa Logan. *Just one!* I wondered who taught her the love of God and who taught the ignorance of hatred. Where does the original seed produce such a harvest of ignorance, totally contrary to the love of God? I have never returned to any school activities associated with the S. H. Blair (Hattiesburg High School) Class of 1968. I pray for them and hope they are teaching love of mankind to their bloodlines, especially those who profess Jesus Christ as Lord.

—*Claudia Polk Bivins*

I feel that attending a segregated school taught me that hard work through good education will bear excellent fruit. It was stressed to work hard on your academics to prepare for integration. Some young people have asked me how you lived through segregation. My response was you really didn't think about it a lot until your paths crossed (such as I previously mentioned before passing the White school and being taunted by students) and you knew there were just two different worlds. This was an acceptable way of life until the civil rights and voting rights movements began.

—*Mildred Johnson Watts*

CHAPTER 8

Bits and Pieces

A Special Moment: Invited to Speak at EURO

On July 2, 2002, I stood at the podium about to address the Ninth Triennial gathering of EURO (Eureka, Royal Street, Rowan National Alumni Association). My classmate, Grady Gaines, had introduced me to the audience. My dear friend, Frankye Johnson, had extended the invitation from the reunion committee to speak at the public and memorial program some months earlier. It was a momentous occasion for me. I felt extremely honored to share with my fellow EUROANS what being a product of the greatest public schools in Hattiesburg meant to me.

The following are excerpts from that address:

> Our theme this evening is "EUROANS United: Remembering Our Roots."
>
> In Isaiah 51:1, the prophet Isaiah says, "Remember the rock from which you were hewn and the pit from which you were dug." In other words, "Remember your roots."
>
> And so, we have come here this week from near and far. We have come standing on the shoulders of some strong, phenomenal men and women who walked ahead of us and left a path for us to follow. And once again, we've come to *remember*. We remember a segregated system which couldn't keep us from excelling.

We remember teachers and principals and mothers and fathers who knew what to do and did it.

We remember a teacher who required us to pass our Black history exam when Black history was not even supposed to be taught. She taught it because it was the right thing to do. And she, Marjorie Chambers, is still fighting the good fight to preserve our history because it's the right thing to do.

We remember teachers who taught us poetry and the classics, teachers who challenged our minds before gifted classes were thought of, and we remember passing standardized tests before we knew workshops to pass the tests were necessary.

We remember parents and families who learned how to take a little bit and make a lot—parents who bowed and scraped and cleaned other folks' houses and then came home and took care of their own and didn't have to pop twenty pills a day to pull it off.

We remember teachers who pushed and prodded us and taught us not only to be Black And Proud, but because they understood the realities of life, taught us that because we were Black we'd have to work twice as hard and be twice as good as a White person in order to achieve success in this world.

We remember a principal, Mr. N. R. Burger, who visualized the building of Rowan High School and whose perception predicted its demise should its standing as a high school be changed. And we remember a teacher, Mrs. Chambers, who as recently as last year, tried to get us to understand a lesson that many of our brothers and sisters have learned too late: that if we neglect to remember the past, we're doomed to repeat it.

When we look to the Rock from which we were hewn, we can see clearly how Eureka, Royal Street, and Rowan have shaped us.

When we look to the pit from which we were dug, we can see that we've come a mighty long way.

We have a Black mayor of Hattiesburg! The Honorable Mayor Johnny Dupree. Who would have thought it thirty years ago? A state representative! The Honorable Percy Watson. (He was afraid to jump in the water when I tried to teach him to swim years ago. Try stopping him now). Laborers, pastors, preachers, nurses, doctors, lawyers, politicians, educators, authors, artists, business people, and on and on. You name it and EURO can claim it!

We have come a long way, but we ought never forget that we didn't make it by ourselves.

Isaiah said, "Look to the Rock." I don't know about you, but my Rock is Jesus. And every day I just try to be sure that my anchor holds and grips the Solid Rock. And when life gets tough, I just go and hide behind that Old Mountain where the chilly winds don't blow.

We've come a long way, but we've still got a long way to go.

You see, as long as one child goes to bed hungry at night, as long as our government continues to build more jail houses than school houses, as long as the median income of Black America is $16,000 less than White America, as long as 26 percent of Black Americans continue to live in poverty, as long as our children and grandchildren remain stranded on the wrong side of the digital divide where quality education is a myth and technology is a fantasy, as long as poverty forces our people to choose between health care and food, between selling drugs and going to school, as long as our children continue to drop out of school, as long as our babies keep having babies, as long as we keep killing each other, as long as those sworn to protect us keep killing us—we've still got a long way to go.

Isaiah said look to the pit from which you were dug. I know you here tonight made it out. But there is still somebody left behind. And the pit is still deep. And none of us can be free till all of us are free.

There are some hurting people down here. There are some lost people down here. There are some broken people down here.

All you have to do is try to help somebody. You reach down, and Jesus will pull them up. Jesus already said, "If I be lifted up, I'll draw all people unto me."

The world doesn't make much sense anymore, and what troubles me is that we are getting used to it.

We fight to keep prayer in the schools, yet we don't have time to go to church to pray and we've taken prayer from the home.

We mumble and complain about how children are today and how they used to be. We like to reminisce with pride about how the adults in our "whole village" really did help raise each child. And we wonder what went wrong.

We went wrong. We forgot to pass on the lessons we learned from our ancestors—from our Abrahams and Sarahs. They learned how to pray and they prayed for us and taught us how to pray.

We used to be dependent on God. Now we are dependent on things. God blessed us to have two socks that match and a change of underwear for every day and we forgot who gave them to us. We forget that not everybody else has access to the things that God blessed us with.

We are so quick to forget the bridge that brought us over—to forget how we got out of our own pits. I don't know about you, but I remember my roots. I remember the pit from which I was dug. Somebody reached down and pulled me out one day. They had to dig deep.

Look to the Rock from which you were hewn and the pit from which you were dug. Remember your roots.

—*Rev. Carolyn Hall Abrams*

These writings are excerpts snatched out of my memories of fourteen of the best years of my life. I describe them as excerpts because it would be an infinite effort to put all my memories in print.

Around the house. I have always been my own person, an individual like no other, with my own mind. I was indeed a very mischievous child around the house. Here are a few chuckle-worthy incidences from my early years.

The rooster and me. We had a chicken yard as far back as I can remember. Every morning I would go out and beat the hens off their roost. Unbeknown to me, Daddy had bought an old game cock. The next morning when I went to beat the hens off the roost, the rooster bowed up at me. Turning to run, I fell face-first, and the rooster pecked and purred me all over my back and my head. The next morning, I went back with a stick, and it was me and that rooster.

Yes, we have no bananas today. I loved bananas. Mama bought bananas to make a pudding for Sunday dessert. Everyone was gone that Saturday. My big sister, Leliar Ann, was watching us or so she thought. I could not resist the urge to have a banana, then another, and another until they were just about gone. Knowing I had a whipping coming, I hid under the house. Night came and the family went all over the neighborhood looking for me to no avail. That night, Mama heard some bumping under their bedroom floor. The mosquitoes were biting me and she found me fast asleep.

Just call me Hobo. One of the older girls on our street, Annie Bee Calbert, gave a yard party. Everybody was having a good time. Once again, sleep got the best of me. Daddy parked his car across the street from the Calbert's house on the church grounds. I decided to take a quick nap in his car. When I woke up about six o'clock the next morning, everybody was gone, of course. Mama said when she looked in on us, it appeared that I was in bed. When a knock on the door woke her up and who but me would be standing at the door. For fear of getting into trouble for getting in his car, I lied to Daddy and said I fell asleep on the church steps. When word got out, Charlie Jr. nicknamed me Hobo.

It's so hard to say goodbye to yesterday: "How do I say goodbye to what we had? The good times that made us *laugh* outweigh the bad. I thought we'd get to see forever, but forever's gone away. It's so hard to say goodbye to yesterday." I wouldn't take anything for my school years. There were some trying times, but the good times made it all worthwhile. For the most part, we had excellent teachers who actually cared about us and our need to get a good education. We were blessed. To all of those teachers, I say, "Thank you!"

—*Randall Williams*

Things My Mother Taught Me

Proverbs 17:22 says, "A cheerful heart is good medicine, but a crushed spirit dries up the bones." All of us use proverbs from time to time. Some are biblical; others are secular. They are simple, concrete sayings that are easily memorized and often repeated.

1. Keep your dress down and your drawers up!
2. One day you are going to wish you could put your feet under this table.
3. You can lie before a cat can lick his ass and his tongue is halfway across it.
4. You need to get a job and marry it.
5. One day you will see those words in boxcar letters.
6. You are just throwing money up a wild hog's ass.
7. A fool and his money are soon separated.
8. One monkey does not stop the show.
9. You must think money grows on trees.
10. A dog that brings a bone will take a bone.
11. Why buy the cow when you can get the milk free?

Our parents and grandparents used these phrases. At that time, I did not understand, but today they are as clear as day.

—*Ella Sue Jackson*

Finale

I have no regrets growing up in Hattiesburg. Hattiesburg is a wonderful place to live.

—*Betty Bournes Hill*

 The "village" were those people in my life who saw the potential in me and did what they could to make it happen. As I attended their "celebrations of life," my mind reflected on just how much they impacted my life. I am grateful for my parents and grandparents who sacrificed so I could have a better life than they did. I really didn't know we were poor until I went off to college.

Sure, I remember "White only" and "Colored" signs and secondhand textbooks, but I would not change the journey. Adversity, trials, and hard times only made me stronger. To God be the glory!

—*Beverly Harris Abrams*

I know that I did not receive the best education that I could have gotten at that time; I really know that I did not receive the worst. I am grateful for what my teachers taught me over the twelve years. The majority of them gave us their best. I write this journal or capstones at the age of sixty-seven. I am a husband, father, and grandfather. I thank God for allowing me to be alive to take part in this project of the Class of 1968 for our fiftieth-year class reunion. God has blessed me, my wife, and my family. A lot of my classmates are dead. I think about them often. For example, I think of Clarence Breland and my friend, Eugene Edwards. They have been dead a long time. They are gone, but they are not forgotten. I give God all the praise and all honor for allowing me to get to this point in my life. To all who read this journal or capstone, I wish you good health, longevity, prosperity, and Godspeed.

—*Willie Sanders*

 After I finished high school, I worked as a teacher's aide at Head Start-Library Center for several years. In 1971, I went to work at Big Yank Corp. in the stitching department. Some of the positions I worked in were running bands on pants, hemming legs, ripping out bands, turning pants, and in repairs. I remained on this job for twenty-two years until the factory closed for the first time. Big Yank reopened in 1993, and I was called back to work for about three months.

In 1993, I enrolled in Pearl River Community College in administrative assistance on the Hattiesburg campus where I graduated in May 1994. After months of applying for jobs in this field, I went to work at CC Sewing factory for one year after which the job closed. In 1995, I went to work at Bedford Care Nursing Home. I was a CNA for five years. I am the mother of two children: Jennifer (Jen) and Benjamin (Ben).

—*Carolyn Atkins*

My Aunt, Lola Mae Brown, made an impact on my life because she was always there for us. Another person that made an impact on my life was Wayne Adam. One day, while I was working as a cashier in the cafeteria of William Carey College, I met him and he changed my life. He told me I can do more with my life, and I made a decision to change my life that day. I went back to school to get my GED, and this was special to me because it was the last class that Fannie Lou Knight taught. After having three kids, I went back to school to get my General Education Diploma (GED). After receiving my GED, I wanted to work in an office. With no experience in business, I knew that I needed to attend college. I went and spoke with Eddie Holloway at the University of Southern Mississippi (USM) to get some advice on the direction that I wanted to take in my life. I spoke with him about only having a GED and no ACT score. He made sure that I took the classes that I needed to get the degree that I was trying to obtain. After getting into college, I landed my first job working in the library under Carolyn Thompson. While working in the library, I met Jack Myers, who also worked at the library. He needed someone to manage some apartments he had on section eight. I worked for him for two to three years, before landing my job at Forrest General Hospital. I went to work at Forrest General Hospital as a lab clerk. Many years later, I applied for the office manager position. Not only did I get the job, I was the first person of color to hold that position. The way that I was raised, I wanted to make sure that my kids didn't live the life I had to live. I made sure that they had a home to live in, food on the table, and their clothes were not hand-me-downs. All of them finished school, and my girls didn't get pregnant. I always wanted to keep my childhood away from them. Now I want to thank the Class of 1968 for arranging for me to get my "Golden Diploma" after all these years. It is something I have regretted not doing all my life. I finally got my diploma!

—*Doris McNeill Collins*

I am proud to have graduated at 16 years old as the salutatorian of the class of 1968—the mighty Rowan Tigers! I attended Dillard University in New Orleans and graduated from William Carey University. Having intended to teach, I went to work for AT&T (until I could find a teaching job) and stayed there for nearly forty years. I'm so glad that God was working it out for me and my life. As I look back, those were some of the most wonderful days of my life. I have been a *blessed* woman all my life. God has favored me in so many ways: my parents, my devoted husband, my three wonderful and beautiful daughters, my true and lifelong friends, my church family, and the many wonderful things that I've experienced along the way. God is good!

—*Doris Townsend Gaines*

After college, I joined the U.S. Navy and really grew up because it was the first time I was really by myself. During my time in the Navy, I really enjoyed myself. I've traveled just about all around the world. I went to Spain, France, Italy, Puerto Rico, South America, and all the southeast and northeast of the United States.

—*Hayes Boles Jr.*

I have no regrets about my years growing up in Hattiesburg. Other than a desire to mature earlier than what I did, all my experiences of growing up in Hattiesburg are part of who I am, the person I have become today. I'm thankful for all of it—good and bad; I feel truly blessed.

—*Ethelyn Fairley Reid*

Many great people came out of adversity, including some of our classmates. I am so proud to be a member of the Rowan Class of 1968 and especially those people that came along with me. We all came through adversity and proved the pundits wrong. No matter what a person's background, personality, ethnicity, or gender, they should not be judged but given the opportunity to succeed. Thank goodness for the leadership that we had in our communities, which always encouraged us and told us that we could be anything we wanted to be. I thank God for being in the Class of 1968 and for the people that influenced our lives.

—*Lionel Peyton*

The years I spent at Rowan were some of the best years of my life. I made a lot of good friends and met my wife. I came up being a part of the village, segregation, and the civil rights movement, and integration. The highlight of my life, other than seeing my kids and grandkids, was seeing the first Black President of the United States, Barack Obama. My life has been complete.

—*Grady Gaines*

After graduating from L. J. Rowan Senior High School, during the summer of 1968, I was employed with Piggly Wiggly on North Main Street until I started college at William Carey College, now William Carey University. The legacy that I would pass on from my parents is to be there for my children, no matter what, respect your elders no matter what, speak to them whether they reply or not. If you know someone that needs help, give them a helping hand whether it is your last because you will be rewarded in the end. To me, I could never say no. My motto is "If I have it and you need it, I will give my last to help someone in need." An example that I will never forget: a lady from the neighborhood just up and left her baby unattended, and I found him and took him in, fed him, and changed him. I cared for him until the authorities came and got him; he was then put in foster care in another county.

—*Hattie Williams Knight*

My message that I would leave in a time capsule about growing up in Hattiesburg would be "Even though you did your best to keep us down, the cream always rises to the top."

—*Hayes Boles Jr.*

Since high school graduation, I've enjoyed a rich and meaningful life, fulfilling my purpose, helping others, and making a difference for causes that are passionate to me. Passionately, I was always drawn to the aspect of becoming a civil rights activist, fighting for those who couldn't find the voice to fight from within. It was then I became a member of the highly accredited organization known as the National Association for the Advancement of Colored People (NAACP) in Forrest County. Having been an advocate for African Americans in our very own community, I spent time educating those on the rights of voter registration. During the 1960s, a typical registration process for an African American was far from smooth and was intimidating and oftentimes humiliating to those interested.

In the year of 1985, I became a victim not because of the content of my character, but because of the color of my skin. Federal, state, and local laws provide protection from discrimination based on certain characteristics; nonetheless, I was degraded by a housing office that discriminated against African Americans and their desire for residency. After obtaining exceptional counsel, I was able to successfully win my lawsuit based on the grounds that Black prospective renters were advertised fewer rentals than other races, that blacks were refused without formal explanation and reasoning, and discriminatory advertisement. As a result, the owner was subjected to pay fines for his renting practices and was forced to revise his advertisements according to the Equal Housing Authority Policy.

In the 1980s, I got married and relocated to the state of Kansas. I felt it was my duty to continue to serve by becoming a member of the local chapter where I operated as the local secretary from 1995 to 2000. During my residency in Kansas, I filed a complaint with the EEOC based on the county's interviewing and hiring practices. Therefore, I was given the consent to sue, and I won damages that were awarded. The county, however, refused to admit any wrongdoings.

In 2001, I relocated to Florida and immediately found myself working in the community. I joined the Democratic Women's Club of Florida and committed to working on several committees. I participated in training workshops about current political issues and advocacy, attended or volunteered for conventions, and attended lobbying opportunities. I was also involved in voter registration and canvassing for local and state candidates and also for the US presidency.

As of today, I currently own and operate my own business, the Linda T Harris Agency where its sole purpose is to create innovative ways to help adults with developmental disabilities reach their full potential.

—*Linda Turner Harris*

 We did not always do what was right, and no, we did not listen to our parents some of the time. But thanks be to God, he kept us. When telling my story to my children about my childhood, I realized they would never experience the closeness and caring of our teachers, church, loving neighbors, and classmates. I enjoyed my school days and growing up in the Deep South with the rich history of the civil rights movement. My children can't relate to how much I valued that time. We had fun without all the distractions kids have today. We grew up in a time when people had respect for one another.

I will always cherish the memories of loving classmates and teachers; they played a big part of shaping who I am today.

—*Margaret Hill Burger*

The L. J. Rowan High School Class of 1968 is a unique class. We have a bond of lasting friendship until death we part. We are a class that loves one another, shows support for each other, whether it is the birth of a child or grand-child, or the death of a loved one. We all support each other. L. J. Rowan High School is a staple in the commu-nity. It is now an elementary school, preparing kids for the high school level. L. J. Rowan is preparing students for the future. I love L. J. Rowan High and my classmates of 1968.

—*Mattie Hudnall Ponder*

It was now the summer of 1968. I had graduated from Rowan, and my plan was to find a summer job, save a little money, and enroll at the University of Southern Mississippi (USM) in the fall. I found employment on the USM cam-pus and managed to save some funds for college. My sis-ters had the same drive and determination. Mildred went to Jackson State College, and Lorma transferred from USM to Tougaloo College. In 1972, we all graduated with bachelor's degrees and started out on our respective careers. And now, fifty years after receiving my diploma, I am a proud alum-nus of Rowan High School and very appreciative of the out-standing academic preparation and training that I received. I am confident that Rowan will live on through the great teachers and staff who taught us, nurtured us, and helped shape us to become men and women of character, courage and competence. The legacy of Rowan will be remembered and strengthened through the dedicated service and stellar achievements of our alumni and friends both near and far. And finally, Rowan will live on through our children, grandchildren, and future generations who carry on the ideals, values, and principles that were instilled in us. Therefore, I am very proud to join with the other members of the Class of 1968 as we celebrate the golden anniversary of our graduation from Rowan High School. I thank God for providing me with the opportunity to be a part of the Rowan family and all that it stands for. Hail to thee, my dear Rowan!

—*Melvin Miller*

My time capsule message would include a short timeline of events describing our lives and educational experiences during the fifties and sixties. It was the best of times because there was no violence, drugs, or guns in our schools. It was the worst of times during the civil rights and Vietnam War era.

—*Mildred Miller Short*

 I appreciate the majority of the teachers that I had. A few were actually prejudiced. I am proud of my accomplishments. Having God's help and blessing and a big want-to, I had a successful journey. I have an advanced degree in nursing. I am an author of two books, a wife, a mother, and a servant of God.

—*Willie Ruth McDonald Sanders*

My parents, raising six children, always taught us to never quit. I saw my Father knocked down many times in his career life, but he picked himself up and continued to leap forward.

Today, when I think on the negatives in my life, Jeremiah 29:11 comes to mind: "I have it all planned out—plans to take care of you, not abandon you, plans to give you the future you hope for." If we only had a glimpse of the future, we would never worry about others' opinions.

Thus, Rowan High School, Hattiesburg, Mississippi, would be challenging, but it opened the door for other opportunities for my family and me. My Father later pursued his doctoral degree at the University of Southern Mississippi, and I would be accepted to enter my first and only choice, Jackson State College.

Many of my Rowan classmates and a friend from my previous school, Jo Bertha Buck Oliver, would meet again at Jackson State. Jo Bertha would become Mildred Watt's roommate for two years.

—*Patricia Berry Blake*

After receiving my high school diploma from L. J. Rowan High School in 1968, I sought out to make a difference by applying to William Carey College. Beyond my own expectation, I was accepted into the Forrest General School of Practical Nursing in 1971. During this time, integration was fairly new. Only two Black nurses were selected from each program class, and I was very fortunate to be chosen.

With this achievement, I began dedicating myself to the nursing profession by continuing to work at Forrest General Hospital as a licensed practical nurse for an indefinite time. Several years later, I was inspired to further my education by taking classes at Louisiana Delta College (formerly known as Ouachita Parish Community College) located in Monroe, Louisiana. There I studied on the basis of intravenous infusion therapy, central line care, and administering IV medications. After relocating to Michigan in 1991, I began working at St. Joseph Mercy Hospital in Pontiac. I continued my calling by specializing in psychiatric mental health nursing and became well versed in surgery and perioperative care plans. I have three inactive licenses (Mississippi, Louisiana, and Michigan) and one active license in Pensacola, Florida.

Deciding it was time to elevate in my profession, I accepted a position at Sacred Heart Hospital where I worked in the cardiovascular unit with emphasis on open-heart surgeries. Additionally, I worked in the cardiac or telemetry unit practicing in the care for patients with heart disease, those that suffered from complications and/or heart failure, or those that needed continuous monitoring. I remained a dedicated nurse and worked hard at my job for over twenty years.

I am a member of the Democratic Party and the local organization "Movement for Change" in the Pensacola chapter. I worked voter registration for presidency, specifically Barrack Obama and Hillary Clinton.

—*Patricia Turner Bradley*

I married Jimmie Harrell Sr. in 1968. We have two girls, Deborah Ann Harrell Yarbrough and Geneva Elizabeth Harrell Allen, and one son, Jimmie Harrell Jr.

I worked at Forrest General Hospital for about eight years. Initially, I wanted to become a nurse but changed my mind. My husband worked mixed shifts and I worked days. After my daughters were teenagers, I left FGH to be close to them.

Wanting to help my niece who became pregnant at an early age, I sought to help her understand what her situation was. After talking to several women, we decided to start a teen pregnancy education program.

Mrs. Joyce Vaughn suggested the name Neighborhood Educational Enhancement and Development Services Inc. (NEEDS).

We began with classes on pregnancy prevention. Our first year, we had forty-five participants. Another need we identified was that no child care was available for them when they wanted to return to school. No child care center would take children under two years of age. With the help of Mr. Johnny Dupree, we were able to open one.

In 1992, we opened a center at Mary Bethune School for infants and toddlers with the help of United Way and other organizations. That year we had twenty participants. Later, the program was extended to include working parents and college students. We presently have two centers. I have served the community through several organizations and received many awards.

I leave this advice with every young man and woman. If you have a vision, see it through. If you can put it on paper, you can also accomplish your dream.

—*Rose Mary Montgomery Harrell*

Nineteen sixty-eight was the beginning of a new season in my life, leaving the comfort zone of home to enter Jackson State University majoring in music. What an adjustment to learn independence among many strange faces. I had two semesters and later changed my major to elementary childhood education with an emphasis in reading. I left school after the Jackson State riot and relocated to Muskegon, Michigan. I later returned to Jackson State and earned my BS in December 1973, after which I gained employment with the Muskegon Heights Public School System as an elementary teacher, administrative assistant, and Title 1 instructor. I retired in 2009 with thirty-seven years of service.

I presently reside in Muskegon, Michigan and have three children, which I have been blessed to parent who are the child and grandson of my deceased sister, Diane: Makisha, forty-three; Ashton, twenty-eight; and my baby Mackenzee, eighteen.

—*Thelma Bacchus*

 I graduated high school and business school in New Orleans. I also took early childhood classes at Delgado Community College and worked in the early childhood field for over thirty years before retirement. I opened my own Beauty Salon, namely,

Beautiful You Salons on Broad, LLC. My childhood friend and beloved brother were there to celebrate with me and did the photography as well as video. I am also the owner of A Step Above Babysitting LLC. I was married to Napoleon Odomes, and then Cary J. Andry Sr. who passed suddenly in 2009. I am the mother of six children, Grandmother to eleven, and great-Grandmother to seven. My life has been filled with ups and downs, good and bad, but I was prepared in Hattiesburg, MS and equipped for battle at DePriest Elementary, Earl Travillion Attendance Center and L.J Rowan Senior High School.

In closing, I am a strong, self-sufficient, independent and courageous Woman of God because of my roots that began on Hwy 49 in Hattiesburg MS at the hands of a midwife.

—*Vernette Wallis Andry*

The Class of 1968 was a community of learning, having fun, and developing lifelong friendships. Rowan High School was an extraordinary place that helped prepare me for the military, being a pilot, entrepreneur, and an elder in the church. This preparation aided me in my life-changing moment.

—*James Chatman*

My most enjoyable time living in Hattiesburg was growing up, because I had the opportunity to meet and be friends with a lot of people I would have never known in my lifetime, and they still exist. In my heart and in my memories, there are still some people there that I think about from time to time. Some of those I grew up with have gone to a better place. Hattiesburg is an extraordinary city, and it has been my pleasure to have been raised there. I have great memories of my friends and my family, especially Mobile Street, which I am sure you've heard a lot about from others as well. It was a learning experience for me because it gave me some idea of a direction. I look forward to coming back to Hattiesburg for a visit. It has been a long time, but it feels as if it were yesterday. Memories fade but are not totally forgotten. I have lived in many parts of the world and I have experienced many things, but I will always be from a small town in Mississippi. So, I say to you and to those who are still there, I am proud of you. I am sure there are a lot of things that have changed, and some that will never change.

—*Teleceno C. Carr Jr*

In closing, I offer my eternal gratitude to our people on behalf of myself and the Class of 1968, which I had the honor of serving as class president. Our people brought us from a mighty long way. As children, I can truly say that we had a great life that was full of happiness in the face of racial bigotry and outright apartheid in violation of our constitutional rights. But we had the entire village raising us: parents, grandparents, relatives, neighbors, the cream of the crop in terms of our teachers, administrators, custodians, cafeteria workers, indeed everybody in the Black community in Hattiesburg. And we had Mr. N. R. Burger, whom I count as one of the greatest education leaders this nation has produced. He presided over the school culture of the Black community of Hattiesburg and fostered numerous deeds of greatness on the part of graduates of Eureka, Royal Street, and Rowan. God is good!

—*Don Denard*

A Special Relationship

I met the love of my life at Rowan High School. We began dating in April, 1967. He was a senior and I was a junior. His name is Robert Lee Abrams. Sometimes I call him Bobby.

The first time he came to my house to see me, I called him crazy. I said he was "crazy" because he told me that night that he was going to marry me. He told me that I was going to the prom with him, also. I told him, "I don't even know you." He said that it didn't matter because he had decided to marry me when he first saw me when he was in the tenth grade, and that he went home and told his mother he had found the girl he was going to marry. She later confirmed his story. I still thought he was crazy. I agreed to go on a date with him, and he took me to the Saenger Theater to see *The Sound of Music*.

Robert made me smile. He made my heart smile. Only God could have put him in my path. He cared about me, and finally, I had someone I could lean on. Suddenly, life didn't seem so hard anymore. I missed him so much when he left for Tougaloo College that fall. But somehow he managed to come home almost every weekend.

Robert was mature, hardworking, and very responsible even in high school. He would sometimes fall asleep in class because he had worked a late shift to help support his family.

He has always been handsome. He still has a beautiful smile. However, what I have always admired most about him is his mind. He is a thinker. It didn't take me long to realize how much I loved him and that he loved me as well.

I joined Robert at Tougaloo College after graduating from Rowan in 1968. I was the first in my family to graduate high school. I was class valedictorian. Robert graduated from college in 1971, with BA degrees in History and Afro-American Studies. He received his Master of Divinity degree from Emory University in 1992.

I graduated magna cum laude from Tougaloo in 1972. I received a Master of Library Science degree from the University of Wisconsin-Madison in 1973, and a Master of Divinity degree from Emory University in 1992.

Robert and I both became ordained elders in the United Methodist Church. He worked in prison ministry and other outreach ministries. I became the founding pastor of H. A. Brown Memorial United Methodist Church in Wiggins, Mississippi, and served the church for fifteen years.

I guess I was the one who was "crazy" that first night he came to call on me. Everything he said came true. He took me to my junior prom in 1967 and married me in 1969. On February 28, 2019, we celebrated our fiftieth wedding anniversary.

Robert told me something else on that April night. He said we would have lots of smart children. He was right about that, too. We had seven children. If Robert were telling this story, this is what he would say:

Our eldest daughter, Andrea, graduated from Agnes Scott College and received her PhD in Cultural Anthropology from Emory University. She is a tenured professor at Centre

College in Kentucky and author of *God and Blackness: Race, Gender and Identity in a Middle Class Afrocentric Church.*

Our second daughter, Veronica, was born on August 17, 1971. She only lived for two days on this earth, but has eternal life with Jesus.

Our third daughter, Stacey, is a graduate of Spelman College, the University of Texas-Austin, and Yale Law School. The former Democratic Minority leader, she is a candidate for governor of Georgia. An author, her most recent book is *Minority Leader: How to Lead from the Outside and Make Real Change.*

Our fourth daughter, Leslie, is a graduate of Brown University and Yale Law School. She is a federal judge, appointed by President Barack Obama to the Middle District of Georgia. Leslie is married to Jimmie Gardner and they live in Albany, Georgia.

Our oldest son, Richard, is a graduate of Paine College in Augusta, Georgia. He works with at-risk children and adults. Richard is married to Nakia, and they have three children—Jorden, Riyan and Ayren.

Our second son, Walter, attended Morehouse College. He is employed in Hattiesburg and has plans to complete his degree at the University of Southern Mississippi. He has one daughter, Faith.

Our seventh child, Jeanine, is a graduate of Duke University and received her PhD in Evolutionary Biology from the University of Texas-Austin. She is employed at the Center for Disease Control (CDC) in Atlanta, is married to Brandon McLean, and is the mother of two boys, Cameron and Devin.

The day our angel, Veronica, died was the worst day of our lives. On July 14, 2006, God brought another angel into our lives who brings us great joy each day. Her name is Faith Ann Abrams. She is eleven years old now, but she has been with us since she was five days old. Robert and I adopted Faith in 2008. She is smart, talented, and is surrounded by so many people who love her, especially her father, Walter.

Falling in love with Robert Lee Abrams was the best thing that happened to me at Rowan High School. Bobby said I should also tell everybody that we are the best thing that happened to each other, period. I agree.

PS: He still makes my heart smile.

—*Carolyn Hall Abrams*

Expectations

Expectations set high to reach for the sky.
Friends, family members and a whole neighborhood from
8th Street to Royal Street (now Martin Luther King).
My English teacher.
My Typing instructor.
Biology teacher.
And, singing in the choir.
Tools and skills I've used throughout my careers—I remember how.
And over the years we still remain close friends.
8th Street to Royal Street family, class members, friends.
I remember you, dear Rowan.

—Janice Walton Foreman

Closing Thoughts

We have now come to the close of our journey back through time. Though many names are mentioned in the preceding chronicles, the primary point and purpose of this meandering tale is to illuminate the memories of the Class of 1968, who actually lived during a pivotal time in the history of the world. It is to leave just a portion of our remembrances for the generations to come so that they can know from whom they are descended—giants who took and used their limited resources to contribute to the world in which we live. Many students that followed us have never given much thought to the segregated South from whence we came, nor do they understand what we mean when we admonish them for not taking advantage of the many new opportunities that were not present in our day. Yet we hung in there and accomplished much. We want you to remember the times we lived in, the events that shaped our lives, and the talented and dynamic people we became.

—Doris T. Gaines, Creator and Editor

Hail to thee, Oh hail dear Rowan
Standing brave and true
How we love your deeds of greatness
Hail, all hail to you!

How we honor all you stand for
Loud your praises sing.
Joyfully we greet you Rowan
Best in all the land!

AFTERWORD

What began years ago as the passionate vision of our editor, Doris Townsend Gaines, has culminated in our memoir, *The Class of 1968: A Thread Through Time.* Her perseverance and passion inspired us all. I am fortunate to have helped launch our project and to serve as co-editor.

In these pages, we have told our tales, shared our memories and preserved for ourselves and our posterity the journey we made through the segregated public schools of Hattiesburg, Mississippi, as well as the neighborhoods and communities that shaped us, shielded us and nurtured us. We have expressed gratitude for our families and our teachers and school staff. We have extended our deepest appreciation for the leadership of our principals, especially Mr. N.R. Burger, who dared us to reach for the stars, but ensured we remained grounded in our commitment to our shared values.

We have written this book together. Still, this is not our first publication. Our memoir had its genesis more than fifty years ago when *PROFILE '68*, our class yearbook, was published. In its pages, we told our story through pictures and narrative that captured not only our senior year, but also the beginning of the end of segregated Rowan High School. In essence, *PROFILE '68* became the first chronicle of our stories, and the first book we completed together as classmates.

Our classmate and Editor-in-Chief, Elaine Anderson Peacock, penned these prescient words in her Editor's Message:

> "Mindful of the fact that the school year 1967-68 was one of importance in the history of Rowan Senior High School, the Profile '68 staff has attempted to design this year's publication in such a fashion that it will portray the highlights of memorable activities during 1967-68 and serve as a means of recalling experiences once shared during this year."

While Elaine led us in chronicling our high school years in our 1968 year book, she will not have her own entry in our memoir. Despite her most valiant effort to participate in our new venture, Elaine became ill and passed away in 2019.

Ever unique and creative, Elaine was very excited about her planned narrative which would have included a dialogue between the two of us, bridging the past and present in light of our segregated high school years and where we are today. I know that our pride in being able to vote and witness the election of President Barack Obama as the first Black President of the United States would have been highlighted in our dialogue.

I believe we would have also continued our frequent conversations about the political future of my daughter, Georgia Democrat Stacey Abrams, who became the first Black American female major-party gubernatorial nominee in the United States in 2018. As we continued our dialogue, we certainly would have rejoiced that on February 5, 2019, Stacey also became the first Black woman to deliver the Response to the State of the Union address.

We would have further recalled that on March 11, 2014, President Obama appointment my daughter, Leslie Gardner Abrams, to serve as the first Black American female Article III federal judge in the state of Georgia, thereby also becoming the first female to serve the Middle District of Georgia. Leslie was confirmed by the United States Senate on November 18, 2014 by a vote of 100-0.

I believe that at the conclusion of Elaine's planned narrative, she would have admonished each of us to always be mindful of the importance of recalling, reflecting on, and recording our experiences. And so, over fifty years later, we still cherish our yearbook as we celebrate the publication of our memoir, *The Class of 1968: A Thread Through Time*.

I am awed by the members of the Class of 1968, women and men who have distinguished themselves in tremendous ways, and a number of whom we wish to pay special mention. We salute those who served in the United States military, particularly those who made the ultimate sacrifice. Forty-nine of our classmates joined the armed forces, including two pioneering young women who enlisted. In gratitude, we call the roll of our military veterans for their dedication to our security, and we are privileged to list their names herein in the section titled, "In Salute."

We also proudly celebrate the lives of our classmates who are no longer with us, and we honor their contributions to the Class of 1968, as they helped make us who we are. Their lives and memories will forever be woven in our thread through time, and their names are inscribed in the section titled, "In Memoriam."

The story of the Class of 1968 could not have been told without each classmate who contributed to this memoir and trusted us to share their tales with honesty and integrity. We appreciate the thought-provoking questions developed by cultural anthropologist, Dr. Andrea Abrams, which helped us to define our focus and begin the writing process. As we compiled this narrative of our journey, we were ably assisted by Dr. Tom O'Brien, professor at the University of Southern Mississippi, and doctoral candidate, Olivia Moore. Dr. O'Brien currently works in the university's School of Education, and specializes in the study of race and education in the U.S. South. Ms. Moore also specializes in the study of race, and is in the process of writing her doctoral dissertation titled, "Fractured Activism: Competing Visions for the Civil Rights Movement in Hattiesburg, Mississippi, 1966-80." The enthusiasm, support and editorial skills of these two individuals have proven invaluable.

Each of us has told our story in our own way, but together we, the Class of 1968, recount a collective experience that binds us one to another. And because we have each had our say, *our thread will continue through time.*

Carolyn Hall Abrams
Co-Editor

IN SALUTE

Adams, Clemmie, Air Force
Archie, David, Army
Ash, Willie, Navy
*Beckum, Tony, Army
Boles, Hayes, Navy
*Bourne, Larry, Army
Brown, Willie D., Navy
Chatham, James, Army
*Dent, Charles, Navy
*Donald, Bernard, Army
*Fairley, Vaughn Wendell, Army
Fautner, Larry, Marine Corps
Gamble, Alvin, Army
Gamble, Earl, Air Force
Garner, Benjamin, Air Force
Garner, Willie, Army
*Godbolt, Harry, Air Force
Harris, Albert, Army
Harris, Harvell, Air Force
Hearn, Aaron, Army
Hollingsworth, Edward, Marine Corps

Jones, James Harold, Army
*Legrone, Jerry, Army
Lindsey, Ronald, Army
Lofton, Michael, Air Force
Miller, Melvin, Army
**Myers, Oliver, Army
Nelson, Jerry, Army
Payne, Wiley C. , Army
*Payton, Louis, Navy
Polk, Ervin, Army
Reid, Jim, Navy
Rogers, James, Army
Short, Howard, Air Force
Stewart, Calvin, Air Force
Strickland, Larry, Navy
Taylor, Richard, Air Force
*Thames, Mack, Army
Thigpen, Willie J., Army
*Thorton, Jerome, Army
Tillman Brown, Carolyn, Navy
Turner, Richard, Air Force
Walker Ford, Annie S., Army
Walker, Leroy, Air Force
*Walker, Levi, Army
Walmon, Oliver, Army
*White, Jasper, Navy
*Womback, Ivan, Army
**Woods, R.C., Air Force

*Deceased
**Ultimate Sacrifice

In Memoriam

Adams Hunter, Georgia Ann
Adams Phillips, Zia Lynn
Adams Smith, Lorene
Allen, Roy
Anderson Peacock, Elaine
Applewhite, Willie
Archie, David
Armstrong, Edsel
Ash Kelly, Bettie S.
Beckum, Tonnie
Bivins, Jackie
Bourne, Larry
Breland, Clarence, Jr.
Brewton, John E.
Brown Hudson, Cathy
Brown, Roy Lee
Coney, Freddie L.
Curb, Lawrence
Curry, James
Davidson, Francis
Davis Jenkins, A. Vidilia

Dedrick Portis, Diane
Dent, Charles
Dillard Heard, Margaret
Donald, Bernard
Donald, Jessie Mack
Doss, Howard, Jr.
Fairley, Isaac J.
Fairley, Vaughn Wendell
Fautner, Larry
Gibson Williams, Mary
Godbolt, Harry
Hall, Tommy, Jr.
Hill, Harry
Hill Burger, Margaret
Howze Mackabee, Bessie
Hughes, Eddie Lee
Jackson, Ella Sue
Johnson Slusher, Betty
Jordan, Donald B., Jr.
Keaton, Haywood
King Coleman, Ethel
Kirkland Hunter, Dorothy
Knight, George E.
Knox, Herbert C.
Legrone, Jerry
Lewis Ray, Betty
Lewis Vaughn, Evelyn
Lindsey, Ronald
Marsh, Hettie
McCree Palmer, Mamie

McCurty, Edward
McDonald, Larry
McKorkle, Jackie
McLeod Agee, Cecillia
Moffet, Leon
Montgomery Smith, Mattie
Myers, Oliver
Payton, Louis
Pittman Smith, Dorothy
Powe Hamilton, Bertha
Ratliff, Jimmie Ruth
Robinson, Stella
Shaw, Emmett
Slay, Johnnie Bea
Stribling Smith, Dorothy
Strickland, Larry D.
Thames, Mack, Jr.
Thornton, Jerome, Jr.
Tillman, William G.
Townes, James
Walker, Levi
White, Jasper
White Temple, Shirley
Williams Blythe, Kay Marie
Williams Jones, Tommie Jean
Williams, Reginald
Williams, Willie Ray
Womback, Ivan
Woods, R. C., Jr.
Young, Wayne

About the Editor

Doris Townsend Gaines is a native of Hattiesburg, Mississippi, and has spent her entire life working and raising her family in the community in which she now lives. The salutatorian of the L. J. Rowan High School Class of 1968, she attended Dillard University, is a graduate of William Carey University, and studied further at the University of Southern Mississippi and St. Leo University. She worked for ATT for nearly forty years and ended her career there as a logistics manager responsible for Mississippi and West Tennessee.

Now retired, Doris works tirelessly in her church and community and has been married to her high school sweetheart, Grady Gaines, for fifty-one years. They are the parents of three daughters and have two grandchildren.

She enjoys singing, fishing, baking, and visiting with friends and family. She reads extensively, is a word enthusiast, and lover of mysteries. Doris is also a member of the True Light Baptist Church where she has served in many capacities including choir director for many years. Over the years, she has volunteered in many organizations including DREAM of Hattiesburg, and the Telephone Pioneers of America.

About the Co-editor

Rev. Carolyn Hall Abrams graduated from Rowan High School in 1968 as class valedictorian. Carolyn has been married for fifty-one years to her high school sweetheart, Robert Abrams, and the two currently reside in Stone Mountain, Georgia. They are the proud parents of eight children and six grandchildren.

Carolyn received a Bachelor of Arts in Political Science and Afro-American Studies with honors from Tougaloo College. She also graduated with honors from the University of Wisconsin-Madison with a Master's in Library Science. She worked as librarian and assistant professor of education for William Carey College on the Coast for thirteen years. Answering the call to preach, Carolyn and Robert each earned a Master of Divinity from the Candler School of Theology at Emory University in 1992.

As founding pastor of H. A. Brown Memorial United Methodist Church, Carolyn served the congregation for fifteen years. Now retired, she continues to enjoy preaching and performing other pastoral duties. Forever a librarian, Carolyn is an avid reader and book collector. She also enjoys spending time with friends and family as well as fishing and traveling with her husband. She is honored to be a member of the Class of 1968.

(Left to right) Dr. Thomas V. O' Brien, Mrs. Carolyn
Hall Abrams, Mrs. Doris Townsend Gaines, Ms. Olivia
Moore at the Hattiesburg Public Library in 2019.

Printed in the USA
CPSIA information can be obtained
at www.ICGtesting.com
LVHW072152130823
755145LV00021B/1160